MAJOR VICES

THE BEELER LARGE PRINT MYSTERY SERIES

Edited by Audrey A. Lesko

Also available in Large Print by Mary Dahiem

The Alpine Gamble
Just Desserts
Murder, My Suite
The Alpine Hero

MAJOR VICES

A Bed and Breakfast Mystery

MARY DAHIEM

BEELER LARGE PRINT
Hampton Falls, New Hampshire, 2002

Library of Congress Cataloging-in-Publication Data

Dahiem, Mary
    Major Vices : a bed and breakfast mystery / Mary
Dahiem.
        p.   cm.—(The Beeler Large Print mystery series)
    ISBN 1-57490-449-3 (alk. paper)
        1. Flynn, Judith McMonigle (Fictitious character)—
    Fiction. 2. Bed and breakfast accommodations—Fiction. 3.
    Aged men—Crimes against—Fiction. 4. Northwest,
    Pacific—Fiction. 5. Birthday Parties—Fiction.
        6. Large type books. I. Title. II. Series.

PS3554 .A264 M35 2002
813'.54—dc21   2002013994

Published in Large Print by arrangement with
Avon Books, an imprint of HarperCollins Publishers.

BEELER LARGE PRINT
is published by
Thomas T. Beeler, Publisher
Post Office Box 659
Hampton Falls, New Hampshire 03844

Typeset in 16 point Times New Roman type.
Printed on acid-free paper, sewn and bound by
Sheridan Books in Chelsea, Michigan.

MAJOR VICES

ONE

JUDITH GROVER MCMONIGLE FLYNN TIPPED HER HEAD to one side, picked up a black marking pen, and drew antlers on the formal portrait of Aunt Toadie. The effect couldn't have pleased Judith more if she'd added the final stroke to a van Gogh.

"Nice," remarked Serena Grover Jones, admiring her cousin's handiwork. "How about blacking out a couple of her teeth?"

Turning the eight-by-ten photograph facedown on the coffee table, Judith grimaced. "Enough's enough. Especially when it comes to Aunt Toadie. I have *never* understood how Uncle Corky has put up with her all these years."

Cousin Renie considered. "He traveled a lot on his job with the engineering firm. Since he retired, he still travels a lot. Separate continents help, I guess."

Judith leaned back on the off-white sofa in the large living room of Hillside Manor. On a Tuesday afternoon in early February, the bed-and-breakfast was empty. Except for St. Valentine's Day, these were the dull months at the B&B, from the second week of January until the third week of March. Judith didn't mind. In the four years since converting her family home into a hostelry, business had increased steadily. The catering sideline was also doing well. She'd never get rich, but with any luck and a great deal of hard work, she'd never be poor. Again.

Setting aside the box of family pictures, Judith picked up her mug of hot chocolate. "Toadie never liked me," she declared, sipping slowly. "When I was a kid, she

1

always said the rudest things to me. My least favorite nickname was Lardbucket."

Renie snorted. "She never liked any of her Grover in-laws. Toadie called me Bucky Beaver. And then she'd laugh, like it was soooo funny. Mean old hag." Leaning forward on the matching sofa, Renie waved a finger at Judith. "She never said things like that around Uncle Corky. He would have yanked her chain."

Judith arched her dark eyebrows. "Would he? Uncle Corky's a dear, and he loves to bluster. But at home, I always figure Aunt Toadie keeps him on a tight leash."

Renie looked pained. "Could be," she allowed. "I'd hate to think it. So what's the drill for Friday night?"

Flipping open a leather-bound notebook, Judith scanned the page. "It's Uncle Boo's birthday. He's seventy-five or a hundred and seventy-five, depending on whether or not he's been legally dead for years."

"He has. Uncle Boo hasn't moved since Truman was in the White House."

Judith nodded, running her long fingers through her silvered black curls. "Right. The only time Uncle Boo gets excited is when he sees a spaceship land next to his gazebo. Anyway, the party starts at six o'clock with cocktails and hors d'oeuvres for the Major Mush employees. If Aunt Toadie has her way, they'll be given glasses of cheap white wine and soggy cheese balls, then hustled out the door around seven after singing an off-key rendition of 'Happy Birthday, You Tight-Fisted Old Coot.' No cake. No punch. No fun. Next comes the family party." Judith rolled her dark eyes while Renie groaned. "This will not be fun, either, unless you enjoy being in the company of our most revolting shirttail relations."

Renie now waved both hands. "Hey, we aren't guests,

2

we're drudges. We can stay in the kitchen and get secretly crocked, which is the only way I can stand Aunt Toadie and a whole lot of Lotts. No wonder Uncle Corky went off on safari! He'd rather be eaten by two-toed sloths than spend an evening with his in-laws."

"They don't have sloths in Africa," Judith remarked absently, her eyes still on her page of notes. "Dinner at seven, followed by feudal warfare, or whatever that quarrelsome bunch of Lotts does when they get together. Hey, coz," she said suddenly, gazing earnestly at Renie, "I'm sorry I got you into this. I thought Arlene would be back from Palm Desert by now."

Renie shrugged. "No apologies necessary. My workload is in pretty good shape right now. I finished all my annual-report graphics last month. The next crunch won't come for another two weeks, when they start going on the presses." Renie's job as a graphic designer allowed her to work at home, but Judith knew that winter was always her busiest time. The cousins had hardly seen each other from New Year's until late January. "It's not your fault that the Rankerses decided to stay on an extra week," Renie went on. "They've got a grandson in southern California now. You can't blame Arlene and Carl for wanting to spend some extra time with the little guy."

Judith inclined her head. Arlene Rankers was a good neighbor and an even better friend. She was also a crackerjack cohostess in the catering business. The original plan had been for Judith and Arlene to cater Uncle Boo's birthday party. But over the weekend, Arlene had called to tell Judith that they wouldn't be returning home to Heraldsgate Hill until the second week of February. Judith had taken the news in stride, even though it meant juggling her Friday night guest

3

list, which so far showed three of her five bedrooms booked. Happily, Joe Flynn had announced he'd fill in for his wife. He was off duty for the weekend and would take an extra day on Friday. He liked to cook, so fixing breakfast for the guests would be no trouble. He would enjoy making appetizers for the five o'clock sherry hour. His job as a homicide detective threw him in with people who were considerably less savory than his wife's B&B guests. In their not quite two years of marriage, Joe's role at Hillside Manor had been limited. But he didn't mind helping out. He loved Judith very much, and the feeling was mutual.

"It's Joe I'm worried about," Judith said. "He'll go nuts. I never told him about the couple last week who brought a kangaroo gerbil along. It got loose and jumped all the way downstairs and landed in the syrup pitcher. What a mess!" Judith shook her head at the memory. "Have you ever tried to shampoo a gerbil?"

"Oh, sure," Renie responded blithely. "I gave Tessie the Turtle a pedicure once, too. After three kids, there isn't much I've missed."

Silently, the cousins reflected on their maternal experiences. Judith had one son, at last a college graduate and gainfully employed as a forest ranger in Idaho's Nez Percé National Historical Park. Michael McMonigle had taken his time finishing his degree in forestry, but at least he had gotten his education. Back in the dark, dreary years of Judith's first marriage, in the Thurlow Street rental, while working two jobs and enduring the verbal abuse of a lazy, ill-tempered, four-hundred-pound husband, she had never dared hope that Mike would go to college. When Dan McMonigle had died at age forty-nine from overeating and underachieving, Judith had felt not loss, but relief. She

4

had recovered her freedom, and with it a future for herself and her son. Now that Judith was remarried and those years were behind her, Dan seemed less loathsome. On occasion, her memory of him was benign. Once in a while she even missed him. There had been some good times, especially in the beginning. Dan had been smart; he had possessed a sense of humor; he could be very generous. His flair for alienating people had grown not out of dislike for them, but from dislike of himself. Nobody—not even Judith's relatives—had despised Dan as much as he had.

"Bill is going to cook dinner for our kids," Renie remarked at last, referring to her husband of twenty-five years.

Judith gave a start. "Bill? Cook? What, for heaven's sake?"

Renie smirked. "Fish and chips. He picks them up on the way home from the university, then warms them in the microwave. For Bill, that's cooking."

Judith grinned at her cousin. "At least he knows how to turn on the microwave."

Renie's round face went blank. "He does? Who said so? I'm leaving instructions."

Judith didn't know whether or not Renie was kidding. Bill Jones, Ph.D., clinical psychologist and tenured professor, knew his way around a textbook better than a cookbook. She gazed at the group family photograph on the coffee table. Bill Jones's square, serious face gazed back. Next to him was Renie, with her thick chestnut hair worn long and about six months pregnant. Bill and Renie each held a toddler. Mike, at two and a half, reposed in Judith's arms. Dan McMonigle loomed behind her, scowling at the camera. The picture had been taken in this same living room at Christmas, some

5

twenty years earlier.

"A lot of these faces aren't around anymore," Judith remarked sadly.

Renie glanced at the photo. "Right. My dad's. Dan. Grandma Grover. But," she added brightly, "we've added a few. Our youngest, Tony. Your Joe. Cousin Sue's granddaughter. The twins by—"

A sharp ringing sound rattled the living room. Renie jumped; Judith sighed.

"I wish," Judith said through gritted teeth, "Mother wouldn't do that unless it's really an emergency." Getting to her feet, she headed for the French doors at the end of the living room.

Renie trotted along behind. "Maybe something *is* wrong," she suggested. "Maybe she fell. Maybe she's sick."

Going down the short flight of stairs that led to the backyard, Judith threw Renie a disparaging look. "Maybe she overdosed on Granny Goodness Chewy Centers. Give me a break, coz—Mother doesn't have emergencies. She just causes them."

The February air was raw. The trio of fruit trees, which were all that was left of the original Grover orchard, stood gnarled and bare. Except for a brave camellia bush with bright buds beginning to unfold, the garden was fallow. There was ice on the birdbath, and the small statue of St. Francis looked as if he could use a sweater. The cousins trudged down the walk to the converted toolshed which was now the home of Gertrude Grover.

"Mother! Yoo-hoo!" Judith banged on the door.

There was no sound from within. Judith leaned her statuesque frame against the door, listening. She called again to her mother. With a trace of apprehension, she

6

tried the doorknob. The door was locked.

"Damn!" Judith breathed. Her strong features puckered in frustration. She turned to Renie. "Check the front window. She must have been alive a couple of minutes ago or she wouldn't have set off that blasted buzzer."

Renie, who was almost six inches shorter than Judith, had to stand on tiptoe to look through the window. "I don't see her," she said, sounding worried. "She must be in the bathroom or her bedroom."

Judith hopped off the single step and headed back to the house, this time toward the entrance to the kitchen. "I'll get my keys," she muttered, seeing her breath go before her on the cold February air.

Judith disappeared inside the big old Edwardian house. Renie was pacing in front of the smaller structure, trying to keep warm, when Gertrude snatched open the front door and made a peculiar noise.

"H-u-u-u-t! Therena! Where did that lamebrained kid of mine go? The'd better be coming back with a think plunger!"

Renie stared at her aunt. "You're okay? We thought you'd had a stroke. Why are you talking like that?"

Leaning on her walker, Gertrude snorted. "Never mind. What if I'd had a throke? Or two of 'em. Who'd care? Not Knucklehead or her dim-witted huthband." Between Gertrude's feet, an orange-and-white cat eyed Renie with little yellow eyes. Gertrude nudged the animal with her foot. "Beat it, you flea-bitten creep! You ate my creamed tuna on toatht!"

Sweetums flew out into the yard, stopped at the far edge of the small patio, arched his back, and hissed. Gertrude hissed back. Sweetums gave the equivalent of a shrug and ventured into the Rankerses' hedge.

7

"Mother!" Judith was poised at the top of the porch steps. "What happened?"

Impatiently, Gertrude gestured with her right arm, her baggy electric-blue cardigan flapping in the breeze. "Come here! Put thome leg in it!"

Running on command, Judith dashed past Renie, who duly followed both of the other women inside the little apartment. The cousins came to a standstill behind Gertrude and her walker. "The toilet," she said, clumping toward the bathroom, which also contained a sink and a shower stall. Stepping aside, Gertrude gave the walker a final bang. "I lotht my dentureth. Get 'em out, and hurry up!"

Standing over the toilet, Judith could see no sign of dentures. "Oh, jeez!" she breathed, rolling her eyes. "How on earth did you do *that?*"

Gertrude drew herself up to her full height, which was diminutive at best. She spoke with dignity: "I sneethed. Tho what?"

Judith's high forehead furrowed. "You . . . ? Oh! You *sneezed!*"

"Thath what I thaid!" Gertrude was getting angry. "Now get my dentureth!"

It took Judith ten minutes to find the plumber's snake and another fifteen to fish out Gertrude's teeth. Renie tried to help, but couldn't provide much more than moral support, which took the edge off Gertrude's nagging. When at last the upper plate had been retrieved, Judith insisted on sanitizing it with a run through the dishwasher. Gertrude demurred: She could rinse her own damned teeth with boiling water from the teakettle. What did people do before there were dishwashers anyway? That was the trouble with the modern generation—they had to have all kinds of fancy-pants appliances, like automatic dryers, clothes washers without wringers, plug-in irons instead of mangles, and stupid telephone answering machines where stupid people left stupid messages because they were too stupid to stay home. Given that Gertrude's litany was delivered in her present irksome lisp, Judith was grateful that she never got to "espresso machine." Before that happened, Joe came home from work early. Gertrude and her walker scampered back inside the toolshed. She was not anxious to see her son-in-law. She never was.

Joe's ruddy round face lit up when Judith told him about Gertrude's mishap. The gold flecks in his green eyes danced. He all but skipped inside the house, with his wife and her cousin at his heels.

"You're mean, Joe," Judith chided as Joe headed for the liquor cabinet in the kitchen. "No wonder Mother thinks you're such a jerk."

"I didn't start out being mean," Joe replied, not bothering to ask, but automatically pouring a bourbon for Renie and scotch for himself and Judith. "I liked your mother. She was crusty, but benign. Since we finally got married, she's just crusty. If I didn't carry a weapon, I'd worry."

Judith's oval face was aghast. "Joe! If you two could get along, it would make life easier for me."

Joe was leading the way into the living room, shedding his raincoat and loosening his tie en route. He paused at the built-in china cabinet in the dining room to catch his reflection in the wavery glass. "Hey," he said, running a comb through his red hair which was going gray at the temples, "I'm not the one who wouldn't live under the same roof. I was perfectly willing to let her stay in the house after we were married. Leaving was her idea, not mine."

It was true. Joe and Judith had a history, dating back a quarter of a century to when they had been engaged the first time. But Joe, in a drunken stupor induced by a vice assignment with tragic results for two teenagers, had fallen prey to another woman. Instead of going home to sleep it off, he had awakened in bed with a new bride. Somehow, Herself, as Judith was wont to call Vivian Flynn, had managed to get Joe on board a Las Vegas-bound jet, off to a justice of the peace, and into legal wedlock. The detour had cut off twenty-five years of Joe and Judith's life together. Judith had forgiven him, but her mother had not. Gertrude Grover disliked Joe Flynn almost as much as she had Dan McMonigle. She had sworn never to live under the same roof with Joe. To her surprise, Joe had moved in. Gertrude had bitten her tongue—and moved out. For several months she and Renie's mother had coexisted in Aunt Deb's apartment. While there was affection between the two sisters-in-law, they tended to get on each other's nerves. Or so the more kindly Deborah Grover would have phrased it. To Judith and Renie, they made everyone, including each other, crazy as bedbugs. Judith had resolved the problem by remodeling the toolshed so Gertrude could come back to her own turf.

But the war wasn't over; the truce was tenuous. Judith knew that the twenty yards of garden that separated Joe and Gertrude was really a demilitarized zone. She wished it were not so.

Over the rim of her highball glass, Renie gave Judith a sympathetic look. Two years apart in age, the cousins were without siblings. A mere three blocks had separated them while growing up, and the emotional distance was even closer. Judith and Renie could almost read each other's minds.

"You've done your best, coz," Renie declared. "It was hell on wheels when we had to move my mother out of her house and into the apartment a few years back. You remember. But we had no choice. She simply couldn't manage on her own once she had to stay in the wheelchair."

Judith nodded in sympathy. While Renie's mother didn't have Gertrude's sharp tongue, she was a world-class whiner. "Getting old is the pits," Judith said, "but being middle-aged isn't always a lot of fun, either. Between Mike at one end and Mother at the other, I feel like sandwich filling. When I was young, I figured that by the time I reached my late forties, life ought to have smoothed out, with some sort of watershed before—"

The phone interrupted Judith. She got off the sofa and went over to the extension on a small cherry-wood table. If her frown hadn't told Renie and Joe that the call wasn't welcome, her words would have conveyed the message:

"Of course, Aunt Toadie . . . Yes, we can do that . . . No, we don't wear uniforms . . . Well, we'd have to rent them and charge you for . . . No, I'm never asked to do that . . . A skit? . . . I don't think so. Why don't you hire a couple of actors? Yes . . . yes . . . yes . . . no. Right, thanks for calling. 'Bye." Judith slammed the phone down and stalked back to the sofa. "Witch. She wants us to wear uniforms and put on a little play about the beginnings of the Major Mush Company. I'll bet she wants to see me dressed up as a bag of oats."

"Oh, Gawd!" Renie collapsed against the sofa and rolled her eyes. "You did say no, didn't you?"

Judith's black eyes snapped at Renie. "You heard me. Of course I said no. If she wants a skit, she can hire somebody—or get her loathsome daughter, Trixie, to do it. If anybody can play a part, it's that phony baggage. She's acted her way through more divorce hearings than the Gabor sisters."

"Trixie!" Renie was now looking appalled. "She'll be there, too?" She saw Judith nod. "Which husband is it now? I stopped counting at Rafe Longrod, or whatever his name was."

"The Porno King?" Judith shook her head. "She dumped him a year or so ago. He was Number Three, officially. Trixie's engaged, as she so quaintly puts it when she's between legal mates, to some guy named Mason Meade. I think he's into concrete."

"That makes sense," mused Joe. "The last time I ate a bowl of Major Mush, it tasted like concrete."

Judith gave her husband a mocking glance. "Your palate is too refined, my darling. The unwashed masses have been slopping up Major Mush since World War One. Uncle Boo's grandfather started out with a few acres of corn in the Midwest a hundred years ago, bought up more land, sowed more crops, and hauled in big bucks during the glory years of the American farmer. Then his son got the bright idea of starting his own breakfast cereal company. Dunlop Major founded his mush business in Minneapolis in 1918, made a killing, and retired to the Pacific Northwest. I guess he couldn't stand the cold winters and the hot summers on the Great Plains. Maybe he couldn't stand the mush."

Renie, who had taken in Judith's recital without batting an eye, yawned. "All I know is that Uncle Boo has never lifted a finger in his life. He's the laziest man I ever met. Talk about sloth being one of the Seven Deadly Sins! It's also a major vice with Uncle Boo— pardon the pun. One Christmas I saw him go to sleep

12

while he was filling his face with my mother's plum pudding. He was snoring when he ate the plastic holly decoration."

Judith shrugged. "I don't doubt it. Uncle Boo has never had to work. Old Dunlop left him millions. He just sits there in his big mansion over on The Bluff and dozes in front of the TV and talks to invisible green spacemen. At least when Aunt Rosie was alive, she made him get out once in a while."

Joe had gotten off the sofa to pile kindling in the fireplace. "Hold it," he said in his mild, mellow voice. "I know that Uncle Boo and Aunt Toadie and Aunt Rosie and the rest of them aren't related to you two except by marriage to Uncle Corky and that you're thankful for it, but how the hell are they related to each other?"

"Easy," Renie replied. "Aunt Toadie's eldest sister, Rosie, married Uncle Boo late in life. Like over forty, though I now consider that later in youth. Uncle Boo never had much energy to do anything, including getting married. I suspect Rosie swept him off his feet. There's another sister, Vivvie, who's a widow. She's the middle one of the three Lott girls, right, coz?"

Judith nodded. "Right. Real names Rosalinda, Viveca, and Theodora. Thus Rosie, Vivvie, and Toadie. They fight constantly. Or at least they did when Aunt Rosie was still alive." She paused, giving Renie a sheepish look. "Uh—I forgot to tell you—Aunt Vivvie is coming to the party. So is her son, Derek, his wife, and their daughter."

Renie's initial dismay turned to resignation. "Oh, well—you said there'd be other family members present. I guess I was hoping they'd be from Uncle Boo's side, not Toadie's."

"There isn't anybody on Uncle Boo's side," Judith said, taking a small sip of scotch. "That's how he ended up so rich and lazy. He was the sole heir."

Finishing her drink, Renie got to her feet. "We'll manage. After all, it's only for a few hours. Got to run and get dinner for—"

The buzzer again shattered the peace of the living room. Joe, in the act of setting off his fire, dropped the match and burned his fingers. He swore. Judith leaped from the sofa, heading for the French doors. Renie followed.

"Maybe she melted her teeth," Renie suggested as they went outside.

"Maybe," Judith responded. "I wish I'd never had the bright idea for that buzzer system. Mother's going to drive me nuts."

At the edge of the walk, Renie started for her car, which was parked in the driveway. "Stop bitching." She grinned. "Thank your lucky stars she's as good as she is."

Halfway to the toolshed, Judith whirled and stared at Renie. "Good? As in good for what?"

Renie shook her head. "Not for what—for who. She's not Aunt Toadie. What more could you ask?"

Judith considered. Maybe Renie was right. By comparison, Gertrude Grover was a gem. "Mother!" Judith called, all but running. "I'm coming! Hey, Mother—have I told you lately that I love you? Mother! Yoo-hoo, you sweet thing!"

In the doorway, Gertrude leaned on her walker, looking astonished. For once she was speechless. Judith gave her a big hug.

"Whath thith all about?" Gertrude demanded, shaking free of her daughter. "You want to borrow money?"

"No," Judith answered with a wide smile. She paused, waving to Renie, who was backing out of the driveway. "It's just that . . . hey, where are your teeth?"

Gertrude snorted. "Thath why I called for you. They're gone."

"Gone where?" Judith shut the door behind her, noting that the apartment was warm and cozy.

"Tholen," replied Gertrude. "Hidden, to be egthact. Under my bed. I can't reach 'em."

Judith eyed her mother curiously. "Hidden under your bed? By—oh!"

The perpetrator sat on a braided rug Grandma Grover had made some fifty years earlier. The long tail curled around the furry body, and the yellow eyes were defiant. Judith made a face.

"You got it," said Gertrude. "Thweetumth. That cat'th a petht."

"Yeth," said Judith. "Ah—*yes*, Mother—he sure is."

TWO

THE TUDOR MANSION ON THE BLUFF HAD ONCE offered a commanding western view of the bay, the islands that sprawled across the sound, and the majestic mountain range on the peninsula. To the north, Dunlop Major had enjoyed gazing at his own gardens, complete with rose arbors and a lily pond. South, and slightly to the east, he could have seen the burgeoning downtown, a pretty, if not impressive sight in 1933. And out of the windows which faced east, he had looked over the rest of the city and beyond, to the towering peaks that split the state in two.

Some sixty years later, if his son, Boo Major, had the energy to get out of his easy chair, he would find the view from the main floor cut off on all sides—except for the garden. Other houses surrounded the block on which Major Manor stood, and while they were costly and handsome, none could compare with the mansion built by mush.

"We're supposed to go in through the tradesmen's entrance," Judith said to Renie as they pulled up across the street on a cold, gray, late Friday afternoon. "Aunt Toadie said to park at least a block away because of all the guests. Only the family can use the driveway. I say screw it, I'm parking the Nissan here. This neighborhood is so stodgy that nobody leaves a car on the street anyway. They all have double and triple garages. We need to be close to the house because we've got so much stuff to carry."

Renie was staring at the imposing brick and half-timbered mansion. "I've never been here before. Have

16

you?"

Judith shook her head. "I've only met Uncle Boo at family doings where we generous Grovers included all the shirttail relations. He and Aunt Rosie used to come for Thanksgiving and Christmas Eve, remember?"

Renie nodded. "How could I forget? All the entertaining with the Majors and the Lotts has been one-sided. They may have the money, but we've got the time. And still we've always gotten stuck paying for everything. Leeches, my mother calls them, though she uses a more tactful word."

Judith nodded agreement as she clicked on the overhead light and lifted the cake-box lid to make sure the frosting hadn't been damaged in transit. She had finally convinced Aunt Toadie that a birthday party required a birthday cake. With ill grace, Toadie had asked Judith to place an order with Begelman's Bakery, insisting that the cake should be baked in the shape of a cereal bowl with frosting that would resemble oatmeal mush. The visual result was repellent, resembling curdled cottage cheese, but the cake itself would taste delicious. The added expense had forced Aunt Toadie to dump her plan for a skit.

"The icing survived," Judith noted. "You're right, coz—we're a long-suffering family. Aunt Rosie hated to entertain and Aunt Toadie hated us."

Renie glanced at the cake before Judith closed the lid. "Gruesome," she remarked, making a face. "But appropriate in oh-so-many ways. If I hadn't loved the rest of our relatives, inviting the Lotts to family gatherings would have spoiled everything, even when I was a kid."

"Grandma and Grandpa Grover were too kind about including strays," Judith said, securing the cake box

17

with extra tape.

"Being imposed upon is a Grover family tradition," Renie observed with a grimace. "We're too well mannered to complain. Remember how Uncle Boo would sit down in Grandpa Grover's favorite chair and never get up? Still, he's kind of sweet. I haven't seen him since Aunt Rosie's funeral three years ago."

"That was something," Judith remarked, checking through the carton on the floor by Renie's feet to make sure she had all of her catering gadgets. "Uncle Boo and Aunt Rosie never went to church, and when Father Hoyle came into the funeral parlor, he thought Uncle Boo was the one who had died. Aunt Rosie looked a lot livelier." She fingered a corkscrew, a sharp knife, a box of cocktail napkins, a blender, and a hand mixer. Judith had learned from sad experience never to count on any kitchen being fully equipped.

Loaded down with boxes, the cousins crossed the street. They would have to go back to the car for the cases of wine and sparkling cider. The neighborhood was very quiet. While Hillside Manor was situated at the end of a relatively peaceful cul-de-sac, the Rankerses, the Dooleys, the Ericsons, the Porters, and the Steins provided enough bustle to give the street a sense of vitality. By contrast, The Bluff seemed moribund. Judith wondered if Uncle Boo wasn't the only one who was asleep on his feet.

The three-car garage was closed up, but a new Buick Park Avenue was parked in the drive. In the wan winter light, Judith studied the mansion. The garage jutted out from the house, with a flat roof discreetly hidden by crenellated masonry. A scaffolding stood at the south end, and it appeared that some brickwork was in progress. A stack of lumber sat at one side of the garden

18

near a huge birdbath fashioned from volcanic rock. The latticed gazebo sported a new shake roof. Judith wondered what had inspired the improvements.

The so-called tradesmen's entrance was actually the back door, which was reached off the small cement porch by a short passageway. Next to the porch itself were two recessed garbage cans. At ground level, concrete steps led into the basement. Evidence of an old-fashioned cooler was at the cousins' left; a carefully stacked woodpile and an empty shelf marked "Deliveries" were on the right. It was tricky to ring the bell while hanging onto the cartons, but Judith managed. Though the lights were on inside, no one responded. Judith tackled the bell a second time.

"I'm coming, I'm coming," shouted a husky female voice. Judith frowned at Renie. The voice didn't belong to Aunt Toadie.

The door was jerked open by a stout, red-haired, middle-aged woman in a purple velour sweat suit. "Whaddya want?" she demanded. "You from the upholsterers?"

Judith's mind raced: The woman was staff, part of a family that had been with Uncle Boo for years. But Judith couldn't remember the name. "No, ma'am," she replied, "we're the caterers."

The woman eyed Judith and Renie with suspicious green eyes. "Caterers? Where's your van?"

"We have a car. It's across the street." Judith tried to smile but failed. The boxes teetered awkwardly in her grasp.

"Caterers have vans," the woman asserted, planting herself so that she neatly blocked the door. "Who hired you? That old bat, Toadie Grover?"

Judith felt a sudden kinship with the redoubtable

woman who barred their way. Renie, however, felt no such thing. She could barely see over her boxes and was now jumping up and down on the small side porch.

"Hurry up, lady," Renie ordered. "I'm about to drop a load of shrimp balls."

"You can drop triplets for all I care," the woman snapped. But she moved aside. "Put your junk on that counter. Don't get the floor dirty. Use the green garbage can for glass, the blue for aluminum, the red for paper, the yellow for—"

"Rubbish!" snapped Renie. "I didn't get drafted into this army, I volunteered! Who are you, and why do I want to beat you up?"

Taken aback, the stout, redheaded woman gave Renie the once-over. "You're kind of puny, but you might be tough," she allowed, then put out her hand. "Hi, I'm Mrs. Wakefield, the Major housekeeper. Weed's resting."

Startled, Judith almost dropped a box of sesame crackers. "What?"

Mrs. Wakefield sneered. "Weed. My husband, the valet and chauffeur and butler and gardener and general handyman. Except he doesn't do much of that stuff because he doesn't like to waste his energy. And who needs it? I work hard enough for both of us."

Judith gazed around the kitchen. It was not big— indeed, it was somewhat smaller than her own at Hillside Manor. The small green-and-white tiles which covered the counters looked as if they were the original craftsmanship. So did the light green paint which was peeling in places on the cabinets. The sink was vintage Depression era, as was the flecked white linoleum. The refrigerator was also old, though large. Only the dishwasher bespoke a more modem age. The effect was tasteful, efficient, and designed strictly for the hired help. No gracious hostess ever whipped up omelettes or pan-fried chicken in this kitchen, thought Judith. She felt as if she'd stepped into a time warp.

Mrs. Wakefield was looking at her watch, a large-faced model with a wide red band. "It's four-forty. The guests'll be here at six. Go to it. You're serving sixty-eight." She started toward one of two doors which stood side by side at the far end of the kitchen.

"Wait a minute," Judith exclaimed. "Aunt Toadie said fifty-five. What's going on here?"

Over her shoulder, Mrs. Wakefield shot Judith a grazing glance. "Don't ask me, honey. Go ask Aunt Toadie. She's in the living room, drinking like a sailor." Wide hips swaying, the housekeeper opened the door with frosted glass and tromped down a flight of stairs. She didn't bother to close the door behind her.

Judith stared at Renie. "What a zoo! Why did I ever agree to this?"

Renie's brown eyes were wide. "Because you're getting paid for it?"

Judith shut the door to the downstairs. "If that's up to Aunt Toadie, I wouldn't guarantee the check won't bounce. You start hauling in the wine. I'll be right back." She headed in what she hoped was the direction of the living room.

It was, but first she passed through a paneled dining room featuring a big bay window, a large entry hall with a handsome staircase, and several doors which led, she presumed, to coat closets, bathrooms, and possibly a den.

Aunt Toadie wasn't drinking like a sailor. She was drinking like Aunt Toadie, which was genteel swizzling, at least as far as Judith could recall from family

21

gatherings. In her late sixties, Theodora Lott Bellew Grover had pale, bleached blond hair, a once-shapely figure now corseted into planes and angles, and a pretty face that owed much to Nature and even more to plastic surgery. She took one look at Judith and began to gush.

"Judith! Dear heart! How sweet of you to come! Where's darling Serena? I always just loved her pug nose and buckteeth!"

Judith tried not to reel in Aunt Toadie's heavily perfumed embrace. "Renie's in the kitchen," she murmured, her chin stuck somewhere in the furls of Aunt Toadie's dye job. "Her teeth aren't buck, they're just big."

Toadie stepped back, but still kept her hands on Judith's shoulders. Two silver charm bracelets jangled at her right wrist. "Of course! Our skinny little beaver! And you! I haven't seen you since you finally landed what's-his-name and put on all that extra weight! Having a man around must suit you, dear heart! How adorable! You look positively pandalike!"

Judith, who was always sensitive about her weight, bridled. "I haven't gained more than five pounds in the last two years," she declared, almost truthfully. "Where's Uncle Boo?"

At last Toadie Grover released Judith. She gestured toward a wing-backed chair which faced the marble fireplace. "There, dearest! He's having a nap! The poor old darling is tired out from smoking a cigar! Would you like to give him a teensy kiss?"

Judith would not, but she approached the chair anyway. It took a while, since the living room was long and stately. The stuccoed walls were fitted with wrought-iron sconces. A chandelier, also of wrought iron, hung from the center of the ceiling. The furniture was old, handsome, and, like everything else in the house, had probably been in place since 1933.

So, it seemed, had Uncle Boo. When Judith leaned over the arm of his chair, he stirred, barely. Bruno Major looked much younger than his seventy-five years, which wasn't surprising, given his lack of exertion and carefree existence. Or so Judith thought as she planted a pristine kiss on his soft pink cheek.

"Happy birthday, Uncle Boo," she said. "Serena and I have come to help you celebrate."

Uncle Boo's gray eyes were vague. "You have? Celebrate what?" He gazed around the living room, his cherubic face wearing the faintest hint of alarm. "Oh! My birthday! Now, isn't that nice of you. Be sure to invite those little green men out on the lawn." He resettled himself into the wing chair and nodded off.

"What a darling," Toadie exclaimed softly. "Come, Judith, let's go into the den and discuss your duties."

Judith thought they already had. After no fewer than nine calls from Aunt Toadie during the past week, Judith couldn't imagine any details left untouched. There was no choice, however, but to humor her.

The den was off the entry hall, its door recessed some four feet, with a coat closet on one side and a cupboard on the other. Aunt Toadie fiddled with a key, then ushered Judith into the room.

"Boo always locks the door," she explained as Judith admired the boxed parquet floor, a bronze chandelier with four candle-shaped bulbs, and the glass-fronted bookcases that lined the walls. Judith wondered if anyone at Major Manor had read the hand-tooled leather volumes of Shakespeare, Dickens, Melville, Hardy, and Hawthorn, among others. As a former librarian, she itched to hold the books in her hands and savor the wonderful words penned by the masters. Toadie didn't seem to notice that Judith's attention was straying. "Boo keeps all his important papers in here," she announced in a smug tone that brought Judith to heel. "Of course, I have access to everything since Rosie passed away. Boo needs a woman to lean on."

Judith refrained from saying that it looked as if Boo could also lean on a telephone pole, a maple tree, or a lamppost. "It's nice of you to keep tabs on him," she remarked cautiously. She wasn't exactly sure what Toadie had meant.

The older woman had seated herself behind a large, uncluttered desk made of Philippine mahogany. Judith observed that it was the wood of choice for Major Manor. The paneling in the den, along with that of the other rooms she'd just seen, was done in the same rich brown wood.

Judith pulled up a side chair, noting that the original radiators still stood in the den. A pair of leaded windows flanked the bookcase behind the desk. Unlike the old leather-bound volumes that were crammed into the shelves along the other walls, the books on these shelves—which were not fronted by glass—appeared to be popular reading. They were mainly bestsellers that spanned some fifty years, with a few biographies and pop culture volumes thrown in. A large cardboard carton at least six feet tall and four feet wide filled a corner of the room. Judith regarded it with curiosity.

Aunt Toadie followed Judith's gaze. "Boo got a new, big-screen TV set for his birthday from Vivvie and her son, Derek." She spoke their names with distaste. "Boo was going to put it in here, but I said it would overwhelm the den. I had it moved upstairs to the master bedroom. So much more convenient, though such a large screen is quite unnecessary. Boo's vision is exceptional for his age."

"Amazing," Judith remarked, marveling not at Boo's eyesight so much as at the generosity of Toadie's sister and nephew. Derek Rush, however, had always been close to Boo, or so Uncle Corky had once revealed.

Aunt Toadie had put on her half-glasses, which she wore on a gold chain. Charm bracelets a-jangle, she opened the desk drawer and took out a single sheet of paper. "The guests from Major Mush are local employees of the company's branch office here. And their families, of course. Some are retired, some are active. We want to treat these people generously. However, we don't want them to gorge." Her voice had changed, from the usual high-pitched gush to a deeper, brisker tone. "Don't pass the food and drink trays more than twice. They're due to stay approximately one hour. If anyone lingers after seven o'clock, Mr. Wakefield will take care of them."

Judith blinked. She had visions of Mr. Wakefield picking up any laggards by the scruffs of their necks and hurling them out into the frosty night.

"Boo is receiving them in the entry hall," Toadie continued, removing her glasses and allowing them to dangle against a black cashmere sweater which sported tiny silver rivets. "Then they'll be ushered into the living room to enjoy themselves with food and beverage." She leaned forward, fixing Judith with her cold blue eyes. "How many jugs did you bring?"

"Jugs?" Judith looked startled. "I didn't bring the wine in jugs. I never do. I brought two cases of Chablis, one of rosé, one Riesling, and one Burgundy. Sparkling cider, too. Nobody said anything about *jugs*."

Aunt Toadie's gaze was reproachful. "Judith! I know

25

we discussed the wine. How on earth could you bring so much? I hope you don't intend to bill us for it!"

Judith's strong chin jutted. "When it comes to beverages, I bill for what's consumed. With food, I charge for all of it, because leftovers usually won't keep."

Frowning, Toadie drew circles on the sheet of paper which lay before her. "How big are the plastic glasses?"

Judith gestured with her hands. "Three inches, I'd say." She wished they were as big as beer steins. "We've also brought along plates and forks and napkins. The appetizers are shrimp balls, pickled herring in sour cream, Bavarian ham finger sandwiches, strawberries dipped in dark chocolate, Norwegian sardines, and smoked oysters. I've got Brie and Gouda and Havarti for cheeses. Oh, and crackers, of course. Four kinds—sesame, water wafers . . ."

Toadie Grover was reeling in Uncle Boo's chair. "Oh, my God! This is outrageous! What are you trying to do—bankrupt us?"

Keeping a rein on her temper, Judith lowered her voice. "Aunt Toadie, we talked often and at length this week. You kept saying you wanted a really nice party for Uncle Boo. I mentioned several of the items I would provide. You never contradicted me. What was I to think?"

Toadie had now assumed a stern air. "The problem with you, Judith, is that you *don't* think. You never have. I remember one Christmas Eve when you were a little girl, and after Santa left, they took down the big curtain that hid the tree and the presents. You acted so impulsively, diving right into the living room and smashing the doll bed your parents had given you. Of course, it wouldn't have happened if you hadn't been

26

such a heavy child."

Judith bristled. "It wouldn't have happened at all if Trixie hadn't pushed me." Vividly, she remembered her younger cousin leaping among the pretty packages, screaming, "Mine! Mine! I want! Now!" Renie, who was never one to suffer fools gladly even in her youth, had put a headlock on Trixie and carried her off to the coal bin in the basement. Renie had been punished for her temerity but always swore it was worth it.

Toadie was still looking severe. "Never mind all that petty bickering. We're in the present, Judith. My estimate of the cost for tonight clearly doesn't match yours. We'll have to hammer it out later. Right now, you've got work to do. And I must change."

Judith was still angry. She'd spent two days and two hundred dollars preparing for Uncle Boo's party. Aunt Toadie was going to squirm off the hook when she got the bill. Judith should have known. There was no point in arguing until push came to shove. Judith also got to her feet.

The phone on the desk rang, a sharp, jarring sound. Toadie picked it up, then grimaced. "It's for you," she announced.

Judith's high forehead creased. She took the old-fashioned black handset receiver from Toadie and heard Joe's voice on the other end.

"Jude-girl," he began, using the nickname that she'd never liked and he refused to abandon, "I've got a problem."

"What? Where are you?" Judith checked her watch. It was after five. Joe should be on his way home. A sense of unease crept over her.

"I'm still at work. I knew it was too good to be true when I got off early a couple of days this week. Now I

27

get stuck on a priority missing-persons investigation. I'll probably work through the weekend."

Judith's heart sank. At the door, Toadie sensed apprehension in the air, and seemed to enjoy it. "But the guests! What shall I do?" Judith wailed.

Joe's voice took on a miserable note. "I don't know, Jude-girl. I feel rotten about this. Believe me, I wouldn't do it if the marching orders hadn't come down from the Mayor's office."

Briefly, Judith forgot her own dilemma. "The Mayor? Who's missing? His campaign manager for reelection?"

Joe's chuckle was jagged. "Not quite. It's his cousin, a city building inspector who disappeared yesterday. Reliable guy, family man, no kinks, no quirks. But he never came home last night. We're presuming he met with foul play. That's why I got assigned, to cover the homicide angle. Ordinarily, we don't consider anybody officially missing until they've been gone forty-eight hours. But this is different—the Mayor and his family are frantic."

Joe had managed to tap Judith's deep well of compassion. "No wonder. That's terrible. Gosh, Joe—it sounds as if the Mayor has a lot of faith in you if you've been assigned to the case. Isn't it a feather in your cap?"

Joe's attempts at modesty rarely succeeded. "Oh, maybe. It was either me or Buck Doerflinger, and I'll be damned if I let that self-serving S.O.B. get ahead of me. He's a showboater, but since life is unfair, the next promotion will probably go to him instead of me. When it comes to complicated investigations, he's a washout. I call him Mr. Obvious."

Among other things, thought Judith, well aware of her husband's contempt for his archrival in the Homicide Division. "You'll do your usual bang-up job," she assured Joe. "And I'll cope without you. Maybe Corinne Dooley can come over and help. With all those kids of hers, she's used to feeding mobs. I'll give her a buzz."

Joe allowed that Mrs. Dooley was a possibility. His voice grew deeper, softer. "I'll be home around eleven. Will you be waiting for me?"

Judith wished Toadie would leave the den. "Of course," she replied.

"In bed?" Joe asked.

"Right, sure, you know it."

"I'll try not to be too tired," he said, and this time his chuckle was more hearty.

"Oh, good, that'd be wonderful." Judith felt her cheeks flush.

"What will you be wearing?" Joe inquired, despite the eruption of voices in the background.

"Uh—something. Yes, something long."

"The hot-pink number?" Joe suggested as the voices grew louder. "Or the black lace?"

"One of the above," Judith responded weakly.

Joe finally caught on, or else his fellow detectives were nagging at him to get going. "Good, great. Got to run. Hey, be careful coming off The Bluff. It's supposed to rain, and if it's cold enough, it could turn to snow or ice up."

Judith promised to exercise due care. She hung up, then informed Toadie she had to make a phone call. She half-expected her aunt to tell her to leave a quarter on the desk.

Corinne Dooley was in the middle of making dinner for her brood. But nine children had given her flexibility in more ways than one. She cheerfully agreed to greet the B&B guests and provide them with sherry and the hors d'oeuvres Judith had already prepared. Relieved, Judith returned to the kitchen.

Renie had already brought in the wine and cider. "It's starting to rain," she announced, running a hand through her damp chestnut curls. "When do we heat the Brie and the shrimp balls?"

Judith suggested they wait until shortly before the guests' arrival. Relating Joe's tale of woe to Renie, she also recounted the interview with Aunt Toadie. Renie shook her head.

"You know how cheap she is," Renie pointed out, slicing Havarti cheese with Judith's sharp knife. "Remember the year she gave me Trixie's outgrown playclothes for my doll? On my tenth birthday, I got an eraser."

Judith nodded. "Same here. But what gets me is that she isn't paying for this party. Uncle Boo is—or so I was led to believe. I mean, it's a legitimate business expense, right? Not to mention that he's loaded. But Toadie acts as if it's *her* money, too. What's going on?"

Renie leaned against the wooden counter. "I don't know. My mother talks to Aunt Toadie now and then. Mom and Uncle Corky have always been pretty close. I gathered that Toadie was keeping an eye on Uncle Boo because she doesn't think the Wakefields are reliable."

Opening a tin of smoked oysters, Judith gave Renie a questioning look. "I've never met the Wakefields before, though I recall that they've been with him forever. In fact, they came here not long after Aunt Rosie and Uncle Boo got married, right?"

Renie shook her head. "No, I don't think so. Old Dunlop was still alive then. The Wakefields came after he died, somewhere around the time you and I went to Europe."

"That's right," Judith responded. "Old Dunlop went to that big barley field in the sky while we were in Vienna. That was 1964." Having set out the oysters, Judith tackled the stove. She studied the dials and smiled. "Wow, is this old! It must be good, though. I'll bet it's the original model." Checking the oven, she found it in need of a good cleaning, and shrugged. "It'll do for heating up. What's this?" She pointed to a steaming pressure cooker atop the stove.

Renie glanced around from her task of placing water wafers on a plate. "Mrs. Wakefield returned briefly to put on some beet greens. I wish she hadn't. I hate pressure cookers." Renie sneezed. "Drat! I got choked up outside getting the wine. There's dust all over the place. It must be from the masonry work. The rain ought to settle it. Hay fever I don't need tonight."

Cautiously, Judith turned on the oven. There was less than half an hour before the guests were due to arrive. Judith was setting plastic wineglasses on a tray when the frosted glass door opened and a languid, auburn-haired beauty drifted into the kitchen.

"Hi," she breathed, not hesitating before slipping a smoked oyster between her full lips. "I'm Zoe Wakefield, the Major maid."

Judith and Renie stared. Zoe did not look like a maid. She was dressed in a white poet's shirt and a tiered green velvet skirt. Her bountiful auburn hair was piled casually on her head, revealing perfect ears with clusters of dangling pearls that couldn't possibly have been real. Judith guessed Zoe's age in the mid-to-late twenties, but couldn't be sure.

Regaining her aplomb, Judith introduced herself and Renie. "Are you helping us, Ms. Wakefield?"

Zoe ate another oyster. "Helping you with what?"

31

Long, curling lashes dipped over riveting big eyes of an uncertain color. Gold? Green? Amber? Judith realized she was staring.

"The party," she replied with forced cheer. "Mrs. Grover hasn't made it clear to us who is doing what."

"Mrs. Grover is an idiot." Zoe Wakefield spoke with scorn, her perfect chin tilted upward.

Neither of the cousins felt like arguing with Zoe. Judith, however, pressed on: "The problem is that we've got to serve the Major Mush guests, then get dinner ready for the family. We thought maybe you or your mother would help us between six and seven."

Zoe's laugh was lovely, a musical cascade of notes that rippled around the kitchen. "This event is in Mrs. Grover's hands. Officially, my parents and I have the night off. In fact," she went on, going over to the sink to gaze through the window, "my drama club meets this evening. I wonder if I should go. That rain looks like sleet." Zoe drifted off toward the dining room and into the entry hall.

"We're the designated saps," Renie declared, giving the cutting board a whack with the kitchen knife. "We're stuck with this whole show, right, coz?"

Judith was chewing on her forefinger and thinking frantically. "Right, right," she answered vaguely. "Let's see—we heat the party stuff; then the rack of lamb can go in just after six. Dinner is at eight, after the relatives have time to get tight as ticks or deck each other or whatever. New potatoes, broccoli with béchamel sauce, cauliflower Allemande, rolls, crème brûlée for dessert." Pointing to the stove, she grimaced. "We might do it. It'll be rugged, but we've got no choice. Mrs. Wakefield will have to remove her beet greens, though. I'll go downstairs to tell her."

32

But first Judith opened the door next to the one that led to the basement. As she had suspected, the stairs went upward. Judith reasoned that the triple garage must be reached through the door in the adjacent wall. She headed downstairs. The part of the basement which she entered by the back stairs was obviously the servants' quarters. A narrow hall was flanked by several closed doors. Outerwear hung on brass hooks at the bottom of the steps. Two jackets, one dark green, the other red, were flanked by a long brown raincoat and a large black loden coat. At the far end of the hallway was a small door about three feet off the floor. Judith guessed it was the laundry chute. She paused, not knowing where to find the housekeeper or her husband.

A strange aroma wafted along the corridor. Judith sniffed. She made a face. She knew the smell from some of her more daring guests. And, in his teenaged years, from Mike. If Judith hadn't figured out much concerning the Major Manor ménage, at least she now knew why Mr. Wakefield was known as Weed.

THREE

MRS. WAKEFIELD WAS WATCHING THE EVENING NEWS on TV. Her husband was sprawled in an overstuffed chair, staring blankly, if happily, at the ceiling. Judith's request to move the pressure cooker was met with hostility.

"You got four burners up there," Mrs. Wakefield asserted. "Why should I stink up the place down here with those beets?"

"It already stinks," Judith responded bluntly. "I need to make sauces, cook the vegetables, parboil potatoes. Come on. If you're not going to help, don't hinder."

With a vexed sigh, Mrs. Wakefield lifted her velour-covered body from the leatherette couch. "I'll use the stove down here," she grumbled. "There's a small kitchen off the saloon."

Judith let Mrs. Wakefield lead the way. Weed Wakefield didn't notice their departure. He seemed to be settling into a fetal position, an awkward collection of lanky arms and legs. The marijuana smell faded; the scent of pine tinged the air.

"That's the saloon," Mrs. Wakefield said, pointing to double doors farther down the hall. "Old Dunlop was a Midwestern boy who longed for the sea. I hear he tried to run away a couple of times when he was a kid, but they always hauled him back to the farm." She began to ascend the narrow back stairs. "When he got out here, where he could see salt water from his new property, he had the architect add a lot of marine touches. You see the rope pattern in some of the rooms?"

Judith hadn't, though she had noticed the coved

34

ceilings and the sailing ships in the stained glass above the first landing. "Did Dunlop go to sea when he got older?"

The housekeeper opened the frosted glass door. "He did. Up to Alaska, mainly, time and time again. His wife wouldn't go with him. She was a German immigrant who'd come to this country when she was a little girl and had gotten so seasick she wouldn't set foot on a ship ever again. I guess she didn't mind Dunlop going off now and then. He always brought her expensive presents like jewels and furs, stuff for the house, too. He hauled back a bunch of that volcanic rock you see in the birdbath and the rest of the garden. From the Aleutians, I think." She marched over to retrieve her pressure cooker. "Got it," she said, taking a firm grip on the handle with a pot holder. "Have a nice night." Mrs. Wakefield started back for the stairs. Suddenly she stopped and gave Judith what could have passed for a kindly look. "You sure you don't need me? I could always take around some trays. Zoe can help, too."

The unexpected change of heart caused Judith to beam. "That'd be great. Thanks, we're really under the gun. It wouldn't be so bad if we were doing only the party, but with dinner following so close . . ."

Mrs. Wakefield's expression was conspiratorial. "It'll annoy Mrs. Grover if we lend a hand. Besides, I like to keep an eye on that old bag. She might pinch the silver." With a wink, the housekeeper exited the kitchen.

Judith was elated. "We won't have to kill ourselves after all," she exclaimed, sliding the tray of shrimp balls onto the lower rack of the oven. "Mrs. Wakefield and Zoe can handle the actual serving while we work out here."

"And avoid the rest of Aunt Toadie's relatives,"

35

Renie pointed out. "Who else is coming besides Trixie, Vivvie, and Derek?"

Judith put the Brie on the top oven rack and closed the door. "Derek's wife, Holly, and their daughter, Jill. Actually, it's not *their* daughter, right? Holly was married before, to some guy in the military. Holly's had a hard life, as I recall, and married young because she'd been orphaned in her teens. Then she was widowed, either just before or after Jill was born. I think Derek adopted her. Jill's real father was an Air Force pilot who was shot down in Vietnam right at the end of the war. She must be about twenty by now. That's the whole lot of the Lotts. Oh, except for Trixie's fiancé, Mason Meade."

"Only seven," Renie mused. "Not bad. Compared with our family gatherings, it's a pretty lean number."

Judith agreed. For the next quarter of an hour, the cousins worked quickly to produce the trays of appetizers. The guests from Major Mush began to arrive promptly at six. Judith peeked out from the dining room into the entry hall, where there was much stomping of wet feet and shrugging off of damp coats. As predicted, the guests were a mixed bag, men and women from twenty to eighty-five. They struck Judith as a grim-faced group, complaining about the chilling rain and looking as if they were faced with an onerous but necessary duty.

"Uncle Boo's on his feet," Judith reported when she returned to the kitchen. "Aunt Toadie put him into a suit and tie. He's welcoming the guests."

Renie rushed off to the entry hall. "This I've got to see! Boo standing up! Wow!"

The frosted glass door opened, revealing Mrs. Wakefield and Zoe, now attired in decorous black

36

dresses and white aprons. The mother wore a limp white cap as well. Judith complimented them lavishly.

"We're so grateful for your help," she enthused, ignoring Zoe's pilfering of the Norwegian sardines. "No drama club, I take it?"

Zoe gave a languid shrug. "I could still go later. It depends on the weather. If it freezes over, there's no getting up or down that steep hill to Major Manor."

Judith and Renie were used to steep hills, but the sharp incline that led up to the top of The Bluff had indeed struck them as precarious. Judith glanced out the window to see that the rain was coming down thick and hard—and possibly freezing. She also looked at the outdoor thermometer, which registered thirty-six degrees.

"So far, so good," she murmured. "There isn't much wind." The last thing she needed was to get stuck at Major Manor. Judith couldn't expect Corinne Dooley to serve breakfast for the B&B guests. "Lord, get us out of here in one piece," she said under her breath.

Mrs. Wakefield's keen hearing picked up the comment. "Lord, get them all out of here. Mrs. G. has been hanging around since noon, driving me nuts. In fact, she's spent a lot of time at the house lately. The rest of them don't come around much, which is good, except the Rush girl. She coaxes old Boo into going for rides in her little white Mazda Miata. If you ask me, she's trying to bump him off."

Judith assumed Mrs. Wakefield was referring to Jill, Derek and Holly's daughter. As for Jill's intentions, Judith didn't want to guess. If there was one thing the family members had in common, it was a knack for malicious mischief. If there was any other trait they shared, it was greed.

Mrs. Wakefield carried off the first trays of wine. Zoe followed, at her own indolent pace, with the hors d'oeuvres. The cousins knuckled down to prepare dinner.

"Uncle Boo is actually *speaking* to the guests," Renie remarked in amazement. "Of course, he's like a windup toy, saying the same things over and over. His employees look like they're going to a hanging."

"Their own," Judith replied. "I gather he alternates these parties with a summer picnic. That must be a scream. Can you see Aunt Toadie and Uncle Boo in the three-legged race?"

The basement door opened once more. Weed Wakefield leaned against the casement, a silly grin on his long, seamed face. "Hi, dolls. What's cooking?"

Judith turned, a saucepan in her hand. "Dinner. You want to help?"

Weed shook his head. He was tall and graceless, over fifty and underweight. His brown eyes were unfocused, and his thinning brown hair was combed straight back over the collar of his denim work shirt. "I want to try out that big new TV gizmo. Nobody'll notice if I mosey on upstairs to give it a look-see." He yanked at the other door, almost falling over the threshold. "Beam me up," he murmured.

Renie arched her eyebrows at Judith. "I take it the Wakefields have the run of the house?"

Judith lifted a shoulder. "There's plenty of room for them to rattle around. Seven bedrooms, six baths, according to Aunt Toadie. It's a shame Uncle Boo and Aunt Rosie never had any children."

"I wonder why it's being renovated. Now, I mean." Renie was serious, wearing what Judith described as her boardroom face. "You can tell it's been left as is since it was built."

"True," Judith agreed, stirring her béchamel sauce over a low setting. "It's a beautifully designed house, and the craftsmanship is wonderful, but even quality requires care. Maybe Uncle Boo decided he wanted to make a contribution of his own before he kicks off."

Renie, however, looked dubious. "That doesn't sound like him. I seem to recall Aunt Rosie nagging him about fixing up stuff and renovating. She'd yak and yak, but he wouldn't budge. Now she's gone and suddenly he's putting what must be a lot of money into the house."

"Maybe that's why," Judith suggested. "I mean, it's *his* idea, not Aunt Rosie's."

"Maybe," Renie responded, but as she unwrapped a big head of cauliflower, she didn't sound convinced.

Mrs. Wakefield returned. "Still a few stragglers coming in," she announced, wrestling with the big, lumpy birthday cake. "Old Boo is putting on his party hat."

Judith glanced at Renie. "Literally?"

"I'll check." Renie went toward the entry hall, almost colliding with Zoe, who was drifting back into the kitchen.

"Boo's juiced," Zoe said calmly. "He wants to do the jig."

Judith decided she could leave her sauce unattended for a few moments. Joining Renie at the foot of the main staircase, she watched Uncle Boo shake hands with an elderly, bearded man.

"Carson Crowley, you old fraud! Didn't we put you away for embezzling the pension fund back in '68?" Boo cackled and took a big swig from the coffee mug in his free hand. His expression was puckish rather than malicious.

"Not coffee," murmured Judith.

"Definitely not coffee," whispered Renie.

A voluptuous woman of an uncertain age ankled up to Boo. He clutched her against his chest. They swayed together on the parquet floor. The woman appeared startled.

"Myra!" Boo sighed in rapture. "You're still in the front office?" He was crooning over the top of her bright platinum head. "Wonderful! No one can put on a front like you do!" He stepped back and stared down Myra's cleavage.

Myra's escort, a tall, muscular man of middle age, did not look pleased. "Mr. Major . . ." he began, but before he could finish, Aunt Toadie, in flowing black chiffon, flew out of the living room. Although she was smiling, her eyes were angry.

"Boo! Dear heart!" Toadie snatched him by the wrist, then wrenched the coffee mug from his hand. "Let me get you a refill. And do say hello to Myra's husband, Biff Kowoski, the former professional-football offensive lineman."

Boo, who was almost six feet when he actually stood on his own two feet, had to look up a good six inches to meet his guest's stormy gaze. "Offensive lineman, huh? Well, well!" He chuckled richly. "You look offensive, all right! Want to wrestle?"

"Boo!" Toadie virtually screamed. She pulled him to one side and whispered frantically in his ear. The half-dozen guests who were waiting to be greeted looked at one another in dismay. Boo's face drained of color as Toadie continued to berate him. Then, like a scolded child, he moved back to his official spot and put out his hand:

"Nice to see you . . . welcome to Major Manor . . .

good to have you . . . kind of you to come . . ." The mechanical responses droned on. With narrowed eyes, Aunt Toadie marched back to the living room, the coffee mug clasped to her chiffon-draped bosom.

A moment later, her voice floated across the uninspired ripple of conversation. "Cake! We're cutting it now! Let's all sing to our dear Bruno Major!"

Judith and Renie straggled into the living room behind the other guests. Uncle Boo appeared to be lost in the shuffle. Aunt Toadie raised a hand, then began singing "Happy Birthday to You" in a shrill voice that had the effect of fingernails raking glass. The others joined in without enthusiasm; the musical salute sounded like a dirge.

Standing under the doorway arch, Judith tried to find Uncle Boo among the crowd that had gathered in the big living room. Renie noticed her cousin's quizzical expression.

"Out there," Renie whispered, nodding toward the entry hall. As the last stanza faded into merciful oblivion, Judith saw Uncle Boo standing alone and not looking sorry for it. When a beaming Toadie began to cut the cake, several guests dashed back into the hallway. Judith figured they had seen the faux mush frosting and were gagging in revulsion.

The cousins were about to return to the kitchen when two more people entered through the main door. The barrel-chested man with the iron-gray temples was a stranger, but the ash-blond woman with the long legs was not: Trixie Bellew Vaughn McBride Longrod spotted her cousins by marriage and pretended she was pleased.

"Judith! Renie! What a treat!" With raindrops dripping from her stylish beige trench coat, she raced

41

across the entry hall to embrace her shirttail relations. "Mummy said you'd be here! It's been ages!"

Judith and Renie felt themselves being half-hugged and semi-kissed. Trixie was almost as tall as Judith, and some three years younger. She was attractive, Judith had to concede as much, but the careful makeup couldn't hide all the wear and tear of three husbands and countless lovers. On the highway of life, Trixie was definitely a used car.

Releasing the cousins and nabbing her companion, Trixie introduced Mason Meade. Mason's smile was thin. He had an unnatural tan for February, and his hazel eyes were wary. His voice, however, was smooth.

"I'm trying to see a resemblance," he said, removing a pair of kidskin gloves from big-knuckled hands. "For cousins, you all look quite different."

"From what?" Renie replied, then decided she sounded too flip. "I mean, Judith and I look like our dads, who didn't look a lot like each other to begin with. For brothers, that is."

Trixie laughed gaily. "They didn't, did they? Not in terms of their features anyway. And I look like my dad. My *real* dad," she added. Seeing the puzzled expression on Mason's craggy face, she petted his damp sleeve. "Didn't I tell you? Mother was married before, to a man named Gilroy Bellew."

Mason didn't seem completely enlightened. "But I thought Bellew was your married name by your former husband—"

Trixie squeezed Mason's arm. "No, no, no," she interrupted, leading him to the coat closet that stood between the living room and the entrance to the den. The receiving line was now gone, and with it Uncle Boo. "Bellew is my maiden name," Trixie rattled on. "I had it changed back legally after my divorce. Now let's go mingle and be nice to Uncle Boo's guests . . ."

Judith and Renie were forgotten. They trudged back to the kitchen, where the béchamel sauce was simmering into oblivion. Swearing mildly, Judith rescued the saucepan. "I'd better add half again as much and start over," she muttered. "Do you remember when Trixie was a red-headed vixen?"

"I remember when she was a brunette bombshell, a raven-haired wench, and a striped skunk," Renie replied. "A frost job gone wrong. But I'll bet she's forgotten to tell Mason Meade all about her seedy past. He didn't even know that Uncle Corky isn't her real father."

Judith stirred in more cream. "He's been real enough. Gilroy Bellew took off like a shot when Aunt Toadie got pregnant. Aunt Rosie told me years ago that nobody ever heard from him again. It was a wartime marriage."

"Poor Uncle Corky," Renie mused. "Cousin Cheryl has turned out okay, but Marty is a dork. I suppose you can't expect much with Toadie as their mother."

Judith's opportunity to comment was cut off by the return of Mrs. Wakefield. "Last call for the wine," she said. "The Grover bat's counting the trays I've brought out."

"How's Uncle Boo?" inquired Judith.

Mrs. Wakefield snorted. "Now that Mrs. G. took away his gin, he's in the dumps. It's his birthday, for heaven's sake! Let the old fart get a buzz on! The rest of the year he just sits around doing nothing."

Judith watched the housekeeper sashay out of the kitchen. She felt sorry for Uncle Boo. Maybe he wasn't lazy so much as bored. But, of course, that was his own fault. No inner resources. Judith felt sorry for him

43

anyway.

"All that money and he hasn't had much of a life." She sighed, checking on the rack of lamb.

But Renie disagreed. "He and Aunt Rosie used to take some trips. She made him do it, because he didn't like to leave home, but at least he got a change of scenery once in a while."

"It's a waste," Judith declared. "He could have been a volunteer. He could have given his money away and done some good. He could have turned this big place into a—"

"B&B?" Renie's grin was mischievous. "Knock it off, coz. He didn't do any of the above. He didn't want to. He and his favorite Martians are like Old Man River—they just roll around heaven all day. Give me a kettle for the broccoli."

Judith was complying when a knock sounded at the kitchen door. She looked out through the window to see Aunt Vivvie and her family huddled in the narrow passageway.

"Egad, more relatives," she muttered to Renie. "I'll bet Toadie told Vivvie she couldn't use the front entrance."

Viveca Lott Rush was an older, somewhat plumper version of her sister. Her blond curls could have been a wig or a bad dye job. False lashes fluttered; so did her gloved hands. She had big blue eyes and an ingenuous expression that made her look like an aging baby doll. By contrast, her son, Derek, evoked images of a ravening wolf. Tall, dark, lean, and vaguely saturnine, he had a crooked smile that showed off a gold molar. Yet the limpid dark eyes were not unsympathetic. Judith had always suspected he might be kinder than he looked.

"I don't think you've seen Jill for quite a while," Derek said after the initial greetings were exchanged. "Hasn't she grown up?"

Jill had grown in several directions since the cousins had last seen her as a gawky teenager. Taller than Judith, Jill Rush had a spectacular figure, wide-set brown eyes, a sensuous mouth, and lush, long brown hair parted in the middle. She eyed Judith and Renie as if they'd crawled out of the garbage cans on the back porch.

"You're the librarian?" Jill asked of Judith.

"I used to be, but now I run a—"

"And," Jill continued, turning to Renie, "you draw cartoons?"

"No, I'm a graphic—"

Jill swiveled her head to look at her grandmother. "Where's Mama? I thought she was right behind us."

Plastic rain bonnet and gloves in hand, Vivvie Rush unfastened her galoshes. "Holly is bringing in our things, dear," she informed her granddaughter. With nervous, beringed fingers, she undid the buttons of her dark blue winter coat. Derek helped his mother remove the garment. "We brought along some nice wine and a box of Spanish cigars for Boo. Oh, and some brandy. My sister is awfully thrifty sometimes when it comes to guests." Her manner toward Judith and Renie was apologetic. As the cousins recalled, Vivvie's manner was always apologetic.

The back door was still open. Coming around the corner of the house was a small, dainty figure carrying a large, heavy box. Judith waited for Derek Rush to help his wife. He didn't. Holly Rush panted up the porch steps, staggered into the kitchen, and set her burden on the counter.

"Oh!" she gasped. "That box weighed more than I realized! Whatever is in there? I thought it was only a couple of bottles and some cigars." Holly leaned against the counter, catching her breath. At just over forty, she retained a girlish air. Her short brown hair was cut close to her head, setting off the delicate bones of her face. She offered Judith and Renie a shy smile. "How good to see you both again. When was it the last time? Not Aunt Rosie's funeral—I mean, a happy occasion. Easter, three years ago?"

"Thanksgiving, five," Judith replied in a friendly manner. She saw the crestfallen look on Holly's face and hastened to make amends. "The years go by so quickly, it's hard to keep track. I remember because it was the first Thanksgiving after Dan died."

Jill had already left the kitchen. Derek suggested that he and his wife and mother also depart so that the cousins could work in peace. Noting that it was just a few minutes before seven, Judith didn't try to detain them. There was still much to be done before dinner was served at eight.

Derek was halfway to the dining room when he turned to his wife. "Don't forget the carton, Holly. We'll put it in the den for now."

Grunting a bit, Holly hoisted the box anew. The trio disappeared. Renie shook her head. "Poor Holly. I forgot how downtrodden she is. Vivvie's oblivious, Derek's callous, and Jill is so self-absorbed that I'd like to shake her until she loses her center part."

"They're a queer family," Judith allowed, then stopped in the middle of measuring out the crème brûlée ingredients. "They'll need a key to get in the den. Should we tell Mrs. Wakefield?"

But Mrs. Wakefield was reentering the kitchen. "I

46

don't have the key," she said, looking a bit sulky. "I used to, but Mrs. Grover took it. Mrs. Rush will have to ask her sister." The sulk became a smirk.

Judith decided not to worry about the key. It wasn't her problem. Making the crème brûlée required all her attention at the moment. She couldn't allow herself to be distracted by petty family quarrels.

Or so she thought until someone started screaming.

FOUR

THE GUESTS FROM MAJOR MUSH HAD BEEN DISPERSED. In the wake of Weed's defection, Derek Rush had taken over the duties of official bouncer. He was still at the double inner doors when Judith and Renie arrived in the entry hall. Jill had Toadie backed up against the door to the coat closet, upbraiding her aunt in strident tones while Vivvie sniffled into an embroidered handkerchief. Trixie tugged with one hand at Jill's cream-colored sleeve and yanked at her long brown hair with the other. Mason Meade stood with his hands behind his back, humming and trying to look as if nothing unusual were going on. Holly clutched the wrought-iron balustrade, making ineffectual keening noises. Uncle Boo was nowhere to be seen.

"Give me the damned key or I'll bust your snout," Jill shrieked at Toadie, even as she tried to fend off Trixie.

"Leave me alone," Toadie rasped, raising her hands in a claw-like gesture. "I'll gouge out your ugly eyes!"

"Stop threatening my mother!" yelled Trixie, pulling harder on Jill's long brown hair.

"Oh, don't!" squeaked Vivvie, wringing her hands. "Please don't! My nerves! I can't stand dissension!"

"What?" Toadie managed to punch Jill in the stomach. "You caused it, Vivvie, you old hog! You're the one who wanted to go snooping in the den!"

Jill staggered, as much from Toadie's blow as from the sharp tugs of Trixie. "Let go of my hair, you cow!" she snarled at Trixie. "Or I'll find a blowtorch and melt your silicone boobs!"

Judith and Renie were watching with a mixture of

48

fascination and horror. "Silicone boobs?" whispered Renie. "When did Trixie have those done?"

Judith gave a shrug. "When she had the liposuction? Or the eye tucks?"

"I thought Toadie had the tucks." Renie leaned against the wall which led to the telephone alcove and the main floor's only bath. "Maybe they got two-for-one on a special mother-daughter deal."

"Could be." Judith winced as Jill got her hands around Trixie's throat. Toadie was fanning herself and straightening her dress. Vivvie was openly weeping. Holly was pleading with Derek to intervene. "How long do these skirmishes usually last?" Judith inquired of Renie.

Renie looked at her watch. "Oh—five, ten minutes, unless they resort to weaponry. Don't you remember the Christmas dinner when they all ended up in my folks' fish pond?"

Judith shook her head. "I missed that one. Dan wouldn't let me come in for Christmas that year. We still owned the cafe then and he'd invited his ne'er-do-well buddies over for a free meal. One of them stole my purse."

"M-mmmm," Renie responded, as accustomed to tales of woe from Judith's earlier life as she was to the fractious Lott family.

Derek, however, had finally interceded, pulling his daughter away from Trixie. "That's it," he said quietly, though there was an underlying threat in his voice. "We don't need the key now anyway. The guests are gone and Uncle Boo can have his cigars. Besides, it's time for cocktails."

"Oh, goodness!" Aunt Toadie's charm bracelets jingled as she checked the time. "You're right! It's after seven!"

"I could use a teeny martini," said Aunt Vivvie, adjusting her hair. Or, Judith noted, her wig, since the entire coiffure seemed to move smartly to the left.

"Make mine wine," said Jill, heading for the living room.

The atmosphere calmed as quickly as it had erupted. Judith and Renie withdrew to the kitchen, where they found Mrs. Wakefield laughing her head off.

"That was great!" she cried, leaning against Zoe for support. "I wish that young gal had decked Mrs. G. Too bad the bleached blond hussy got in her licks."

"Stay tuned," said Renie, going straight to the stove to check the cauliflower. "That was merely the opening round."

Judith was putting the crème brûlée cups into a pan of water when a buzzer sounded. "Yikes!" she cried. "I thought I left Mother home."

Mrs. Wakefield had gotten her mirth under control. "That's the living room. There're buzzers all over the house." She pointed to a series of colored lights above the back door. "Old Boo never uses 'em, except when he falls out of bed. But Mrs. G. plays those things like an accordion. My guess is that they want their booze."

"Oh." Judith shook herself. "Silly me, I thought there must be a liquor cabinet or a bar in the living room. Shall I?" She threw the housekeeper a questioning look.

"Somebody shall, and why not you?" Mrs. Wakefield responded. "Zoe and I'll get the dining room table ready."

Reluctantly, Judith headed back to the living room. Uncle Boo, who might or might not have noticed the melee in the entry hall, was dozing in his wing chair. Jill was picking out notes on the grand piano at the far end

50

of the room, Derek Rush was poking at the fire in the grate, Trixie was showing Mason Meade what was left of the once-sweeping view to the west, and Toadie and Vivvie were sitting on the tapestry-covered sofa as if they were indeed the closest of sisters.

Martinis, of vodka as well as of gin, seemed to be the family's favorite beverage. Except, of course, for Jill, who gleefully remarked that since she was still under age and considerably younger than anyone else present, she'd settle for a glass of wine. A Barolo, preferably from Casa Vinicola Bruno Giacosa.

"How about a rosé from the state liquor store on Heraldsgate Hill?" Judith suggested. Jill turned up her nose, but she didn't turn down the offer. Instead, she played "The Drinking Song" from *The Student Prince*.

"This," said Judith, after Mrs. Wakefield had shown her where the liquor was stored in the kitchen, "reminds me of my second job tending bar, at the Meat & Mingle. These customers are better dressed, but they don't have any more class."

Uncle Boo had been permitted a glass of wine. Apparently he'd managed to guzzle enough gin to satisfy his thirst. Opening his eyes, he accepted the finely cut Czechoslovakian goblet from Judith.

"Thank you," he said with a wan smile. "Did you talk to those fellows with the extra eyes?"

Judith blinked. "The . . . oh, you mean the men from Mars? No, I didn't, Uncle Boo. They were unloading gamma rays from their spaceship."

Uncle Boo nodded. "Weed'll see to them. He always does. Good man, Weed. He knows an alien when he sees one."

Judith didn't doubt it for a minute. She finished serving the drinks and fled to the kitchen.

With Mrs. Wakefield and Zoe arranging the table service, Judith and Renie were able to bring dinner off on time. A second round of drinks had been served shortly after seven-thirty, this time by Renie, who reported that all was calm, if not all bright.

"Dumb," Renie declared as the cousins began carrying out the serving dishes. "The Lotts are *dumb*. How can Uncle Corky stand being married to a stupid woman? He's really smart."

"Toadie's shrewd, though," Judith said under her breath as the family made its procession into the paneled dining room. "Don't underestimate her."

Uncle Boo sat at the head of the table, with his sisters-in-law on each side. Mason Meade was next to Toadie; Derek Rush sat beside his mother, Vivvie. Holly and Jill filled out the rest of the table. The place at the far end was vacant. Judith could picture Aunt Rosie, a squat, belligerent figure with bright gold curls, presiding in her favorite shade of pink. As the eldest of the Lott sisters, Rosie had always managed to get in the last word.

The sterling gleamed; the crystal glittered. The Wedgwood china was handsome, formal, Florentine black on white. The linens were edged in handmade lace, probably from Ireland, Judith thought. A pair of lamps with small navy shades sat on either side of a dried floral arrangement in a silver tureen. It was a table fit for a king. Instead, the gathering was made up of knaves, jokers, and a pretender-queen.

Or so it seemed to Judith. "They look out of place," she muttered to Renie as the cousins finally had a chance to relax by the sink.

"Aunt Toadie doesn't think so," Renie replied, pouring them each a glass of wine. "She acts as if she's

52

running the show."

Having temporarily completed their serving tasks, Mrs. Wakefield and Zoe returned to the kitchen. Renie put a question to the housekeeper:

"We've been wondering—whose idea was it to fix this place up?"

Mrs. Wakefield unpinned her cap and smoothed her graying red hair. "Mrs. G.'s. Who else? Old Boo'd let it fall down around his ears."

Judith and Renie exchanged swift glances. "So why do it?" asked Judith.

The housekeeper snorted. "Dumb question. The old Toad figures she'll get everything when Boo kicks off. Why do you think she's been hanging around him like flies on a horse's behind?"

At the stove, Zoe lifted the lid from a pot and forked out a mouthful of new potatoes. "Boo's so lazy he lets Mrs. G. do anything she wants. He has no spunk. And there's no 'No' in his vocabulary."

"You got that right," huffed the housekeeper. "When Mrs. G. showed up this afternoon, she said the masons had been screwing off. I told her to tell the master. As usual, he just sat there like a lump. Guess who had to fire them?" She stabbed her bosom with her thumb. "Now I suppose I'll get stuck finding another bunch of bricklayers. Mrs. G. comes in and raises all sorts of hell-oh-bill, then waddles away and expects somebody else to pick up the pieces."

Judith gave a slight nod. "That's Aunt Toadie, all right. But is Boo actually going to leave her everything? What about Derek? He's always been the favorite. Aunt Rosie and Uncle Boo helped raise him, especially after Uncle Mo got sick."

Mrs. Wakefield looked blank. "Who's Mo?"

"Mo—Maurice—Rush," Judith explained. "He was Aunt Vivvie's husband. He owned a plumbing company, which was a good thing, because he was chronically ill and never did much real work after he hit forty."

"Right," Renie chimed in. "Mo Rush was a hypochondriac who finally had to die to prove he was really sick. Of course, he was almost eighty at the time."

The blank expression remained on Mrs. Wakefield's face. "Maybe I met him once. I don't remember."

"Probably not," said Judith. "He was always too sick to go anywhere. That's why Aunt Rosie and Uncle Boo hauled Derek along on their trips. The poor kid would never have gotten out of the house otherwise."

Zoe had buttered one of the extra rolls and was munching away in her unconcerned fashion. "When I was a little kid, Derek would hang out here a lot. He was years older than I, but he didn't mind horsing around with me. We spent a lot of time hiding in the bushes."

Judith tried not to look askance. Zoe's remark didn't seem to perturb Mrs. Wakefield, however. "Derek Rush can be a pain sometimes, but I figure it was his upbringing. It looks as if he expects that poor wife of his to spoil him silly. Maybe he's making up for lost time."

The housekeeper's assessment struck Judith as credible. From what she knew of Derek, he was selfish, thoughtless—and yet likable. The hint of menace in his lupine manner was born of a wily determination to get his way. With a coddled father and a distracted mother, young Derek had learned to go it alone.

The buzzer sounded from the dining room. Glancing through the door, Judith could see Aunt Toadie with her lips pursed and an expectant expression on her face.

Renie wrinkled her pug nose. "Refills for the trough?"

Judith nodded. "That's my guess, unless they're complaining about Uncle Boo's face falling into his potatoes."

"He passed out?" Renie joined Judith at her vantage point. But Judith had been joking: Boo was contentedly munching away on a meaty lamb bone. He had a linen napkin tucked into his collar and appeared to be ignoring the rest of the diners.

Mrs. Wakefield bustled past the cousins. "I'll handle this. You'd better get your dessert ready to roll."

The crème brûlée was done to perfection, with its amber crackle shining under the oven light. Judith set the cups on a tray, then checked to see if the coffee had finished perking.

"More rolls, seconds on the broccoli," Mrs. Wakefield reported, returning to the kitchen. "Hit it, Zoe."

Zoe did, though she took her time about it. Five minutes later, the entree plates were ready to be cleared. The Wakefields were hauling dishes from the dining room when Weed strolled in from the back stairs.

"Great TV set," he declared, hands in his pockets and a rapturous look on his face. "Next time I'll plug it in." Weed Wakefield wandered off to the servants' quarters in the basement.

Mrs. Wakefield and Zoe had delivered the crème brûlée, coffee, and tea when the buzzer sounded again. Judith was ready to tear her hair. "Now what?" she demanded in an impatient tone.

The housekeeper wheeled around, heading back to the dining room. A minute later, she returned, relaying the message that Toadie wanted to speak with Judith.

Gritting her teeth, Judith entered the dining room.

Toadie was spooning the last of her crème brûlée into her mouth. She held up a hand while she finished swallowing. "Ah, there, mustn't talk with one's mouth full." Toadie gave Judith a smile that went only as far as her nose. "By and large, the meal was rather good, Judith. However, you might want to cook the lamb a bit longer next time. I found some pink meat close to the bone. The potatoes were a trifle overdone—they should have a bit of snap and never, never, any squish. The same with the broccoli. As for the cauliflower, you should come up with a new sauce. The Allemande and the béchamel are too similar. Are you sure you used fresh Parmesan cheese for the cauliflower? Did you add one egg yolk or two for the béchamel? When I simmer sauces, I always . . ."

Since Judith had never eaten a meal prepared by Aunt Toadie that hadn't come out of a box, a can, or a package, she couldn't stand any more criticism or questions. Toadie's garnishing standby was an envelope of dehydrated Mr. Sauce. Indeed, Judith suspected that Toadie had looked up the béchamel and Allemande recipes in a cookbook.

"You ate everything but the centerpiece," Judith broke in. "We hardly need to wash the dishes. I think you licked them clean." Judith turned on her heel and went back to the kitchen. Derek looked startled; Holly appeared crushed; Aunt Vivvie seemed on the verge of tears; Uncle Boo had crème brûlée all over his chin.

"That does it," Judith muttered, black eyes flashing at Renie. "Let's clean up this place and get out of here."

Renie was more than willing. To the cousins' surprise, Mrs. Wakefield and Zoe offered to help. The dishwasher had already finished one cycle. Zoe

56

removed the clean items; her mother reloaded. Renie scraped plates; Judith scoured pans. The diners retreated to the living room, except for Uncle Boo, who headed for his den.

Peeking out into the entry hall, Mrs. Wakefield chuckled. "He's had enough of that crew. I'll bet he finagled the key out of Mrs. G. and is going to lock himself in. Old Boo's no dope."

"W-e-ll . . ." Judith hedged, then laughed as she turned out the lamps on the dining room table. "Maybe not. When do the rest of them go home?"

Mrs. Wakefield removed the lamps and began stripping the table. "Not a minute too soon," she muttered, then glanced out the window. "In fact, if I were them, I'd leave now. The wind's coming from the north. Look at those trees."

Judith went to the leaded bay window, from which she could see the tall yew trees swaying next to the brick wall that separated the property from the sidewalk. The hard rain was now coming down on a slant, its freezing drops punishing the expanse of lawn between the house and the herbaceous borders.

"It looks miserable out there," Judith agreed. "Let me check the thermometer by the kitchen window."

The mercury had fallen to thirty-four. Judith urged Renie to hurry. They were loading the cartons when a loud noise made them jump.

Zoe, who had been putting clean dishes away, almost dropped a stack of butter plates. "What was *that?*"

Her mother's head darted in several directions. "Damned if I know, kid. It sounded like an explosion."

Still looking startled, Zoe twitched her lips in a smile. "Maybe Mrs. G. blew up."

"Dream on," muttered Mrs. Wakefield.

Zoe's wish was in vain. Toadie appeared in the kitchen door, bug-eyed and apprehensive. She did not, however, cross the threshold. It occurred to Judith that even in a time of anxiety, Toadie Grover wouldn't deign to put her fine foot down on serf turf.

"Did you drop something and break it?" she asked, her voice a trifle hoarse.

Judith shook her head. "The noise didn't come from in here."

Toadie scanned the kitchen, apparently to make sure. "Then what was it?" she inquired. Her charm bracelets jangled as she nervously fingered the half-glasses which hung around her neck.

Mrs. Wakefield's aplomb had returned. "A car, maybe. Or somebody ran into a pole. Who knows?" She shrugged her stout shoulders. "It's a nasty night out there. You folks ought to be heading home."

Toadie's nerve hardened. So did her expression. "We're finishing Derek's brandy. His taste is deplorable, but we're drinking it to be polite."

She was about to sweep away when the downstairs door opened. Weed Wakefield entered the kitchen. His body was plastered with beet greens. He stared vacantly at his wife.

"Your pot blew up." He patted his shirt pocket. "It's a good thing I've got mine." Weed broke into uncontrollable laughter.

The housekeeper gaped at her mate, then whirled in his direction. "Oh, for God's sake! You mean the pressure cooker? Hell's bells, what a mess! Weed, are you scalded? What were you doing?" She pushed him back toward the open door to the basement.

"Watching it, just like you told me . . ."

"Get below, let me see if you're all right . . ."

The Wakefields disappeared down the stairs. Toadie uttered an indecipherable exclamation, threw up her hands, and stomped off. Zoe giggled while the cousins returned to their tasks. Renie scrubbed the durable one-inch tiles on the counters. Judith swept the linoleum, then wiped it down with a damp rag. Cantankerous voices were raised in the living room: Aunt Vivvie emitted a wail; Trixie's laughter verged on hysteria; Derek's low voice rumbled with warning; Jill drowned them out with a few chords from Chopin. More faintly, a soft thud emanated from somewhere in the house.

"Poor Pop," Zoe remarked, eating the last roll. "I'll bet he fainted. He can be really ineffectual sometimes."

Judith didn't comment, but Renie made a face. "Does he ever do anything around here?" she asked.

Zoe had propped herself up on a kitchen stool. "Oh, sure, he does what he has to. Handyman stuff. Errands. Driving to doctor and dentist appointments for the old coot a couple of times a year." She stuck out one long, slim leg and admired its shapeliness. "Pop's not stoned all the time. He usually smokes only before and after meals. Oh, and in the evening."

That covered most of Weed's waking hours, as far as Judith could tell. If Weed's self-induced euphoria could indeed be considered a state of consciousness. Master and servant were well suited. Neither was in sharp focus.

"Who," Renie asked, stuffing the last of Judith's plastic containers into the cardboard box, "hired your parents?"

Zoe tugged at her earlobe. "Mrs. Major, I guess. Rosie, Boo's wife. I was a baby at the time. Dunlop had servants, but they were as old as he was. They died, too, all about the same time. Boo didn't want to bother getting new staff, but Mrs. Major must have convinced him. She usually did."

Judith nodded. "Rosie Major was a forceful woman. She could be a nag, but I always thought she was the most agreeable of the three Lott sisters."

With a languid toss of her head, Zoe sniffed. "Isn't that like choosing your favorite disease? Those women are all awful, if you ask me."

The cousins didn't argue. Haste was imperative if they were to beat the falling temperature. There were few leftovers, except for the wine. Judith had the feeling that if she hadn't kept the cases in the kitchen, they, too, would have disappeared along with all of the food. Aunt Toadie probably had a secret cache. Judith wouldn't put it past her to return the unopened bottles to the liquor store.

Flushed and fanning herself with her hand, Mrs. Wakefield returned. Zoe expressed mild interest in her father's welfare.

"Did he get burned or does he know the difference?" Zoe seemed inured to Weed's mishaps.

Mrs. Wakefield cupped a hand around her ear. "What? Oh, he's okay, except for a couple of places on his face. I fixed him up with some ointment. Maybe that'll teach him not to peek into a pressure cooker."

"They're dangerous," Renie declared, closing up one of the boxes. "My mother's blew a hole in the ceiling once."

Judith gave Renie a sidelong look. "That's because your dad put a cherry bomb in it. He didn't like pressure cookers, either."

"He didn't like chokecherry jam, which was what Mom was making," Renie replied. "I didn't blame him, but nowadays it's sold as a delicacy up at Falstaff's—"

Another loud noise jolted the four women. "Now what?" Mrs. Wakefield sighed. "I put what was left of the beets in a kettle."

Zoe swiveled on the stool. "What about Pop?"

"I put what was left of him to bed." The housekeeper peered out through the dining room and into the entry hall. "Jill and that low-life fiancé of Trixie's are out there, nosing around. I can hear Vivvie Rush sniveling all the way from the living room."

Judith was closing the last of the cartons. "That almost sounded like a firecracker. Was it outside or in the house?"

Mrs. Wakefield was removing her white apron, which was now stained with meat juices, beets, and a good many patches of dirt. "Hard to tell. With that wind blowing, sound gets distorted. You need some help with those boxes?"

The offer was accepted. With Zoe joining in, the car could be loaded in just one trip. But as soon as they reached the cement steps on the back porch, they realized that it was beginning to ice up outside.

"Be careful," Mrs. Wakefield urged. "It's getting ugly outside."

"It's ugly inside," Renie retorted. "At least in the living room. Those lamebrains better button it up and head home."

The street was still mainly wet, but the sleet was blinding. The quartet trod cautiously, feeling the wind bite into their faces. For the return trip, everything could be loaded into the trunk. Judith slammed the lid shut and spoke through half-closed eyes:

"Thanks so much for helping us. We honestly couldn't have done it without you two."

Mrs. Wakefield had allowed her daughter to take her

arm. "No problem," she said, raising her voice to be heard over the howling wind. "Be careful."

"Right," Judith responded, unlocking the car door. " 'Bye, now." Heads lowered, the Wakefield women started back toward the big house.

Renie swore. "I forgot my purse."

Judith swore, too. "You're an idiot."

"I'll be right back," said Renie, stepping off the curb.

Judith shut the car door. "I'll go with you. You'll fall down. And we really should say good night to Uncle Boo. Three minutes won't make any difference."

The cousins clung to each other as they picked their way back across the street. There were definitely icy patches, but Judith had studded tires on her blue Japanese compact. Once they got to the bottom of the steep hill that led up to Major Manor, there should be no further problems.

Zoe let them in. "What's wrong?" she asked, her auburn hair now loosened and falling over her shoulders. Mrs. Wakefield was emptying the most recent load of dishes.

Renie explained, then espied her handbag sitting on the floor next to the refrigerator. "We wanted to say good night to Uncle Boo," she added.

"Get in line," said Mrs. Wakefield, gesturing toward the entry hall. "The goon squad is about to leave. They're making nice in the den."

But they weren't. The guests had gathered in the little corridor between the entry hall and Boo's sanctuary. Derek was pounding on the door; Toadie was shouting. Uncle Boo obviously didn't want to be disturbed. The cousins couldn't blame him.

Toadie was looking vexed. "He took my key and now he won't open the door."

Vivvie shot her sister a reproachful look. "You wore him out with all this partying. I'll bet he's taking a nap."

"Some bet," remarked Jill, her brown leather jacket hanging over one arm. "I like the odds."

Trixie eyed Jill. "Don't be snide, you little snip. Uncle Boo is so thoughtful—he wouldn't smoke his cigars in front of us because they make your grandmother sneeze."

Jill returned stare for stare. "*You* make Grandmother sneeze. A lot of people are allergic to you, Trixie, including three out of three of your ex—"

"Ohhh!" Trixie clutched at her throat and staggered. "I feel strange! All weak and shivery!" She allowed Mason Meade to take her in his arms.

"Menopause," muttered Jill. "It's probably a hot flash. You *are* almost fifty, aren't you, Aunt Trixie?"

Trixie started to bolt out of Mason's embrace, then remembered her allegedly fragile state. "Hardly! I turned forty just a short time ago."

Renie rolled her eyes. "Oh, brother!"

"Trixie's three years younger than I am," Judith said out of the corner of her mouth.

It was Holly, however, who set the record straight: "Let me think—I was born in '51, and you're seven years older than I am, Trixie, so that makes you—"

"Unconscious!" cried Mason Meade as Trixie collapsed in his arms. "Quick! Do something!"

Mrs. Wakefield did. She marched up to the recumbent Trixie Bellew and slapped her across the face. Trixie's eyes flew open, her body recoiled, and she glared fiercely at the housekeeper.

"You fool! How dare you! That *hurt!*"

Mrs. Wakefield shrugged. "Brought you around, didn't it? Ever try a dose of smelling salts? They're nasty."

Angrily, Toadie wedged herself between her daughter and the housekeeper. "That's grounds for dismissal, Mrs. Wakefield! I'm going to report this incident to Mr. Major!"

Mrs. Wakefield yawned extravagantly. "Go ahead. I'll bet he gets real excited, especially if you tell him he got a birthday card from Saturn."

At the door to the den, Derek was still trying to turn the knob. He pushed, he shoved, he wiggled and jiggled. He also shouted. There was no response, either from the door or from Uncle Boo.

"I wouldn't come out, either," Renie whispered to Judith. "If Boo stalls long enough, they'll all go home."

"Us, too," Judith whispered back, then frowned. "You don't suppose he's sick?"

Renie made a face. "Hardly. He's asleep, as usual. If everybody shut up, we could probably hear him snore."

Derek turned to Aunt Toadie. "Is there another key?"

Toadie shook her head. "No. The one I gave him was the only key to the den. The lock for every room is tooled differently."

Mrs. Wakefield guffawed. "A lot you know! There's a master key for all the rooms."

Everyone stared at the housekeeper. Trixie, now recovered from whatever had been ailing her, glowered at Mrs. Wakefield. "Well? Where is it? Go get it so we can open the blasted door."

But Mrs. Wakefield suddenly looked blank. "I'm not sure. Weed had all the keys on a big ring he kept downstairs by the furnace room. But I haven't seen it in weeks. Shall I ask him?"

Derek's dark eyes narrowed. "You shall indeed. And if he can't find those keys, tell him to bring a crowbar."

With a sigh of resignation, Judith stepped forward. "Hold it," she said, feeling all eyes now upon her. "That's a beautiful Philippine mahogany door, and I'd hate to see it ruined. Has anybody got a crochet hook?"

No one replied. Finally, Mrs. Wakefield recalled that there was an old sewing cabinet in the third-floor attic. Mason Meade volunteered to go look for it. Trixie insisted on accompanying him.

"I know the way," she said, clutching his arm and heading for the main staircase. "Now, Mason, don't pay any attention to what Jill and Holly say about ages and . . ." The pair disappeared above the first landing.

Toadie confronted Judith. "What do you intend to do?"

Judith attempted a smile. "I hate to admit it, but I've always had a knack for picking locks. I used to do it when I was a kid. You know, just for fun." She didn't add that she had also done it, more recently, out of necessity. There had been occasions in the past few years when Judith had needed to gain access to locked rooms, not for fun or even idle curiosity. Judith and Renie had usually been on the trail of a killer. Of course, this was not the case now.

"Snooping," breathed Toadie. "Really, Judith, now I know it was you who took my topaz brooch back in 1951. I always suspected as much. Then there was the twenty-dollar bill that went missing from Corky's wallet a couple of years later. I shall have to deduct those amounts from your catering bill."

Judith couldn't believe her ears. She knew Trixie had taken the brooch for a game of dress-up and Cousin Marty had swiped the money to buy a model airplane. What had become of the brooch was not known to

Judith, though she supposed that Trixie had lost it in her usual brainless manner. As for the airplane, Uncle Corky's Siberian husky had sat on it. Judith turned away and counted to ten.

Derek was still fiddling with the door. "We could take it off its hinges," he said.

Holly put a hand on her husband's arm. "Stop, darling. You'll wrinkle your nice suit." She brushed at some dust on his pin-striped jacket. "Wait and see if Judith can't pick the lock. I think it's very clever of her."

With her wig sliding backward, Aunt Vivvie's forehead had grown higher and was seamed with deep lines. "I don't know—if Boo wanted to see us, he'd let us in. Why don't we leave the poor dear alone? He's not used to so much company. Rosie could be very antisocial."

But before anyone could debate Vivvie's advice, Trixie and Mason reappeared, armed with not one but two crochet hooks. "That sewing stuff must have belonged to Boo's mother," said Trixie. "There's a picture of Mussolini in her darning kit."

"Darning kit?" muttered Renie. "Why would anybody that rich need to darn?"

"Darned if I know," retorted Mrs. Wakefield. "Maybe she was bored. Hey, let's see your cousin strut her stuff."

Everyone backed off as Judith knelt next to the lock. The audience made her nervous. On the first four tries, nothing happened. Then, as she concentrated on her work rather than on those dubious eyes, Judith felt something give. A click followed, and the doorknob turned. Jill, Zoe, Holly, and Mrs. Wakefield cheered.

Judith stepped aside to let Derek into the den. Indeed,

the entire crew stampeded at his heels. Judith exchanged a look of dismay with Renie. They were straggling in together when Aunt Vivvie screamed. So did Aunt Toadie. And Holly and Jill and Zoe and Mrs. Wakefield. Derek and Mason groaned.

The cousins tried to peer around and through the crowd which had gathered at Uncle Boo's desk. "What . . . ?" Judith began, then saw Jill turn away, her hands pressing against her pale face.

"He's dead," she gasped out. "It looks like he's been shot! I can't believe it!"

Judith could.

FIVE

THE COMMOTION IN THE DEN SET JUDITH'S TEETH ON edge and frayed Renie's temper. Toadie shrieked; Vivvie howled; Holly moaned; Derek groaned; Trixie again fell in Mason Meade's arms. This time her collapse seemed genuine. At last the cousins were able to get a closer look. Neither wanted to, but they felt the call of duty. After all, Judith was a policeman's wife. She was also well acquainted with murder. Violent death had crossed her path too often. Some people were lucky at winning lotteries and contests and door prizes. Others were accident-prone, breaking bones and limbs like so many dishes. Then there was Judith, whose life-style constantly brought her into contact with strangers. And with murder.

But Boo Major was no stranger. He was distant kin, and the cousins felt an obligation. Side by side, they gazed at his body, slumped forward on the desk. His gray hair hung lankly, with a smear of blood and a large, ugly hole in his right temple. His profile was turned to the wall, eyes wide, mouth agape. Judith winced; Renie swallowed hard.

Derek had gone around behind Boo's chair. He stooped to retrieve a book which had fallen out of the case between the two windows. "We've got to do something," he said, his voice thick. "What is it?"

Mrs. Wakefield was fending off Aunt Vivvie, who was leaning heavily on her. "Call the police? Isn't that what people do when somebody gets whacked?"

Trixie, who was now half-sitting, half-lying in one of the two side chairs, brightened. "The police! Of course!

Let's do that!"

Jill reached for the black handset on the desk, but Judith restrained her. "Wait—let's call from the phone in the entry hall," she urged. "We shouldn't touch anything. In fact, we all ought to get out of here right now."

Whatever resentment the others might have shown earlier toward Judith seemed to fade in the face of death. Obediently, the family members, as well as the Wakefields, trooped out of the den. Judith and Renie lingered briefly.

"Look at the floor," Judith said in a low voice. "Is that dust or ashes?"

Renie bent down. Small gray particles were scattered all over the boxed parquet floor. "Ash?" Reluctantly, she moved back to the desk. There was more of the same residue in the brass-and-wood ashtray. "Uncle Boo's cigar, maybe. When he fell forward, the ashes were scattered around the room."

Judith nodded. "Could be." She stared at the big carton which had contained the new TV set. Her eyes traveled to the windows flanking the bookcase behind Uncle Boo. The casements were latched from the inside. The floor itself revealed no wet footprints, no stains, no heel marks. A key, presumably to the den, lay innocently near the brandy snifter. The cousins bowed their heads in Uncle Boo's direction, crossed themselves, and closed the door behind them.

It was Derek Rush who seemed to have taken over as head of the family. He had commandeered the phone in the entry hall alcove. Holly stood next to him, wiping at her eyes with a tissue. The others had returned to the living room. They were arguing about when it would be appropriate to leave, but for once, their manner was low-key, almost reasonable.

"We can't leave until the police come," Vivvie asserted. "I watch TV. I know that's how it works with shootings."

Aunt Toadie had recovered her nerve. She had no compunction about sitting in Uncle Boo's favorite wing-back chair. Her posture was very straight, her demeanor that of an empress seated on a throne. "The weather is getting terrible. It must be freezing outside. If we don't leave now, we'll never get out of here."

Mason Meade stood at one of the four mullioned windows that looked out over the front lawn. "Mr. Major seemed so cheerful. Why would he kill himself?"

Still agitated, Aunt Vivvie darted a look at Mason from her place on the sofa. "Kill himself? Who said he did?"

Mason turned, a startled expression on his craggy face. "Why, what else could it be? The den was locked."

Caressing the brandy glass with its fresh refill, Trixie scoffed at her fiancé's pronouncement. "Mason, darling! That's crazy! You don't know Uncle Boo! It was an accident! He must have been cleaning his guns."

"What guns?" demanded Mrs. Wakefield, as she warmed her broad backside in front of the fire. "Boo Major was in the infantry in World War Two, but he gave his guns away a long time ago."

Toadie's and Vivvie's heads swung around simultaneously as Derek Rush returned from using the telephone. "What is it? Why are you staring at me?"

Vivvie gestured nervously with her beringed hands. "Boo's guns. He gave them to you when you turned eighteen."

Derek tipped his long, narrow head to one side. "He

did?" His lean features were pained. "Poor Uncle Boo," he said, more to himself than to the others. "He was always so good to me . . ." Getting a grip on his emotions, he gazed at his mother. "I rather remember it now. I suppose I put them away. I don't recall where. Do you?"

Vivvie put a fluttering hand on her bosom. "Oh! No, I don't. Your father would have . . . But he's gone, too. And now Boo is dead . . . oh, my!" She burst into a new spate of tears.

"Wait a minute," said Jill from the piano bench. Her face was still pale and her usual panache was missing. "What's all this suicide-and-accident crap? If Boo shot himself, where's the gun?"

Judith and Renie, who were sitting on a striped settee near the piano, kept quiet. By mutual, silent consent, they had decided to withdraw from the fray, at least until the police arrived.

Toadie seemed to agree with her daughter. "It must have been one of those freak mishaps. The gun fell on the floor. It's probably under the desk."

Jill made a slashing gesture with her hand. "That's bull, Aunt Toadie. Boo had a lot to look forward to. Believe me, he had no reason to kill himself." She paused, her brown eyes traveling from face to face. "Well? Don't you get it?"

Judith watched curiously; Renie shifted impatiently. The only light in the room came from the candle-shaped wall sconces and the dying fire in the big grate. Long shadows played against the cream-colored stucco walls. The small, leaded-glass panes were streaked with rain; the big house had grown quite chilly. All of the faces turned toward Jill were anxious, strained, and wary.

Finally, the truth descended upon the room, from the

71

coved ceiling with its nautical rope decor to the lush pattern of the handsome Oriental carpets. It was Derek who was the first to comprehend. His wolf like features sagged, his hunted eyes bulged, and his long, thin fingers clawed at the back of the sofa on which his mother sat.

"You mean—*murder?*" His voice was incredulous. "Jill, my dear, how could you think—" Derek bit his lower lip, unable to continue.

Vivvie stopped weeping, but turned on the sofa to grab at her son's hand. "Derek! No! It's too awful!"

"It's silly," Trixie insisted. "Why are you always so grim, Derek? Lighten up."

Derek stiffened, a lock of black hair falling over his forehead. He removed a pack of cigarettes and a book of matches from the inside pocket of his suit coat, and defiantly began to smoke. "You're a fool, Trixie. For once, don't dodge reality. Somebody killed Uncle Boo."

In the arched doorway, Zoe reeled. "Wow! This is heavy! This is grimmer than Ibsen! In fact," she went on with a catch in her voice, "this is horrible!" With her hair streaming behind her, she fled out through the entry hall.

Jill seemed transfixed. "The maid's right. This is more than I can handle. Poor Boo!" Flinging a hand over her face, she leaped off the piano bench and also raced away.

Holly Rush's face crumpled. "My poor baby! I must go to her! Jill!" Holly hastened after her grieving daughter.

"I can't believe this." Aunt Toadie spoke in an unusually thin voice. "Imagine! Murder! It's so embarrassing!"

"Now, Mummy," soothed Trixie, "look at the bright

side. We may get our pictures in the paper or even on TV. It'll be good publicity for my home fashion business. Women can't resist buying clothes from a celebrity. Look at Arnold Palmer."

"What?" Renie couldn't contain her dismay. "Good God, what has Arnold Palmer got to do with women's fashions? And when did you start peddling clothes?"

Trixie shot Renie an indignant look. "You know—those golf sweaters. They've been the rage for years. For men. But women wear them sometimes. I've been a Wear-House Dressing rep for almost two years. It's really great. Want to see my catalogs?"

"Oh, egad," groaned Renie. "*No*."

Trixie looked offended, but before she could challenge Renie, Mason Meade held up his hands. "Listen! I hear sirens. Here come the police."

Trixie and Derek joined Mason at the window. On the settee, Judith could hear the faint wail of the approaching squad car. The little group waited in silence. It seemed to be taking a long time for the police to arrive. Judith craned her neck to look out the window. To her surprise, the rain had blown out across the bay, and the wind had died down. A bank of fog was rolling in over The Bluff. Anxiously, she wondered about the driving conditions.

At last the red-and-blue flashing lights were spotted at the corner. The police car crept up the street. So did the ambulance that followed. A third vehicle skidded at the intersection, then veered into the curb. Judith's heart sank. She knew the pavement must be covered with black ice. Her chances of getting home plummeted.

Straining to see, Toadie got to her feet. "They're coming in the *front?* Oh, good heavens! They should use the tradesmen's entrance! Don't they have any sense of decency?" She whirled on Judith, who was still sitting next to Renie on the settee. "Aren't you living with a policeman? You must speak to him about this breach of conduct."

"Actually, I'm married to—" Judith broke off as the front doorbell chimed. Derek had already gone into the hall to greet the police. The living room again fell silent. A booming masculine voice bounced off the walls. Some sort of protest issued from Derek Rush, then was drowned out by the much-louder new arrival.

The voice belonged to the man who now filled the doorway. Tall, broad, and bellicose, the homicide detective wore white. His woolen overcoat, his Stetson hat, his stiffly starched shirt, his crisply pressed pants, his calf-high boots, were white. Only his red tie and black driving gloves broke up the monotone color scheme. When he whipped off the hat, his hair was white, too. Or at least a very pale blond.

"Buck Doerflinger here," he bellowed. "Where's the stiff?"

Everyone but Judith cringed. She groaned and grabbed Renie's arm. Renie looked puzzled.

Derek was fighting hard to keep his dignity. "My uncle's body is in the den," he said, pointing to the small passage that led off the entry hall. "Come, I'll show you—"

Buck Doerflinger brushed Derek off as if he were a gnat. "You stay put," Buck admonished. He glared around the living room. "The rest of you, too. We need fingerprints from all of you. I'll be back." Buck thundered away. The footsteps of the other police officers and the ambulance attendants could be heard traipsing to the murder scene.

Renie unfastened Judith's deathlike grip from her

74

arm. "That hurts, coz. What's wrong?"

Judith lowered her voice. "Buck Doerflinger is what's wrong. He's Joe's archrival at headquarters."

Enlightenment dawned on Renie. "Oh! I remember! Joe's always bitching about what a grandstander Doerflinger is. Lots of noise, not much action. The Master of the Obvious."

"That's the one." Judith fell back against the settee. "Damn! Why couldn't Joe have been assigned to this case? Instead, he's off on a wild-goose chase, looking for the Mayor's cousin, who's probably holed up in a motel with cheap champagne and an expensive hooker."

"It might be a conflict of interest if Joe had gotten this case," Renie said in what she hoped was a calming tone. "Hey, it's after ten. I'd better call Bill before he goes to bed. We may be stuck here for a while."

That, Judith feared, was putting it mildly. She accompanied Renie to the hall phone, noting en route that two uniformed officers stood outside the den. The door was closed, but she could still hear Buck Doerflinger.

Renie's conversation with her husband was not as brief as usual. Bill Jones did not like the telephone. He used it as seldom as possible. But Renie's news was such that Bill was forced not only to hear her out, but to ask some questions as well.

"Maybe I should call Mother," Judith said after Renie had finally hung up.

Renie dissuaded Judith. "She'll worry. She won't admit it, but she will. Wait until Joe gets home and phone him. Then he can go out to the toolshed and tell her in person. That'll make her feel better."

Judith looked askance at Renie. "Talking to Joe will make Mother feel better? Are you nuts? That's like asking a man sitting on a keg of dynamite if he's got a match!"

Renie shrugged. "Go ahead. Call her. Tell her Uncle Boo's been shot to death in a locked room, a big-mouthed imbecile is handling the investigation, and we're iced in on The Bluff with Aunt Toadie and the rest of the loathsome Lotts." Renie smiled thinly. "Well? Dial away, coz."

Judith stomped off toward the main entrance. "Later. Let's go check on the weather. Maybe it's not as bad as we think."

Without their coats, the cousins felt the damp cold straight through to the bone. Unfamiliar with the front of Major Manor, they carefully picked their way down the walk that led to the street. Another uniformed policeman standing next to one of the squad cars told them to go no farther. They must stay within the grounds.

Annoyed, Judith marched along the grass, which was frosty but not as dangerous as the icy pavement. Through the drifting fog she could make out the half-timbered overhang above the dining area, the crenellated staircase tower which matched the design of the extended entrance, and the fine old oak door lighted by a ship's lantern. The beacon also illuminated a coat of arms depicting a lion rampant clutching a spoon. Wheat, oats, barley, corn, flax, and rice symbols flanked the lion. The name MAJOR was etched at the top; the date 1933 was at the bottom.

Despite the chilling cold, Judith turned to head for what she presumed was the lily pond. "Let's see if it's iced over. If it is, we're sunk."

Judith and Renie clung to each other as they proceeded slowly down a short flight of flagstone steps.

The pond was large, circular, and surrounded by brickwork. Some of the bricks had been removed, presumably to replace damaged masonry in the house. Three curved wrought-iron benches would provide restful relaxation in better weather. But now the lily pads were submerged under a sheet of ice. Judith made a choking sound.

"It's got to be thirty degrees or less," she fretted. "We're doomed, coz. If the police can't take us home, we're stuck here for the duration."

"The police barely made it here themselves," Renie reminded her as they struggled back up the flagstone steps. "Black ice screws up everybody in this town. Too many hills."

Irritably, Judith nodded. She began to worry about how Joe would get back to Heraldsgate Hill. Or how the guests would fare at the B&B. And if Gertrude was keeping warm and snug in the toolshed.

"Stop fussing," Renie urged. "If Joe has to, he can walk home from the bottom of the hill. Your mother's already spent one winter in her new place, and she was just fine. The guests can fend for themselves. It serves them right for taking a vacation in February. Nobody can predict the weather around here, especially at this time of year. We can have a false spring, with lots of shrubs in bloom, or a blizzard with two feet of snow. Remember what Grandma Grover used to say about buying primroses before St. Valentine's Day? 'Fools' flowers,' she called them, because we'd have a frost and they'd die."

"Yeah, right." Judith only half-heard Renie's monologue. Shaking with cold, she tried to open the front door. It was locked. Renie rang the bell. One of the uniformed policemen who had been standing by the den let them in. He didn't seem too happy about it.

"I'd advise you two to remain inside," he said with a trace of a Texas accent as he led them through the double inner doors with their stained-glass panels. "There may be a killer lurkin' around out there."

"Yeah, right," Judith repeated. Her indifference to danger made the policeman frown. The cousins headed back into the living room.

Buck Doerflinger had not yet reappeared. Aunt Toadie was again ensconced in the wing chair, now drinking a stiff gin martini. Mason Meade was trying to get the fire going. Aunt Vivvie twittered on the sofa while Derek tried to pacify her. Trixie played "Chopsticks" on the piano, possibly for the tenth time, since Derek finally asked her to desist.

"Music lightens the mood," Trixie pouted. "You're such a sobersides, Derek. It's all right if Jill pounds away at this old keyboard, but you always want to spoil everybody else's fun."

"Fun?" echoed Judith, going to the hearth to warm herself. "Trixie, you are unbelievable."

Trixie slid off the piano bench. "Look," she admonished, waving a manicured finger. "It's sad that Uncle Boo is dead, I'll give you that. But he didn't have to suffer. If he'd lived longer, he might have gotten some awful disease and lingered and been in pain and writhed around in bed forever. Try to see the bright side—he's out of all that misery."

"But he was never in it," protested Renie, joining Judith by the rekindled fire. "Furthermore, the man was murdered. Doesn't that bother you, Trixie?"

If it did, Trixie didn't let on. She straightened the ruffle on the low neckline of her red crepe jacket. "Gloom and doom," she murmured, "doom and gloom.

What good does it do?"

The rhetorical question went unanswered. Buck Doerflinger blew into the room like a winter storm. "First we get fingerprints. Then we'll be interrogating suspects in the dining room," he announced. "The den's off limits for a while."

Behind Buck, Judith could see Uncle Boo being wheeled away in a body bag. She closed her eyes briefly, saying a mental prayer. The intention was there, but her concentration was demolished. Aunt Toadie had leaped to her feet and was shrieking like a harpy.

"Fingerprints! Suspects! What are you talking about!"

Buck's steely gaze would have mowed down almost any hardened criminal. But Aunt Toadie was made of sterner—and meaner—stuff. She headed straight for the detective, matching shriek for bellow. Judith and Renie returned to the settee.

"We'll take you first, lady, since you're so anxious to make trouble," Buck shouted. He signaled to the Texan. "Rigby! Get a move on! Where's your fingerprinting kit?"

Officer Rigby responded with alacrity. Despite Toadie's outraged protests, she was subjected to the inkpad. "I'll have your badge!" she rasped at Doerflinger. "The chief of police is my hairdresser's next-door neighbor's sister-in-law!"

Buck ignored the threat. He waved a majestic arm in the direction of the dining room. "Okay, lady, get in there and start answering some tough questions. This isn't no birthday party."

"But it is," Trixie called after the detective and her mother. "You know, we should have had balloons. Why didn't I think of that?"

Even Mason Meade seemed put off by his fiancée's

remark. "Uh, Trixie—we shouldn't worry about the past. What's done is done. Or not done, in this case." Mason hadn't left his station by the window. "What's bothering me is how we get out of here," he fretted, with one eye on Officer Rigby, who was making the rounds with his fingerprinting kit. "I have an early appointment in the morning."

Trixie gave an unconcerned shrug. "Whoever you're meeting is probably iced in, too." She stroked the arms of the sea-green chair in which she was lounging. "Besides, you need to take a good look at the outside of the house if you're going to bid on the masonry work." Trixie favored the room with an ingratiating smile. "It's such a coincidence that you should be here on the very day that the masons were fired!"

Mason Meade didn't look pleased. "Yes, yes," he replied edgily, "but I'd rather it hadn't also been the same day your uncle got killed."

Trixie was unmoved by her fiancé's quibbles. She submitted to Officer Rigby with a flirtatious smile, and when he had finished his fingerprinting task, she began to hum tunelessly. "You know, we could decorate Uncle Boo's casket with balloons. Since he died on his birthday, that would be a really nice touch."

Next to Judith, Renie began to splutter. Officer Rigby completed his job and hurried from the room. Judith didn't blame him for beating a hasty retreat. In an effort at keeping the fragile peace, she got to her feet. "Say, it occurs to me that this is a family matter after all." Judith paused, not only for the baffled faces that had turned toward her, but for the return of Holly and Jill Rush. Both women's fingers were stained with black ink and their eyes were rimmed in red. It occurred to Judith that they, along with Derek, might be the only people present who were genuinely grieving for Uncle Boo.

Vivvie's blue-eyed gaze followed her daughter-in-law and her granddaughter as they both sat down on the piano bench. Mother and daughter appeared to be seeking mutual support. Vivvie asked her daughter-in-law to fix her a teensy vodka martini.

"You're not related to us," Vivvie said to Judith, then made a quavery gesture with her hands. "That is, not by blood. You needn't feel any . . . responsibility."

"But we do," Judith averred. "We were in this house when Boo was killed." She saw Vivvie shudder and Holly shiver as the vodka martini was passed from daughter-in-law to mother-in-law. "Naturally, I have the utmost confidence in Detective Doerflinger," Judith went on as the lie tripped glibly off her tongue, "but having had some experience with police investigations, I can tell you that the officers won't tell us much, at least not right away. I think we owe it to ourselves to do a little sleuthing on our own."

Derek Rush glumly shook his head; Aunt Vivvie waved her handkerchief in a negative manner; Holly turned away; Mason Meade looked alarmed; Trixie screwed up her face in a disgusted manner. Only Jill expressed agreement.

"You're right, Judith. The police have procedures and forms and a ton of paperwork. It's going to take them forever just to talk to each one of us. If nothing else, we can help pass the time by trying to sort all this out on our own."

Trixie now looked puzzled. "You mean like playing Clue?"

"Right, Trixie," Renie replied in a condescending manner. "Like, 'Uncle Boo was killed in the den with the revolver by'—fill in the blank."

81

Trixie's eyes grew round. "He was killed by *blanks?* Is that possible?"

Judith gritted her teeth. "Actually, it is, but I don't think that's what happened here. The first thing we should establish is where everybody was when the murder occurred."

Derek's initial opposition faded. "But we don't know exactly when it happened."

"True," Judith agreed. "Let's try to narrow down the time factor. When did Uncle Boo go into the den?"

Vivvie batted her blue eyes with their false lashes. "Oh, dear! It was after dessert—why, I've no idea!"

Jill, however, had the time nailed down to the minute. She held out her wrist with its digital watch: "It was nine-oh-one."

Trixie tossed her bleached blond head. "Now, how would you happen to know that, Miss Smarty-Pants?"

Jill gave her first cousin once-removed a venomous look. "I was trying to figure out how much longer everybody'd have to stick around this place. Do you think I enjoy family get-togethers? I'd rather be attacked by killer bees."

Trixie stiffened, but it was Holly who spoke. "Jill, dearest, don't say such things! Especially now that Uncle Boo is dead."

Jill appeared unfazed by her mother's criticism. "I'm not referring to Boo. He was . . . lovable." She lowered her dark eyes, stared at the piano keyboard, then softly played a few bars of "Can't Help Lovin' That Man," ending on an off-key note. "This thing's out of tune," she complained. "It's as if when Boo died, the strings lost heart. If pianos have souls, this one senses tragedy and evil."

Holly patted her daughter's shoulder. "You're

distressed, Jill. Don't take it out on the piano. Or your family. We're all undone."

Jill's eyes darted around the room. "Some more than others," she said in a brittle voice.

"So," Judith noted before further wrangling could break out, "Boo went into the den at one minute past nine. What did the rest of you do then?"

Derek, who had been slowly pacing up and down the hearth, stopped and regarded Judith thoughtfully. "I believe we lingered at the table for another five minutes. Then we adjourned to the living room for brandy."

Judith nodded. "Did anyone leave the room after that?"

It seemed to her that covert glances were exchanged around the room. Aunt Vivvie was the first to speak: "Heavens, no! We didn't budge until it was time to leave."

"Which was . . . ?" coaxed Judith.

"Nine-thirty-seven," Jill replied promptly. This time, no one questioned her accuracy.

"So," Judith mused aloud, "Uncle Boo must have been killed in that time span. Did anyone hear the shot?"

"My, yes!" Vivvie avowed excitedly.

"No," Trixie stated emphatically.

"I'm not sure," Derek replied hesitantly.

"The pressure cooker," Holly put in. "Aunt Toadie said the loud noise was a pressure cooker exploding in the servants' quarters."

"'There was more than one noise," Jill insisted. "In fact, I heard at least three distinct sounds—including that dumb pressure cooker."

"Three?" Derek gave his daughter a dubious look. He moved away from the hearth to gaze across the room.

"Mason? What did you—"

Derek stopped, his long face a mask of puzzlement. The others followed his eyes to the front windows.

Mason Meade was gone.

SIX

IMMEDIATELY AFTER TRIXIE WENT TO SEARCH FOR HER fiancé, Aunt Toadie returned, and Aunt Vivvie was summoned by Buck Doerflinger. The debate over what had happened to Mason Meade was cut short by Toadie's charges of police brutality. She was enraged; she was outraged; she intended to sue the city.

"There is no excuse," she seethed, "for treating innocent people as if they were axe murderers! That dreadful man did everything but beat me with a rubber hose!"

"Too bad," murmured Renie, nudging Judith. "You bring your thumbscrews?"

"I wish," Judith whispered back.

When at last Aunt Toadie had run out of steam, Holly expressed the thought that had been bothering everybody: "How did Mason leave without us seeing him?"

Judith considered. The room was large, long, and in deep shadow. All attention had been fixed on whoever had the floor at the moment. Mason Meade hadn't said a word after Judith began her round of questions. No doubt he had taken the opportunity to slip out unnoticed. Judith said as much. The others didn't disagree.

Trixie returned looking subdued. "My car's gone," she said in a hollow voice. "I looked all over the house and couldn't find Mason; then I went outside, and the Lexus is gone." She sank into the sea-green armchair, chin on her semi-bared chest.

"Your car keys," Toadie snapped. "Did he take them, too?"

85

Trixie gave her mother a sullen look. "Mason drove. He had them all along."

At the piano, Jill played the opening bars of "What Kind of Fool Am I?" "Hey, Trixie, your new man's a car thief! You sure know how to pick them. Didn't Rafe Longrod own all the porno-flick theaters in town?"

"They were art houses," Trixie replied indignantly. "Rafe showed only the finest foreign films. Of course there was some nudity and that meant they were often X-rated, but that's because a lot of prudes run this country. Look at Ronald Reagan!"

"Why?" said Renie.

Trixie took her seriously. "He was never in an X-rated movie, so he started up this censorship thing. And the reason he didn't do scenes in the nude was because who would want to see Ronald Reagan naked?"

"Certainly not Nancy Reagan," Jill retorted. "You're full of it, Trixie. You call movies like *An Affair with My Member* and *Ben Hur, Ben Him, Too* art films? How bogus!"

Again Judith saw the need to intervene. "We're not getting very far," she warned the others. Noting Toadie's curious as well as hostile gaze, she explained what had taken place in her absence.

Toadie scoffed. "You're playing detective, Judith? How absurd! Just because you're living with a policeman—what does he do, direct traffic for football games? Honestly!" She folded her arms across her chiffon-covered breast and turned away.

Derek, however, ignored his aunt's carping. "Go ahead, Judith. We might as well do something constructive."

"What about Mason?" Trixie wailed. "What if something's happened to him!"

"It did," Jill responded. "He stole your car."

Judith's peace plan seemed to be unraveling. "Maybe," she suggested, "we should break up into smaller groups. Some of us could go into the breakfast nook."

"But we can't," Derek protested. "We'd have to go through the dining room to get to it, and the police are in there. With Mother." He grimaced.

"Nonsense." Toadie, who obviously was now siding with Judith just to be ornery, glared at her nephew. "We could go outside or through the garage and come in through the kitchen. There are two doors in the breakfast nook—one to the dining room and the other to the kitchen."

"I'd rather be in here," Holly said in her small voice. "I feel safer." She gave her husband an imploring look. "You'll stay, won't you, Derek?"

Derek looked uncomfortable but agreed. So did their daughter. Judith realized she was about to exile herself to the breakfast room with Aunt Toadie and Trixie. The idea appalled her.

But Renie saved the day—or at least what was left of the evening. Sensing Judith's dread, she offered herself as a viable alternative. "I could use a snack," she admitted, finally giving in to her ever-voracious appetite. "In fact, I could eat a cow. I'll take Aunt Toadie and Trixie out to the kitchen and we'll forage."

As Renie and the other two women trooped out of the living room, Judith offered her cousin a grateful smile. Renie smiled back.

"There're steaks in the fridge," she said in passing. "I'm going to cook two. Both for me." Renie patted her stomach and continued on her way.

With only the three Rushes left, the big living room

seemed virtually empty. Judith decided to make the most of the relative calm.

"Jill," she began, moving over to the vacant sofa, "you said you heard three different noises. I did, too. Could one of them have been a gunshot?"

Jill considered. "I don't know. I'm not sure what a gunshot sounds like. Not in real life, I mean."

Holly rose from the piano bench, wandering over to a Duncan Phyfe table near the sea-green armchair. "All I remember was that pressure cooker. That happened right after we came back into the living room."

Derek nodded. "There was at least one other noise, now that I think about it. Much quieter, though. These walls are so solid and the wind was up—it would be impossible to tell where the sounds came from."

Jill's fingers hovered over the keyboard as she gazed first at her father, then at her mother. "Let's cut the crap, okay?" Anxiously, her parents stared at her. "Grandma lied about everybody staying in this room after Boo went into the den. I don't know why she said such a thing, but it's not true."

Holly blanched. "Oh, Jill! I'm sure your grandmother just wanted to avoid trouble. You know how she hates a fuss!"

Judith had doubted Vivvie's words at the time, since she knew Mrs. Wakefield had seen Jill and Mason Meade in the entry hall. Naturally, her curiosity was further piqued. "Who left besides you, Jill? And Mason, of course."

"I had to get out of here for a few minutes," Jill replied. "Grandma and Aunt Toadie were making me crazy, and Trixie is such a dork. Trixie's fiancé followed me into the entry hall, and I thought he was going to come on to me—he looks the type—but he didn't. He said he had to go outside and get something in the car. Maybe he moved it to make his getaway."

"Maybe," Judith conceded. "You didn't see or hear anything unusual while you were in the entry hall?"

Jill snickered. "Everything's unusual with this bunch of weirdos. No offense." She nodded at her parents. "But no, I didn't. I just wandered around, admiring that mirror with the flower design outside the den, the stained glass on the first landing of the stairs—nice ships, pretty colors—and the rest of the decor. I like this house. It's old and dowdy, but it's comfortable." She started to smile, then her lips quivered. "Oh, damn! I hate it when I get all sentimental!"

To cover Jill's embarrassment, Judith turned to Holly. "Did you notice who else left?"

"I went to the ladies' room," Holly answered primly. "So did my mother-in-law, a few minutes later." She looked at her husband. "You went out for a bit, didn't you, Derek?"

He nodded. "I had a cigarette in the garage." As if by reflex, he removed the pack from his suit coat and lighted up again. Through the cloud of smoke, he gazed questioningly at Holly. "Didn't Aunt Toadie go check on Uncle Boo?"

"Yes, I believe she did. That was right after I came back from the bathroom." Holly put a hand to her cheek. "And Trixie—she went to make a phone call. To her brother, Marty."

Judith frowned. "In other words, everybody in this room was gone at one time or another while Uncle Boo was in the den."

Jill had regained her composure. "Great. In other words, nobody has an ironclad alibi." She shot Judith a wry glance. "What about you and the rest of the kitchen crew?"

Momentarily taken aback, Judith stared at Jill. The question was valid, however. "We were working together the whole time. Except when Mrs. Wakefield and Zoe were back and forth cleaning up the dining room. And, of course, Mrs. Wakefield had to go patch up Mr. Wakefield." She frowned again, more deeply. "Shoot, the only people who can alibi each other are my cousin and me."

Derek's expression was sardonic. "And as I recall, you and Renie would—excuse the phrase—kill for each other. Or so it seemed to me when I was a child."

To Judith's chagrin, the bond between the cousins appeared to be well known among the shirttail relations. Flustered, she gave a halfhearted laugh. "We're close, that's true, but all the same we—"

Aunt Vivvie stumbled into the room, her wig askew. "Oh, dear! Such an ordeal! You'd think I was a serial killer!" She collapsed on the sofa, her tiny feet swinging above the carpet. "Derek, dearest, do pour me a bit of brandy. I feel faint."

Derek, however, discovered that the bottle was empty. He volunteered to fetch some other spirits from the kitchen. Aunt Vivvie revived sufficiently to inform Judith that she was wanted next in the dining room.

"I almost forgot," Vivvie said apologetically. "I'm so undone, as you can see. But that terrible detective said he had to speak to whoever was in charge here this evening. It is you, isn't it, Judith?" The false eyelashes flapped over the baby-doll blue eyes.

"I guess," Judith said with a touch of grimness. Resolutely, she left the room and headed through the entry hall.

Buck Doerflinger had restored the pair of lamps to the

dining room table but had removed the shades. The effect was bright, stark, and sinister. Judith blinked as she sat down between Buck and the round brown officer who was assisting him.

"Mrs. McMonigle," Buck began in his too-loud voice, "I hear you put on this shindig for the deceased."

Judith fingered her upper lip. Buck had called her Mrs. McMonigle. Perhaps Aunt Toadie's obstinacy had played into Judith's hands. Not only did Toadie refuse to acknowledge that Judith and Joe were married, but the wretched woman still called her by Dan's last name. Given the animosity between Buck Doerflinger and Joe Flynn, the mistake was providential.

Judith gave Buck a flinty smile. "I catered the event, yes. Mrs. Grover organized it, though."

Buck grunted. He proceeded to ask Judith for her age, address, phone number, and occupation. None of the responses seemed to ring any bells for Buck. His knowledge of Joe undoubtedly was limited to the professional arena.

"You're some kind of relative, I hear," he said, leaning back in the chair at the head of the table and affecting a casual demeanor. His voice had dropped to a dull roar.

Judith explained the relationship between herself and Renie, as well as their connection with the Lott family through Uncle Corky. "Boo Major isn't—wasn't—related to us in any way, not even by marriage," she emphasized.

Buck grunted. "Nepotism."

"Huh?" Judith looked startled.

Buck gave her a conspiratorial look. "You got the job because your uncle Corky is married to this Theodora Grover, right? That's nepotism."

91

"That's a shame," Judith retorted. "If you want to know the truth, I didn't want to do this. Toadie—Mrs. Grover—twisted my arm."

Buck nodded to his subordinate. "Use of force. Make a note, Foster." His seemingly bland gaze resumed to Judith. "Now this coercion—what did Mrs. Grover have on you that she could *force you against your will* to cater this party?"

Fleetingly, Judith wondered how many times her patience could be tried in a single night. "It wasn't exactly against my will. I don't like mixing business with family."

"But you said Boo Major wasn't family." Buck wore a triumphant air.

"Look," said Judith, gripping the edge of the dining room table, "I didn't want to get into a row with Aunt Toadie and I didn't want to hurt Uncle Boo's feelings. I came, I served, I tried to go home. Then Uncle Boo was found shot. That's the whole story in a nutshell, as far as Renie and I are concerned."

Buck Doerflinger was scanning a page of notes. "Renie? Who's Renie? I don't see any Renie listed among the suspects."

Judith winced at the detective's terminology. She explained that Renie was no doubt listed as Serena Jones. Buck lifted one white eyebrow. "An alias?"

Judith sighed. "A nickname. Renie—Mrs. Jones—is my first cousin on the Grover side. She came along to help. Ordinarily, my neighbor, Arlene Rankers, is my assistant caterer, but Arlene's husband, Carl, retired in December and they're in California visiting—"

For reasons unknown to Judith, Buck Doerflinger was scribbling furiously and nodding at Officer Foster to do the same. "Hey," she said, interrupting herself, "why are

92

you taking all this down?"

Buck snorted. "Don't question police procedures. How do we know these neighbors are really in California? It's a big state. They could be anywhere."

"But . . ." Judith's feeble protest died aborning. Resignedly, she waited for the next outrageous question.

This time, however, Buck Doerflinger was right on target: "Did you hear the shot?"

Judith explained about the exploding pressure cooker and the other two noises. Buck listened impatiently, obviously already having heard similar accounts from Toadie and Vivvie.

"Did you see anyone go into the den after Mr. Major entered?" he asked.

The brightness of the lamps and the events of the evening were giving Judith a headache. "No. But then, I wouldn't have. I stayed in the kitchen. You can't see the door to the den from there. At an angle, you can look out from the kitchen through this room into the hall, but the den door is recessed several feet. I didn't see any of the guests go near it, though."

The detective waited for his assistant to catch up. Foster finished writing, then turned an earnest round face to his superior. "That's true, sir," he said, pointing to the two closed doors which led out of the dining room. "I checked the line of sight earlier."

Buck mumbled something which might have been approval. "What happened when the deceased didn't respond to the knocking on the door?" he inquired of Judith.

Judith wanted to be accurate. "Uncle Boo had taken the key into the den," she recounted carefully. "There was a master key on a ring, but it had disappeared a while ago, according to the housekeeper. The men were about to break the door down—or so it seemed—when I volunteered to try to pick the lock."

Buck settled back in the chair and sadly shook his head. "How unfortunate. For you, I mean."

Startled, Judith's black eyes stared. "Huh?"

Buck shrugged carelessly. "If you can pick the lock after he's dead, why not before?"

"Oh, good grief!" Judith twisted around in the chair, making a helpless gesture with her hands. "With what? I had to have somebody go find a crochet hook to do it at all. And how could I pick a lock in plain sight of the others?"

Buck leaned forward, shaking a finger at her. "But you just said yourself that anybody at the door to the den couldn't be seen because the entrance is recessed." He nodded abruptly at Foster. "Make a note of that."

"If somebody walked by, they'd see me," she countered. "Who'd take a chance like that?"

Buck's expression was impassive. "Somebody took a chance. A big one."

"True," Judith allowed. "But I doubt if whoever took that chance did it by picking the lock."

"You got a better idea?" Sarcasm dripped from the detective's voice as he tipped his big head to one side.

Judith considered. "Well—no. There are windows on either side of the bookcase in back of the desk, but they're not very big. And they were latched from the inside."

"Aha!" boomed Buck. "You noticed that, did you?"

Judith ignored his insinuating remark. "Was the key on the desk the one for the den?"

He looked affronted by her temerity in asking such a question. "Sure it was. What else would it be for? You got a noticing kind of nature, lady. How come?"

In the distance, more sirens could be heard. Foster's ears pricked up, but Buck paid no heed. Judith waited until the wailing noise wound down before she spoke again. "Given the circumstances, it would be peculiar not to notice," she said, sounding a bit cross. "What I didn't check on was whether or not those bookcases hide a secret panel. That would explain everything."

Buck's mouth expanded across his wide face, a rumbling guffaw emitted from his chest, and then he threw back his head. "Ha-ha! A secret . . . panel! That's . . . rich!" He was laughing so hard that he could barely speak. Officer Foster chuckled in a manner that was more embarrassed than amused.

Given the eccentricities of the Major family, Judith hadn't found the suggestion inconceivable. "It's possible," she began, "if old Dunlop had wanted to . . ."

Buck's uproarious laughter drowned her out. At last he regained control and wiped his eyes with a large white handkerchief. "This isn't . . . some old manor house in . . . England, or one of those . . . places where they have manor houses. This," he continued, suddenly sober and pounding on the table, "is *The Bluff!* If you're looking for a hiding place, what about that big carton?"

Judith frowned. "The . . . oh, you mean the box the new TV came in? What about it?"

Buck resettled himself. The chair creaked under his weight. He folded his hands across the expanse of his stomach and twiddled his thumbs. "That's right, the box. An adult could hide in that thing. I don't suppose you noticed that."

Judith reflected on the presence of the large carton. Buck Doerflinger was right: It certainly was large enough to conceal a full-grown adult. It could even have concealed one as huge as Buck Doerflinger. But the idea didn't make much sense. Judith decided not to say so. "It's a big box, all right," she allowed as a knock sounded at the door between the dining room and the entry hall.

The officer with the Texas drawl put a deferential hand to the brim of his cap. "Sir, there's been an accident."

Buck scowled at the policeman. "So?"

"It happened at the bottom of that steep hill leadin' from The Bluff. New Lexus, went into a lamppost. The driver's kind of messed up. He's bein' taken to Bayview Hospital. Name of Mason Meade. Isn't he one of the suspects we fingerprinted? Sir?"

Buck Doerflinger flew out of the chair, which toppled to the floor. The table shook; Buck shook, presumably with rage. "Meade's a suspect, dammit! What was he doing, fleeing the premises?" He whirled on Judith. "Did you know about this? Did you aid and abet Meade's escape?"

Judith gulped. "I knew he left the living room," she replied in a feeble voice.

Buck's eyes narrowed to the thinnest of slits. He seemed incoherent with anger, glowering at Judith and wagging his finger. At last he composed himself and turned back to the Texan. "Rigby—once this perp gets to the hospital, have a round-the-clock guard kept on him. I don't want him running off again."

Rigby nodded, his big ears turning pink. "It's not likely, sir. Meade's got a broken leg and arm. Ribs, too. And probably a concussion. He skidded down that steep hill and really slammed into the lamppost. The car's a mess."

"Serves him right," muttered Buck, picking up the chair and sitting back down. Rigby left. Judith was

96

urged to do the same. Buck Doerflinger wanted to see Renie next. Judith hoped Renie had a full stomach. Her cousin could be testy when she was hungry. And with Buck Doerflinger, that wouldn't do. No, thought Judith as she went out through the door that led to the kitchen, that wouldn't do at all.

Renie was just sitting down to her steak, new potatoes, and what was left of the cauliflower. Buck's summons was not met with good grace.

"Tell him to screw off," Renie snarled. "Except for a few samples while we were getting dinner, I haven't eaten since lunch. I'm starved."

"I don't think you can put Doerflinger off," Judith coaxed. "He's kind of awful." Suddenly she gazed around the kitchen. Except for Renie, no one else was present. "Hey, where's Toadie and Vivvie and Trixie?"

Renie gave a slight shrug and tied into the steak. "The old girls went upstairs to bed. I guess Trixie went with them. Or else she's pining for Mason. Who knows? Who cares?" Renie put extra butter on her potatoes.

"Mason wrecked Trixie's car," Judith said, fretting over how to part Renie from her meal. "He's off to the hospital."

"Serves him right," Renie replied with her mouth full. "The food won't be very good there."

"Coz," Judith said slowly, "the cops are waiting for you. Don't aggravate Buck Doerflinger."

Renie tasted the cauliflower. "Why couldn't Woody have gotten this case? He's not working with Joe on this missing-perons thing, is he?"

Anxiously, Judith folded her hands together in a prayerful attitude. "No. Woody's been breaking in a new recruit," she explained a bit distractedly. "He and

Joe will be working again as a team in a couple of weeks. But not now. Unfortunately." Judith knew how much her husband missed his partner, the taciturn, knowledgeable, engaging Woodrow Wilson Price.

"Woody's great," Renie commented, forking in more steak. "Wee Woody must be going on two. Did you say Sondra was expecting again late this summer?"

"Yes, yes, late July or early August. I forget exactly." Judith didn't have time to spare for the growing Woody Price ménage. Her head was throbbing, and she knew it was only a matter of seconds before Doerflinger sent his lackeys after Renie. "Coz," she pleaded, "get in the dining room before Buck busts a gusset!"

"*Sheesh.*" Rolling her eyes, Renie got to her feet, plate and utensils in hand.

"You can't eat in there," Judith said sharply.

"Why not? It's the dining room, isn't it?" Renie huffed her way out of the kitchen.

Judith grabbed her cousin's purse. Her own was in the living room. She knew Renie always carried a small bottle of aspirin. Judith needed some. She had a feeling she'd need more before she left Major Manor.

SEVEN

RENIE HAD BEEN RIGHT ABOUT AUNT TOADIE AND Aunt Vivvie: Claiming exhaustion from their ordeal, they had retired for the night. The Lott sisters had commandeered the bedrooms off the main staircase which were directly opposite each other, but shared a common bath with the other two guest rooms down the hall.

Renie had also been right about Buck Doerflinger: When she emerged from the dining room ten minutes later, empty plate in hand, she reported that Buck had been quite amiable.

"He kept asking questions and I kept saying I didn't know. Which I don't," Renie asserted, rinsing off her dinner plate in the kitchen sink. "I think he's beginning to get tired, too. After all, it's going on eleven-thirty." To underscore her point, she yawned.

Trixie was now in the dining room with Buck. The cousins tried to listen at the door but could hear only muffled voices.

"I suppose," Judith mused, "we should make sleeping arrangements of our own. Why don't you check it out while I call Joe?"

Joe had just gotten home after a harrowing drive. He had taken the long way, going to the north end of Heraldsgate Hill, then creeping through the fog that blanketed the neighborhood's commercial district.

"I left the MG at the top of the hill," he reported, sounding weary. "I walked the last four blocks, but I almost fell on my butt about six times."

"How's Mother?" Judith inquired, not quite ready to

99

admit that anything other than the weather was preventing her departure from The Bluff.

Joe chuckled, a bit weakly. "I pounded on the toolshed door. She was watching an old Western and rooting for General Custer. She told me to go soak my head."

"Oh, good," Judith exclaimed, "she's fine, then. Say, Joe, we've had a little problem over here with—"

"Corinne Dooley left a note," Joe went on, apparently not having heard his wife. "She said everything was okay with the guests. They all went out after sherry and hors d'oeuvres."

Judith frowned. "Did they all come back?"

"Damned if I know," Joe replied unconcernedly. "They always take a key, so they can let themselves in. Since when did you start worrying about curfew?"

"Since the streets got covered with black ice," Judith retorted.

"So? If they're marooned somewhere, it's not your fault. You won't have to worry about getting them breakfast."

Judith rubbed at her head, which was still aching despite Renie's aspirin. "If they *do* come back, can you fix some eggs and bacon and toast and coffee?"

"Sure," Joe answered, his enthusiasm forced. "Sounds good. For me. I've got to be back at headquarters by seven A.M.—if I can make it. The Mayor is in a real tizzy. We haven't turned up a single significant lead on his cousin."

"But, Joe . . ." Judith ran a hand through her short silvered hair. Irrationally, she felt as if Joe were letting her down. "Have you checked to see if the guests are in their rooms?"

"Jude-girl." All buoyancy had gone out of Joe's

100

voice. She had a mental image of her husband sitting on their bed in the third-floor family quarters. Probably his tie was undone, his shirt was unbuttoned, and his loafers were already off. No doubt his sport coat and .38 Smith & Wesson revolver were flung across the back of a chair. "It's going on midnight. I have to be up in six hours. If your guests don't have enough sense to come in out of the ice, I can't help it. I'll give Corinne a call in the morning before I leave. She's a good kid; she'll bail you out again, okay?"

Judith leaned against the wall where the old-fashioned black telephone was situated. She pressed the separate earpiece against her aching skull and tried to think her way through this latest dilemma. Perhaps the guests were safely ensconced in their beds. Maybe Joe was right. Corinne Dooley was always up before seven. She could fix a half-dozen breakfasts without batting an eye. Judith would deal with the next crisis when she felt more rested.

But she still had to tell Joe about Uncle Boo's murder. Or did she? He was worn out; she was feeling ragged. What was the point? He'd be upset, maybe worried enough to risk his neck by coming to rescue her from a murderer—and Buck Doerflinger. It was hard to say which would distress Joe more. The most important thing was to tell him she loved him.

"I love you," she said into the separate mouthpiece.

"The feeling is mutual," Joe replied, sounding less frazzled but more sleepy. "Go to bed. I'll see you tomorrow. I hope."

"Me, too," Judith said fervently. " 'Night."

" 'Night. Miss you," he added, his voice even lower. "Bed's empty. Cold, too. Brrrr." He chuckled again, then suddenly gained momentum. "By the way, don't go

101

for any walks. I heard on the scanner that there was a murder tonight over on The Bluff. I don't remember the address, but I think it was kind of close to Major Manor."

Judith gulped. "I heard about it, too. It *was* pretty close."

Too close, Judith thought as she hung up the antiquated phone.

On the second floor, Toadie and Vivvie both had their doors closed. Trixie informed the cousins she would join her mother.

"There are two other rooms down the hall, but Derek and Holly will take one, and that little snot of a Jill has dibs on the other," Trixie declared, not without a hint of pleasure at the cousins' discomfiture. "Maybe you two can sleep in the furnace room."

Renie gave Trixie a snide look. "That would beat sleeping in Intensive Care, which is where your fiancé is about now. How come he did a bunk? Bad conscience? I hope your car was insured, kiddo."

Trixie blanched. "Serena! You've got a nasty tongue! How can you talk that way when poor Mason is in Unsatisfactory Condition?"

Renie sniffed. "Upgraded from Unstable? Or was that the condition he was in when you two got engaged?"

Trixie looked as if she were about to pummel Renie. The sight of two middle-aged women facing off on the staircase landing beneath Dunlop Major's luminous stained-glass clipper ships was too much for Judith.

"Knock it off, guys," she ordered. "Haven't we had enough trouble tonight?"

As the evening wore on, Trixie's carefully made-up face had lost its bloom. She looked haggard and depleted. While Renie retained her belligerent stance, Trixie folded up, like a fading flower.

"Of course I'm worried sick about Mason," she murmured. "I'm crazy about him." She ignored Renie's snicker. "But," she went on with a hint of her usual bravado, "I don't care about the car. It's insured, and in any event, I don't have to worry about money." Tossing her head, she started up the final flight of stairs. "Uncle Boo's death is a terrible blow," she said over her shoulder, and for a moment her face took on a fresh, youthful glow. "But everything has its up side. He left all of his fortune to Mummy and me."

Trixie swished on up the stairs and disappeared at the top of the landing.

Derek was the most recent member of the family to be interrogated by the police. He emerged from the dining room shortly before midnight, his long face sallow and his eyes sunken. Judith and Renie approached him as he walked slowly across the entry hall.

"Excuse me," he said in a hollow voice. "I must send my daughter into the inquisition. Then Holly and I are going to bed."

Holly, apparently, had been questioned by Buck Doerflinger in between Trixie and Derek. "What about the Wakefields?" Judith asked.

Derek shrugged. "They're not family. Maybe the police will wait until morning to talk to them. It's very late." He headed toward the living room.

Renie had started back up the stairs, but Judith detained her. "Where are you going? There's no room left up there. Besides, I want to ask Derek something."

Renie bridled. "No room? What about the master suite? Uncle Boo isn't using it tonight."

Judith winced at Renie's apparent callousness. But her cousin wasn't unfeeling so much as she was realistic: Renie was a pragmatist who was also a victim of her own creature comforts. For all practical purposes, she was right. Judith and Renie might as well sleep in Boo's empty bed. It was better than the furnace room.

Jill's shoulders slumped as she trudged into the dining room. "This is silly," she commented as she went past the cousins. "Why would anyone kill Boo? He was utterly harmless."

"But," Judith murmured after Jill was out of earshot, "stinking rich." She turned to Derek, who was standing in the entry hall with a protective arm around Holly. "Well? Is it true about Uncle Boo's will?"

Both Rushes looked affronted, as if Judith had insulted them. It occurred to her that maybe she had. Certainly she was invading the family's privacy.

"Wait," she said hastily. "I'm sorry. I'm tired, and so are you. I spoke out of turn."

Holly smiled wanly. "It's all right. This has been a terrible night. We're all on edge."

Derek nodded. "Many unfortunate things have been said in the course of the evening. Given what's happened, your question is natural enough. It would be in poor taste for us to discuss it, though." He touched Judith's arm; his long fingers were very cold. "You understand."

"Yes, sure," Judith replied, though she sounded uncertain.

Renie wasn't inclined to play the agreeable stooge, however. "Understand what? That when it comes to Boo's will, you folks got screwed?"

Holly's expression was startled. Derek arched his thick dark eyebrows. "What?" he said in a very soft

104

voice. "No, no. Hardly that. My uncle left me everything. Rest his soul."

Holding Holly close, Derek led the way upstairs. Judith and Renie watched them go out of sight, then stared at each other.

"Weird," breathed Renie.

"Crazy," muttered Judith.

Renie tapped her chin. "I wonder who Boo's attorney is."

Judith reflected. "Years ago, when some neighbor's kid jumped in the lily pond and concussed himself, Aunt Rosie hired Ewart Gladstone Whiffel," she said, referring to the lawyer who had served not only the entire Grover clan, but many of their friends and relations as well. "I suppose whoever took over his practice also took over Uncle Boo."

"Mom would know," Renie said, relying as she often did on Deborah Grover's legal background. Renie's mother had worked for years as Whiffel's legal secretary.

"Call her in the morning," said Judith as they started up the stairs. "Money is such a wonderful motive, and in this case, there seems to be some . . . ah . . . confusion."

The door to the master bedroom was just off the upstairs landing. Judith felt for the light switch. Overhead, a brass chandelier went on, its amber bulbs bathing the room in a soft golden glow. The suite was furnished with more Philippine mahogany, including a bed with a carved sunburst on the headboard, a chaise lounge covered in rust-and-bronze-striped satin, a dressing table with a triptych mirror, and a bureau with brass nautical accents. There were two closets faced in etched glass, and an ironing alcove where the new, large-screen TV now stood. A fireplace decorated with wildlife mosaics stood on one side of the room, presumably directly above its mate in the living room. The master bath featured mahogany steps to the tiled tub and a separate shower with a frosted glass door depicting King Neptune. The cousins were charmed.

"Nice," Judith remarked, closing the door to the master bathroom. "But it's cold up here. This whole house is drafty. It's too bad there's no wood or kindling up here. I'll bet Boo hasn't used the fireplace in years." She peeked out through the drawn beige drapes. The fog was right up to the windows.

Renie, who was admiring the handsome but faded floral wallpaper, shivered. "You're right. If we got wood for a fire, we'd probably burn the place down. Maybe we should have slept in the furnace room. It would have been warmer. I'm wearing my socks to bed."

Judith had gone to the big bureau, searching for sleepwear. "I feel ghoulish," she said, sorting through orderly piles of shirts. "Maybe we could sleep in all of our clothes."

Pajamas were found, however, as were robes. The bathroom was so large that the cousins could both use it at the same time. Emerging in a quilted maroon robe, Judith eyed the door. "We'd better lock it. This house isn't exactly safe."

Searching in the pockets for the tie to her silk paisley robe, Renie came up empty and grimaced. "It *should* be safe. It's full of cops."

Judith's expression was skeptical. She turned the old-fashioned latch. "Does every room have a separate lock? Who has the master key? The resident space-case, Weed Wakefield? If I could open the den with a crochet hook, how hard would it be for a determined killer to get in here?"

Renie, however, scoffed. "Who would determine to kill us? We're hired hands. We're the people who get 'friendly reminders' from our creditors. We're poor, coz. We're not worth killing."

The argument was convincing, but nonetheless, Judith insisted on putting a heavy nightstand in front of the door. It took some doing for the cousins to shove the solid piece of furniture across the floor, but they finally managed to get it in place. It was almost twelve-thirty when they crept into the big, comfortable bed. They felt safer, but they were still cold.

"Good night," Renie said, tugging the handmade quilt up around her chin. "Wake me if I turn blue."

"Right," Judith replied. "It's not bad under the covers. 'Night."

"Uh-huh," Renie replied, apparently already half asleep.

Silence had enveloped the big old house. Judith wondered if Buck Doerflinger had finished his interrogations for the night. If so, she speculated about where the policemen would sleep. Perhaps some of the officers would try to get off The Bluff. But Buck, she reasoned, would have to stay on for fear of not being able to return in the morning. Unless the temperature began to rise, the black ice would remain on the streets until the following day.

"It's impossible, you know," Judith said suddenly.

"M-mmmf," Renie murmured.

"Everybody else, including Buck Doerflinger, must realize it, but no one has said so out loud," Judith declared, propping herself up on one elbow. "Why not? Are the Lotts too stupid? Can the Rushes be so obtuse? Is Buck purposely avoiding the crux of the case?"

"Uhnnnn," Renie mumbled.

"Buck's reputation is for fixating on the obvious and running with it, no matter where it leads him," Judith went on, her voice gaining momentum. "But he's not even mentioning the obvious with this case. The most important fact to establish is *how Uncle Boo was killed.* Only when that's been determined can you figure out who did it."

Renie said nothing.

"The room was locked from the inside," Judith continued, her tone now musing. "There is the possibility that the master key and the ring it's on aren't really lost. But we have to take Mrs. Wakefield's word for it that they are. Plus, even if that key had been used, how did the door get locked again from the inside? And the windows—they were also latched from the inside, though I doubt that most of the people involved could have gotten in or out that way. The casements are too small. Jill and Zoe and maybe Holly are the only ones who could get through. Buck laughed at my idea about a hidden passage, but I can't help but wonder if there isn't one. It's the kind of thing an old romantic like Dunlop Major might have thought of."

Still Renie said nothing.

"It would have to lead from the little hallway that goes past the telephone alcove and the main-floor bathroom, then into the garage. Unless"—she paused, sounding dubious yet excited—"it came out of the cupboard or the coat closet on either side of the recessed doorway. I should make a diagram."

After fumbling for the switch on the lamp next to the bed, Judith reached for her handbag. Renie whimpered. Using the back of the paper on which she'd written her catering list for the party, Judith began to draw a crude floor plan of Major Manor. Renie groaned.

"There's one exterior wall behind the desk, with the windows," Judith said, more to herself than to Renie, which was just as well because her cousin had put the pillow over her head. "Then there's the south wall, which is also an exterior, because the den juts out from the house on that side. We have to rule out those two as possibilities. We're left with the north wall, which is off the garage, and the west wall, which faces the entry hall but is actually fronted on one side of the den doorway by the coat closet and on the other by the cupboard. I haven't seen the cupboard, but I'll bet it's got shelves. I'd opt for the coat closet." Her voice had risen, and she sounded exhilarated.

With a mighty lunge, Renie leaped up and pounded Judith with the pillow. "Will you shut up?" she yelled. "I was asleep and you kept talking like a damned Congressman going for a filibuster!"

Rubbing her head, Judith gave Renie a sheepish look. "Sorry, coz. How can you go right to sleep with an unsolved murder under our roof?"

Renie replaced the pillow and punched it back into shape. "Easy," she retorted. "One, it's not our roof. Two, why would you want to help your husband's arch-rival solve a murder investigation? Three, Boo's not your uncle. Good night." She hunkered down under the covers, turning her back on Judith.

Feeling her headache returning, Judith stared at the drawing she'd made. "This would be a good time to check out the den," she said in almost a whisper.

"This," Renie said in a muffled voice, "would be a good time to turn out the light."

Judith got up and shrugged into the quilted maroon robe. "I'm going downstairs." She started for the door.

"Damn!" The word exploded out of Renie.

With her hands poised to push the nightstand out of the way, Judith waited. She could hear Renie scrambling around, swearing, and apparently trying to find her paisley robe. A moment later, she was at Judith's side, helping to give the nightstand a hefty shove.

"Oh," Judith said, trying to keep the amusement out of her voice, "you're coming, too?"

"I could use a snack," Renie muttered. "There was some leftover pickled herring."

Noiselessly, the cousins descended the main staircase. A light had been left on in the entry hall, but there was no sign of life. Still holding onto the wrought-iron balustrade, Judith reached the main floor. She could hear the sound of heavy snoring emanating from the living room.

"Buck?" she mouthed at Renie, who gave a shrug.

To Judith's relief, no policeman stood on guard outside the den door. A strip of yellow-and-black crime-scene tape stretched on the diagonal from lintel to threshold. Judith tried the knob; the door was locked.

"How . . . ?" Renie said in a puzzled whisper.

"Toadie's key," Judith murmured. "Or actually, the one that belonged to Uncle Boo. Toadie must have given it to the police."

Moving stealthily, the cousins came out of the small, recessed passageway. Judith tried the cupboard first. As she'd guessed, there were shelves, six in all, filled with various household items, from floor wax to carpet cleaner. The construction was solid and first-rate, like the rest of the house. Angling an arm inside, Judith tried to judge the depth of the shelves. They seemed to reach the wall. She could see no way there could be a secret

110

entrance into the den from the cupboard.

To her disappointment, the closet seemed even less likely to hide a concealed passage. It was wider, but no deeper. At present it held the guests' wraps, including Trixie's chic trench coat, Aunt Vivvie's good blue wool, and a beaver-trimmed Chesterfield that Judith recognized as belonging to Toadie.

Judith rapped; she measured; she poked and pried and pushed. There was, she realized, no space for a hidden entrance. Disconsolately, she made one last attempt, around the corner in the short hallway which led to the second garage entrance.

The six-foot expanse seemed quite innocent. At least half of the other side housed the cupboard. A Canaletto print of Venice was the only adornment. Judith looked under the picture. She found nothing suspicious.

"Doesn't the den jut out from the house?" Renie whispered. "I mean, it has to, because on one side it's next to the garage."

Judith didn't have much hope that the garage door would be unlocked. But it was. An ancient Rolls-Royce in mint condition sat next to a newer but equally well maintained Cadillac. The third car was a battered Ford, which probably belonged to the Wakefields.

Again Judith and Renie could find no sign of a passage out of the garage. The brick wall common to the den was exposed. Indeed, it appeared that this was a part of the house where the masons had left off when they were dismissed. On the far wall, Judith saw sporting gear ranging from ancient skis to bamboo fly rods. There was also a big calendar featuring Pacific Northwest scenery. Judith moved down the row of cars for a closer look. The calendar was dated 1964, the year Dunlop Major had died. His son hadn't bothered to

111

change much of anything, including the calendar.

"It was a thought," Judith said in defeat as the cousins made a cautious return to the hallway. "Now I'm really stymied."

The phone rang just as they passed the main-floor bath. Judith jumped and Renie squeaked. On the second ring, Judith dove for the telephone alcove.

She expected the caller to be from the police, the undertaker's, or possibly even the hospital where Mason Meade had been taken. She was surprised to hear instead the voice of her cousin, Marty Grover. He, in turn, sounded disturbed.

"What's going on over there?" he asked, his usually boyish tones deepened by apparent concern. "I thought the birthday party was going to break up early. Mum and Trixie aren't back yet."

Judith paused, clutching the two sections of the phone in each hand. She mouthed Marty's name at Renie, who nodded and gave a shake of her head. Though in his forties and twice married, the muddleheaded Marty still lived at home. "They're here, they're fine," Judith said at last in a rush. "I thought Trixie called you earlier."

A sense of relief filled Marty's voice. "Oh, good, they're safe. No, Trixie hasn't called this evening. That's why I was worried. I didn't move from the phone after nine o'clock. Then I heard on the news that the weather had gotten pretty rotten over on your side of the lake. I thought they might have been in a wreck on the way home."

Marty, like the rest of the Lotts, lived in the sprawling suburbs across the lake. Though less then ten miles separated them from Heraldsgate Hill and The Bluff, the weather could differ as if the two places were in different climate zones.

Judith leaned into the alcove. Now that she had satisfied her curiosity about the secret passageway, exhaustion was setting in. "Look, Marty, there's been a disaster." Carefully, she explained what had happened to Uncle Boo. The complicating factor of the weather. Mason Meade's accident with Trixie's car. The arrival of the police. The locked room.

"Wild," Marty breathed when Judith had finished. "I've never heard anything like it! Wait'll Dad gets back from Tanzania!" He paused, as if to collect himself. "He warned Trixie never to let anybody else drive that Lexus! I'll bet she's teed off big-time!"

Replacing the receiver on the hook, Judith shook her head. "Every time I think that Marty's smarter than Trixie, he manages to convince me otherwise. And to think he *is* a Grover!"

"Half Grover, half Lott, they cancel each other out and leave us with a Half-Wit," Renie replied, shivering in her oversized bathrobe. "Let's grab the rest of the pickled herring and go back to bed. I'm freezing."

The kitchen looked immaculate. Judith guessed that Mrs. Wakefield had finished the last of the cleanup, including emptying the final load of dishes. The pickled herring, however, was gone.

"Zoe ate it, I'll bet," Renie fumed. "That girl's a hog." She stuck her head in the refrigerator, foraging for a snack. "Here's some ham. I'm making a sandwich. You want one?"

Judith decided she was hungry, too. Renie found some leftover Havarti cheese and a jar of dill pickles. She also poured them each a glass of milk. It was warmer in the kitchen than it was in the master bedroom, so they decided to eat downstairs.

"You're right about one thing," Judith said as they

leaned against the counter and munched their sandwiches. "It's not in Joe's best interest for me to help solve this case."

"You're not a detective," Renie reminded her cousin. "Oh, you've got a knack for puzzles and you're great at getting people to open up. But this isn't your job. I'd advise you to keep out of it. For one thing, you don't want Buck to know you're Mrs. Joe Flynn."

"I sure don't," Judith replied fervently. "If it thaws by tomorrow, we'll get out of this place and never look back."

Renie nodded emphatically. "That's the spirit, coz. Even if Uncle Boo hadn't gotten killed, I wouldn't want to spend any extra time with this crew."

Judith sipped her milk. "Jill isn't so bad," she allowed, "and I've always kind of liked Derek. I feel sorry for Holly—she's so put-upon. Still, they're not *our* sort."

"They're not family—not *our* family," Renie noted. "Besides, Jill has a superiority complex, I don't trust Derek, and Holly is too good to be true. She's either repressed or—" Renie stopped speaking as the basement door opened and Mrs. Wakefield popped into the kitchen. Her hair was done up in big rollers and her bulky blue bathrobe looked as if it could have been used as a cover for Uncle Boo's Rolls-Royce.

"You two still up?" she inquired without much pleasure. "I thought everybody'd be out for the count by now."

Judith explained, somewhat truthfully, that Renie had required a snack. Mrs. Wakefield snorted as she put the teakettle on and went to the refrigerator. "So does Weed. He doesn't eat all day; then he gets starved this time of night. Hey, what happened to the ham?"

114

Renie pointed to what was left of her sandwich. "It was real good," she added with a touch of malice.

The housekeeper's eyes narrowed at the cousins. "There better be some breast of turkey roll left in here," she said in a warning tone.

"There probably is," Renie shot back. "I hate turkey roll. It tastes like paper towels. Say," she went on, resorting to offense as the best defense, "why aren't you using your stove in the basement?"

Mrs. Wakefield found the turkey roll and began making her husband a sandwich. "Because it's full of beets. Weed'll have to clean it up tomorrow. You got any more bright questions?" The amiable attitude that the housekeeper had displayed during dinner had fled. Given what had happened since, Judith didn't much blame Mrs. Wakefield for her change of mood.

"Actually," Judith replied in what she hoped was a conciliatory tone, "I do. How do you figure Uncle Boo got shot in a locked room?"

The teakettle began to boil. Mrs. Wakefield reached for a jar of instant decaffeinated coffee. "I don't," she answered abruptly.

"But it happened," Judith said doggedly. The idea wasn't logical, yet it seemed to be true. Logic was Judith's byword, but it seemed to be failing her regarding Uncle Boo's death.

Putting the sandwich on a plate and the plate on a tray, Mrs. Wakefield plodded over to the counter and extracted two dill pickles from the jar next to Renie. She then placed a coffee mug on the tray and got four chocolate chip cookies out of a package from the cupboard.

"Did it?" she asked in an enigmatic manner. Balancing the tray on her knee, she opened the door to the servants' quarters. "Don't forget to put the pickles back in the fridge," she said, and disappeared down the stairs.

"Now," Judith said with a frown, "what did *that* mean?"

Renie looked blank. "Beats me."

Finishing her milk, Judith dutifully returned the pickle jar to the refrigerator. The cousins put their glasses in the dishwasher and wiped off the counter. They were heading back to bed when Judith stopped suddenly at the foot of the stairs, almost toppling Renie, who was right behind her.

"What now?" Renie asked wearily.

"Marty," Judith replied, signaling for her cousin to keep her voice down. Buck's loud snores could still be heard from the living room. He was now joined by a wheeze that might have been Officer Foster or Officer Rigby. The orchestration was not pleasant.

"What about Marty?" Renie demanded in an impatient whisper.

Judith started up the stairs. "He called." Over her shoulder, she gave Renie a meaningful look.

It was lost on her cousin. "So? Marty can dial a phone. For him, that's progress, but what . . . Oh!"

They had reached the landing. "That's right," Judith said softly. "Trixie claimed to have left the living room to call her brother. But she didn't. So what was Trixie doing? And why did she lie?"

EIGHT

MORE THAN ANY OTHER CALL, THIS WAS THE ONE THAT Judith most hated to make. There were so many reasons, including guilt, anxiety, and fear. But it was seven-thirty in the morning, she was still a prisoner of ice and fog on The Bluff, and there was no way out. Literally and figuratively. With enormous trepidation, Judith manned the old-fashioned rotary dial on the phone in the alcove off the main hall.

The initial response was not reassuring. Gertrude Grover wasn't sympathetic about Boo Major's demise. Boo's passive nature had always annoyed Gertrude. Rosie's aggressiveness had been downright maddening. It would have served them both right if they'd been shot by a sniper twenty years ago. It would also have saved the Grovers a lot of time and trouble. Gertrude had no time for any of the Majors or the Lotts. "Listen, you lamebrained idiot," rasped Gertrude, concluding her tirade about the victim and his relations, "how do you expect a crippled old lady to fix breakfast for a bunch of ne'er-do-wells who ought to stay home in the first place? Why can't they eat out? Haven't they ever heard of a *diner?*"

As usual, her mother's Depression-era lexicon tried Judith's patience. "Hillside Manor is a bed-*and*-breakfast. Get it? My guests pay for both. Corinne Dooley left before it iced up last night to take her kids skiing. Joe had to go to work. He called a few minutes ago to let me know what had happened. Please, Mother—it's only six people, and you can make coffee and some toast and bacon and maybe scrambled eggs.

Oh, and juice—just pour it."

"Toast! Bacon! Scrambled eggs! *Juice!*" Gertrude made it sound as if Judith had asked her to commit four of the Seven Deadly Sins. She was fairly screaming into her daughter's ear. "What next, *fruit compote?*"

"Mother, what's the walk like between the toolshed and the house?" Judith must let her mother know that her first concern was for Gertrude's safety.

"How would I know? I can't see it. We've got fog here, you knothead."

Judith knew that Joe had put down rock salt before he went to work. She also knew that her mother could use the grass, which would be merely wet and perhaps a bit frosty. The distance was very short. Even on her walker, Gertrude ought to manage perfectly well.

"Look," Judith said in what she hoped was a calming voice, "I can call the house and ask one of the guests to come over and get you. They might not pick up the phone right away, but I'll keep ringing. If you don't want to make the eggs, that's okay, too."

"What's wrong with bran?" Gertrude growled. "I eat bran every morning. And you know why—it keeps me . . ."

Judith didn't want to hear about bran or her mother's bowels. She didn't want to hear anything except that her mother would provide the barest subsistence for the B&B's six guests.

"I'll be home as soon as I can," Judith said, still fighting for patience. "Believe me, I don't want to stick around with this bunch."

Gertrude's tone shifted slightly. "Boo Major. If there was ever a more worthless man, other than your first and second husbands, I'll put in with you. Who'd bother to shoot him? Why didn't they just wait until he died of

118

boredom?"

Uncle Boo, it seemed, wasn't receiving much sympathy from any quarter. Except from the Rush family. Judith, however, didn't think it wise to argue with her mother. She'd already suffered through Gertrude's earlier indictment. "He didn't get a lot out of life, I'll admit. Hey," she added more brightly, "I wish you were here to needle Aunt Toadie."

There was a snarl at the other end of the line which was probably Gertrude but might have been Sweetums. "Toadie! I used to call her SOS—for Selfish Or Stupid, and boy, is she both! Cheats at bridge, too. Does she still wear enough rouge to paint a barn? If she entered a beauty contest, she'd finish fourth to a horse's behind. And her sister Vivvie! I remember the time she sat down in one of those little kiddie chairs and got her fat butt wedged in between the armrests. She wore that thing around the house for ten minutes until your uncle Cliff greased her backside with Crisco."

Judith relaxed a bit. It was reassuring to listen to her mother rant and rave about someone other than her own daughter. Somewhere before Gertrude referred to Trixie as a brainless, bowlegged tramp, but after she had called Holly a dim-bulb, spineless doormat, a grudging agreement was reached about breakfast at the B&B. Judith proceeded to call her business number, but no one answered, not even after six tries.

"Mother will either make it or not make it," Judith fretted. "The guests aren't picking up the phone."

Renie looked up from the telephone directory she'd been perusing. "I'll wait a while to call my mother, but I think most of Ewart Gladstone Whiffel's practice was taken over by Douglas de Butts. At least that's who Bill and I use."

"Aunt Toadie would know," Judith remarked, seeing Zoe Wakefield approach. The Major maid was attired in jeans and a sweatshirt, but she was carrying a coffee carafe.

"We're on the job," she announced. "Breakfast is being served buffet-style in the dining room. Dig in. There's quite a line already. Of course, it's mostly the police."

Renie immediately headed for the food, but Judith detained Zoe. "Your mother said something odd last night," she began, attempting a confidential smile. "She suggested that . . . well, I'm not sure what she suggested, but it sounded as if she didn't think Boo was killed in a locked room. Do you have any idea what she was talking about?"

Zoe's response was exasperated. "My mother can be a trip sometimes. She'll say anything, just to confound people. No, I can't even guess." The maid started for the living room.

Judith called after her. "You don't know who Boo's attorney is, do you?"

Zoe laughed. "What did he need an attorney for? Mr. Major never got involved in legal hassles. How could he? He didn't *do* anything."

"But . . . all of this." Judith waved a hand to take in the entry hall, the whole house, the family fortune. "Somebody must manage the money. What about his . . . will?"

Zoe became thoughtful. "The money—that is, both his and the Major Mush Company's—is handled through the corporation. He turned his bills over to the head office and they paid them. As for a will," Zoe added with a shake of her head, "he didn't really have one." Again she started for the living room.

This time Judith ran after her. "Then who inherits his

money? He was childless. There are no heirs."

Zoe stared at Judith, her green eyes like a cat's. "Says who?"

Judith gave an erratic shrug. "Says everybody. I mean, he was Dunlop Major's sole heir. That means there wasn't anyone else in the family."

The maid's mouth turned down. "That means there wasn't any other *heir*." She waited for Judith's show of surprise. "Boo Major had a brother. His name was Reuben—Rube, he was called. I take it you didn't know. Excuse me, Detective Doerflinger is dying for a cup of coffee. If you can figure a way to send out for doughnuts, let me know."

Zoe marched with purpose through the arched doorway. Her sweatshirt seemed to flounce behind her. Openmouthed, Judith stared.

Mrs. Wakefield and Zoe had prepared a more-than-adequate breakfast. Indeed, as Judith approached the buffet, she wished the housekeeper and her daughter had been serving the guests at Hillside Manor. There was white and whole wheat toast, French toast, bacon, sausages, scrambled eggs, coffee, tea, and two kinds of juice, orange and tomato. Mush wasn't on the menu. With a full plate, Judith sat next to Renie, who was across from Holly and Derek. The other four diners were uniformed police officers, including Foster and Rigby. Judith wondered if they'd all slept at Major Manor.

"How are the streets?" she inquired of the two policemen she didn't recognize.

The Hispanic officer shook his head glumly; the Asian-American made a disparaging gesture.

"Terrible," said the Hispanic.

"Scary," said the Asian-American.

"Worst black ice I've ever seen," Officer Rigby put in. "The fog's so thick you can't see past the front porch. The forecast is callin' for a high of thirty-one with no burn-off until late afternoon."

Judith's spirits fell. It appeared that she and Renie were imprisoned in Major Manor for at least another seven or eight hours. Perhaps they should try to walk home and retrieve the car later. The four miles would be treacherous, but they could take their time. She turned to Renie to make the suggestion, but before she could say anything, Mrs. Wakefield entered the dining room to announce that there was a phone call for Mrs. Jones.

"Bill," Renie said, getting up. "Or my mother." She exited the room.

Holly was toying with a rasher of bacon. "We're marooned," she lamented. "We might as well be on a desert island."

Judith gave her a half smile. "We'd be warmer at any rate."

The policemen finished their breakfast and left in a group. Judith seized the opportunity of having the Rushes to herself. She wanted a clarification of Zoe's remark about Reuben Major.

"I didn't realize," she began in a casual tone, "that Boo had a brother. Is he still alive?"

Judith had expected to drop a bombshell. Her question turned out to be a dud. Derek and Holly exchanged mildly puzzled glances.

"Rube died a long time ago, didn't he?" Holly said to her husband.

Derek nodded. "An automobile accident killed Reuben and his wife. It happened in Arizona, I believe. I was away at college and didn't pay much attention."

122

He gave Judith a self-deprecating look. "You know how it is when you're young and utterly self-absorbed—you hear about the death of someone you don't really know and it goes right over your head."

"But you knew Rube Major?" Judith asked, trying not to sound eager.

Derek resumed eating his French toast. "No, I don't recall meeting him. Uncle Boo spoke of him now and then. Rube was very bright, he spoke three languages, and he thought about becoming an actor. But he was a maverick. As the elder brother, he should have taken over Dunlop's position in the business. But that strange streak in Dunlop that lured him to the sea surfaced much stronger in Rube. When he was twenty-one, he—as they say—'hit the road.' It was right after the family moved West. Rube kept on going. That's why Dunlop disinherited him and left everything to Boo."

Holly dimpled, creating a charming effect that made her look much younger and less frazzled. "It's fascinating, really. Dunlop Major and his father before him were such ambitious, hardworking men. Then along comes Rube, who wanted nothing more than to see where the next road took him. And Boo, who was content to just sit and doze. Aren't people interesting?"

Judith couldn't argue the point. She, too, found people intriguing, mystifying, stimulating, and amazing. But, amusement factor aside, Judith wasn't quite satisfied with the Rushes' answers.

"Was Dunlop an only child?" she inquired, still keeping her tone conversational.

Derek's forehead puckered. "Yes, I think so. In fact, I'm sure of it. I remember Uncle Boo saying once that his grandfather's neighbors were astounded by his success as a farmer when he had only a son to help him.

123

So many farm families in those days had several children, you know."

Judith inclined her head. "Yes, certainly it saved on hired hands." She took a sip of tomato juice and phrased her next remark carefully: "Rube and his wife had no children, I gather." Noting the curious expression on Derek's face, she hastened to amend her comment. "I mean, I never heard Uncle Boo talk about nieces or nephews other than you, Derek." As far as Judith knew, Trixie and her half-siblings had little connection with Boo until Toadie jumped into the void left by Rosie.

Derek's voice turned cool. "I couldn't say, actually. I only know what I heard of Reuben Major—and that he died too soon." Somewhat savagely, Derek stabbed his sausage.

Judith decided to back off. Before the silence could become awkward, Renie returned, glowering at her cousin.

"What's wrong?" Judith asked, beginning to feel as if the morning were off to an even worse start than she'd imagined.

Renie was tight-lipped. "Later," she snapped, and re-sumed eating.

Aunt Vivvie twittered into the dining room next, her wig a trifle wilted and her makeup applied with what must have been an unsteady hand. A streak of lipstick ran awry from the corner of her mouth; one false eyelash hung at half-mast. Judith wondered how she could see.

"Oh! I couldn't sleep a wink last night! I was so frightened—at any minute I expected someone to strangle me in my bed!" Vivvie Rush dithered to the buffet, where she shoveled bacon, French toast, and eggs onto her plate. Her nerves apparently hadn't affected her appetite.

"The worst of it," she said, plopping into a chair next to her son, "is that I heard all sorts of strange noises. Boo's ghost, I'm sure." Vivvie began to eat, then suddenly looked up. "Oh! Holly, dear, be a pet and fetch me some of that nice orange juice. And coffee. Sugar and cream, no substitutes. You know how I like it." She smiled coyly at her daughter-in-law.

Renie and Judith finished at the same time, choosing not to linger in the dining room. Instead, they took their coffee refills into the breakfast room off the kitchen and closed both doors.

"Well?" Judith sighed, expecting disaster.

Renie ran a hand through her uncombed chestnut curls. Her round face was a mask of annoyance. "Phone calls. My breakfast got cold while I took your phone calls."

"My . . . ? What're you talking about?"

Renie scooted her chair up closer to the round breakfast table and relaxed a bit. "The first call was from Joe. He didn't want to ask for you for fear of alerting Buck Doerflinger. Joe got to work and found out about Uncle Boo's murder. He's absolutely *wild*."

Judith became indignant. "Whatever for? I didn't shoot Uncle Boo."

"You might as well have. Joe can't believe you got yourself involved in another homicide and didn't tell him about it last night. To make matters even uglier, Buck's assigned to the case, which is making Joe tear his hair. I told him Buck didn't realize you were Mrs. Joe Flynn. Joe said that figured. The only reason Buck's gotten where he has on the force is because he's lucky. 'Lucky Buck,' they call him." Renie paused to drink her coffee.

Judith hung her head. "I didn't tell Joe last night because he was tired and I knew he'd worry. So how," she demanded, regaining her spunk, "was I to know we'd get iced in over here on The Bluff?"

Renie snorted. "Bill says we should have known. He's as mad at me as Joe is at you. I called him after I talked to Joe, and he was in one of his one-syllable moods. You know, where he says, 'Yes,' 'No,' and 'Good-bye.' "

"That's two syllables." Judith couldn't resist the needle.

Renie let out a big sigh. "You know what I mean. He says we should have realized what the weather was going to be like and left immediately. The problem with Bill is that he's always right."

"The problem with Bill is that he doesn't allow for human error unless he's getting paid to hear about it from his wacky patients," Judith replied, not without a touch of anger, directed more at Joe and Bill than at Renie. "Is that all of it?" she asked warily.

Renie sighed again. "No. I checked in with my mother. She's having a world-class tizzy. She'd called your mother who didn't answer. Then she called the B&B. Your mother finally picked up the phone on the ninth ring, apparently having screwed up your machine so that it didn't switch over to the tape. She'd also screwed up your guests by serving them—guess what?—mush."

"Mush!" Judith was aghast. "They'll ask for a refund!"

Renie ignored the comment. "My mother is sure we'll be murdered along with Uncle Boo. She thinks a homicidal maniac must have sneaked into the house to keep warm. I told her that was ridiculous—the furnace doesn't work that well."

Judith smiled thinly, then glanced at her watch. It was just after eight-fifteen. "Gee, with all those calls, you did well. How did you get your mother off the phone so fast?"

"I told her somebody was sneaking up on me with a meat cleaver. It took only two or three more minutes to get her to hang up." Renie stared out the window. There was nothing to see but fog. "Oh," she added, "Mom had no idea who Uncle Boo's attorney is. She said Douglas de Butts would be as good a start as any. She also said she and your mother got into an argument on the phone this morning over whether or not Flabby was one of the Seven Dwarfs." Renie shrugged. Arguments, no matter how inane, were a common occurrence between the sisters-in-law.

Judith made an indifferent sound. "Mush," she murmured, still dwelling on Gertrude's aberration. "How could she? And how could Joe go off to work and leave me in the lurch?"

"Mush is filling," Renie said in an encouraging voice. Trying to put aside problems with husbands, mothers, and guests, Judith recounted what she had heard about Boo Major's brother. Renie listened with mild interest.

"If Reuben—Rube—had kids, it would a make a difference," Judith pointed out. "That is, if Boo really didn't have a will. But Derek says he did, and it leaves everything to him. Trixie also says Boo had a will, but that she and Aunt Toadie are the heirs. And Zoe says there is no will. How would Zoe know? She's the maid."

Renie frowned at Judith. "Don't maids always know stuff like that? In books, they listen at keyholes."

"If anyone knows," Judith theorized, "I'd say it

127

would be Zoe's mother. If Uncle Boo went to see a lawyer, Weed Wakefield would have had to drive him. Or if a lawyer came to the house, Mrs. Wakefield would know about it."

"True," Renie agreed. "But why do we care? You aren't going to solve this one, remember?" Her expression was wry.

Judith, who had been gazing with unseeing eyes at the mahogany paneling that went halfway up the wall before it met a border of wallpaper pansies, uttered a truncated laugh. "I can't help myself. Do you want to walk home?" She saw her cousin's horrified reaction. "I thought not, but a while ago, I was desperate enough to consider it. What else is there to do except sit around and speculate? Would you prefer chatting with the rest of the guests?"

Renie admitted that what she would really like to do was put on her jacket. "At home, I'm warm enough in this sweatshirt," she explained, indicating the blue University of Michigan number she had chosen from her extensive, if ratty, collegiate and sporting-logo wardrobe. "But it's so damned cold in this place. I'm going to ask Mrs. Wakefield what goes with that furnace."

Judith followed Renie into the kitchen. Mrs. Wakefield was at the stove, turning out a fresh batch of French toast. This morning she was wearing another sweat suit, of emerald-green, bright blue, and jet-black velour.

"It's an old house, and a big one at that," she replied with a shrug. "You get used to it in the winter. Try working as hard as I do—you'll warm up real quick." She flipped the French toast with a spatula.

"Say, Mrs. Wakefield," Judith said, deciding to

shelve any more complaints for fear of losing the housekeeper's good humor, "what's all this talk about Boo's will? Did he or did he not have one?"

Mrs. Wakefield opened the oven and removed a broiler pan of bacon and sausage. "A will? Oh, sure, he had one." She drained the meats on a paper towel. "Of course, I don't know if it'll stand up in court. The heirs he named probably won't show up to back their claims." Bacon and sausage were scooped into a serving bowl; the French toast was put on a plate. The housekeeper chortled as she cocked a devilish eye at the cousins. "Boo Major left everything to Space Aliens. Excuse me, I've got to get this out for the next round of rum-dum relations."

NINE

"THIS IS CRAZY," RENIE DECLARED AS THEY continued their exhaustive search of the master bedroom. The door was locked for secrecy as well as safety. "If Boo really did make a will leaving everything to men from Mars, wouldn't it be on file in his attorney's office or in a safety deposit box at a bank?"

"Probably," Judith agreed, searching through the last shelf of the second closet. "It might even be in the den, which we can't get at. But it doesn't hurt to look."

So far, the cousins had turned up nothing more interesting than memorabilia. Uncle Boo had several bound volumes of *The Stars and Stripes* Army newspaper from World War Two, a boxful of infantry combat medals, and a few souvenirs from France and Germany. There was also a shoebox filled with photographs. For lack of anything better to do, the cousins decided to go through the snapshots.

In sepia-tinted pictures, they found Grandpa John on the farm in Minnesota, behind a plow, riding a tractor, loading a truck. Grandma Alice was a shadowy corseted figure on the wide front porch. There was Dunlop and Helga Major's wedding picture, in all the Edwardian splendor that a Midwestern farmer could muster. Then came the children, and sure enough, there were two boys, both dark-haired, handsome, and looking as though they didn't enjoy sitting for the camera.

"So that's Rube," Renie remarked, fingering a photograph that had probably been taken in the twenties. Reuben Major stood next to his younger brother, Bruno. They appeared to be about twelve and nine, respectively. Both were barefoot and wore overalls but no shirts. The snapshot had obviously been taken in the summer.

"Here he is when he was older," said Judith, handing her cousin a photo of the brothers in front of a stone church set among evergreens. "This must have been taken after they moved out here, but before Rube ran away. The boys are all dressed up. A wedding, maybe?"

Renie nodded once. "Could be. Rube looks close to twenty—Boo's in his mid-teens. I'd recognize Boo from this one. His face never changed that much."

"That happens," Judith replied, "when you don't leap into life with both feet. Rube did, though, in his way. I wonder what he looked like after he got older. There's quite a resemblance when they were kids."

Rube Major's pictorial history seemed to end with the church photo. The cousins perused numerous shots of Major Manor while under construction and after completion. There were photos of Dunlop and Helga Major, now middle-aged, and of Boo in his Army uniform. Dunlop looked like a taller, thinner version of Uncle Boo. Helga was pretty, but without character. As she grew older, her clothes became more lavish, as did her jewels. The last picture, probably taken when she was close to seventy, showed a wrinkled, tiny dowager in layers of lace with a diamond-studded tiara on her white curls and a choker with rows of gems covering her throat. Next came buxom, bellicose Aunt Rosie, in a beige suit with a double strand of pearls, and carrying a spray of orchids. The contrast between mother-in-law and daughter-in-law was remarkable, in substance as well as in style.

A single snapshot was stuck to the side of the box. Judith fished it out and gave a start. "Egad," she

131

exclaimed, "it's a Nazi!"

Renie adjusted her reading glasses and gazed at the photo. "It's a German soldier, all right," she said in a thoughtful tone. The picture showed a uniformed man smiling blankly at the camera. In the background was a shelled-out stone building. Renie peered more closely. "For Pete's sake," she murmured, "this looks like Rube Major!"

Judith snatched the photo away and thoroughly scrutinized it. "You're right," she said in awe. "It sure resembles Rube. No wonder he got disinherited! He wasn't just a free spirit, he was a German sympathizer. Wow!"

"That's really weird," Renie said in a voice of wonderment. "But Dunlop's wife was German, wasn't she? Maybe she filled Rube with a lot of bunk about the Homeland and *Deutschland über Alles.* Didn't somebody say she had a picture of Mussolini in her darning kit?"

Judith was slowly shaking her head. "People are very strange. And in the Midwest, they still have those little ethnic farming communities. I wonder if Helga Major was a big Hitler fan. It's funny we never heard any mention of it."

Renie's expression was ironic. "By the time our family got hooked up with the Lotts and the Majors, the war was over. If you were Helga, would you hang a pinup of the Führer on your living room wall? He lost, remember?"

"Right." Judith's reply was vague; her thoughts were obviously elsewhere. She fingered the snapshot before placing it on the pile of pictures they'd already viewed. "Well, I guess that explains Reuben Major. Let's sort through the rest and see if we can come up with something else of interest, like Dunlop Major in fishnet stockings."

Dunlop Major, however, appeared in various poses with his employees at office parties and company picnics. As he grew older, his face became more stern. Dunlop's rigid posture, stiff neck, and tight lips presented a portrait of unyielding determination.

"One tough old coot," Judith remarked as she reached the Age of Aunt Rosie. "Here, see how grim Dunlop looks at Boo's wedding." She handed Renie a colored snapshot of the bridal party.

"I remember when Rosie and Boo got married," Renie recalled. "Somebody spiked the punch and your father danced with the wedding cake on his head."

Almost forty years later, the memory embarrassed Judith as much as it amused her. Donald Grover had been a quiet, dignified, scholarly man. His escapade with the Majors' wedding cake had been out of character—and thus, endearing. Judith smiled at the memory.

"Mother threatened to divorce him," she said, remembering the anxiety over what her youthful mind had understood as a serious threat by Gertrude. It hadn't been, of course. Donald and Gertrude Grover had been devoted. Sometimes Judith felt that her mother's crankiness was the result of an inability to forgive her husband for dying before she did.

"Who's this?" Renie tapped another snapshot, also taken at Boo and Rosie's reception in the Cascadia Hotel.

Judith stared at the picture. There was Boo, his arm around Rosie. At their sides stood the best man and the matron of honor, longtime friends who had introduced them. But in back stood another couple, a handsome man in his forties who resembled Boo, and a woman whose head could barely be seen above Aunt Rosie's shoulder.

"Rube?" Judith guessed. "Do you remember him being at the wedding?"

Renie, who was older than Judith by two years, bit her lip. "No. But there were so many people there. Gee, I was what? Fourteen? I was trying to bat my eyelashes at Cousin Denny. I showed cleavage. But Denny always disdained my attempts at seduction. I was heartbroken when I caught him necking in the hotel freight elevator with some auburn-haired hussy. Denny turned beet-red, and I stuffed a cocktail napkin down my sensuous bosom. The napkin was inscribed 'Rosie and Boo—Love, Like Wine, Takes Time.' "

"Gack," said Judith. "I don't remember that. I wish you hadn't. If Rube was there, his wartime escapades must have been forgiven. But why didn't Derek remember meeting him?"

Renie calculated on her fingers. "Because he would have been about four at the time?"

Judith gave a shrug of assent. She went through the rest of the wedding pictures but found no more recognizable shots of Reuben Major and his wife. They progressed to the late fifties. Derek showed up, first as a small boy, then on vacation as a teenager, and eventually as a college student. There was another wedding, Derek and Holly's, with a very small Jill as flower girl. Jill grew up; her parents matured. Uncle Boo was shown at a Fourth of July picnic by the gazebo. Aunt Rosie was lighting firecrackers under his lawn chair.

Only one other picture excited the cousins' interest. Judith fingered it in a tantalizing manner. The

134

photograph was in color, but the images weren't clear. Whoever had held the camera had possessed an unsteady hand.

"I think it's Rube and his wife," Judith said as Renie finally grabbed the picture. "Who's the young woman?"

Renie studied the photo. "She's wearing a poodle skirt and white bucks, so it's got to be the fifties. Her face is turned, and the damned thing's fuzzy. What's that in the background?" Renie handed the snapshot back to Judith.

It took Judith a while to figure it out. "Advertising," she finally said. "Billboards, like in a baseball park." She turned the picture over. Her black eyes lighted up. " 'March 1955.' Spring training in Arizona. Want to argue?"

"Heck, no," Renie replied. "But so what? We know that Rube and his wife died in a car crash in Arizona. It must have been circa 1970, because Derek said it was while he was in college. Rube and his wife might have lived in Arizona. At least they got out of war-torn Germany, as we used to call it."

Judith was leaning on the bed. She thrust her chin at Renie, who was lying with her head against the sunburst. "They had a daughter, coz. Where is she now?"

Renie's eyes devoured the snapshot. "A teenager. Our generation. Shoot, she could be anywhere. Are you saying she could be Boo's legitimate heir?"

"It beats being a Space Alien," Judith replied. "I think we should call Tucson or Phoenix."

Renie sat up and bounced on the bed. "Oh, I'd like that! An heir who Toadie and Trixie don't know about! Let's do! Where's a phone where we won't be heard?"

Judith's bubble of excitement burst. "Drat. I don't

135

know. There's no phone upstairs that I know of. The basement, maybe? We could go down and sneak in a call. But to who, on a Saturday?" Judith sounded discouraged as well as deflated.

Renie, however, was off the bed and heading for the door. "*The Arizona Republic.* It's the Phoenix daily. We'll have them check the obits for a Reuben Major. Maybe his daughter was married by then and they'll list her as a survivor." Over her shoulder, she gave her cousin a reproachful glance. "Hey, you're a librarian by trade. You ought to know how to do these things."

Judith gave Renie a dour look. "I used to. Now I'm just a B&B hostess who serves her guests *mush.* I'm a failure, coz."

Renie patted Judith's shoulder. "Nonsense. Your mother probably made terrific oatmeal. At least you don't buy Major Mush."

Shaking her head dejectedly from side to side, Judith followed Renie down the staircase. "My mush isn't Major, but Mother has made me a minor. Hostess, that is. Word will leak out. My reputation in the hostelry business will be ruined."

Before Renie could try to console Judith further, Trixie appeared at the bottom of the stairs. Her red crepe pantsuit looked tired in the wan morning light. So did her face, which was devoid of cosmetics except for a dash of scarlet lipstick. She seemed disappointed when she saw the cousins.

"I thought you were Mummy coming down," she said, starting to pout. "I have good news for her. Mason spent a restful night."

Renie made as if to click her heels together on the stairs. "Oh, wow! I'm thrilled! And here I was afraid he'd die from lack of character!"

136

Judith craned her neck to give Renie a warning look. "Knock it off, coz," she muttered, then offered Trixie a weak smile. "Good, good. Glad to hear it. By the way, I forgot to tell you that Marty called late last night. He wondered why he hadn't heard from you."

Trixie seemed unperturbed. "Marty's such a goose. He worries too much. I talked to him just a few minutes ago. The sun's out over on the other side of the lake."

It was apparent that Trixie didn't realize someone had mentioned her alleged phone call to her half brother. Judith decided on tactful confrontation.

"Uh—Trixie . . . I heard you told some of the others you left the living room last night to telephone Marty. Couldn't you get hold of him?" Immediately, Judith bit her tongue. She'd been *too* tactful; her own words had supplied Trixie with an alibi.

"That's right," Trixie replied after a slight pause. *"That's right!* He didn't answer. I suppose he was . . . in the bathroom." She giggled. "You know Marty—he keeps a magazine rack in there!" She ran up the stairs.

"Butt," muttered Renie. "Liar, too."

Judith gave an absent nod. Looking into the living room, she glimpsed Buck Doerflinger conferring with Officers Rigby and Foster. Presumably the dining room was still being used to serve breakfast. The cousins dawdled in the entry hall. Judith eyed the door to the den.

"If only," she murmured, "we could get in there."

"What for?" Renie asked in a cantankerous voice. "We *were* in there, last night. What else do you expect to find?"

Judith drifted off toward the kitchen. "Think about it. Really think, coz."

They passed through the dining room, where Aunt

137

Toadie was the last to finish breakfast. She glanced up, a scowl on her face.

"You're both still here? I thought you'd get a police escort home. Doesn't your live-in handle parade crowds, Judith?"

"Only the elephant patrol," Judith replied, moving on to the kitchen.

Mrs. Wakefield was scraping plates. "The old bat slept in till nine," she grumbled. "Where've you two been?"

Judith opted for candor. "Upstairs, going through Uncle Boo's souvenirs. Do you know if he had a niece on his side of the family?"

The housekeeper halted, a frying pan in her hand. "A niece? No. Never heard of her. How could that be?"

"He had an older brother," Judith responded. "We think the brother had a daughter. She'd be a more serious contender for the family fortune than those men from Mars."

"So she would," Mrs. Wakefield agreed. She chuckled richly. "And wouldn't that fix old Toadie? Oh, I'd like to see that!"

"Maybe you can," Judith said in a mild voice. "Is there a phone in the servants' quarters?"

Mrs. Wakefield's gaze was suspicious. "Yeah, it's down there in the kitchen off the saloon. Who're you going to call?"

Judith assumed a smug expression. "Someone who might know where to find Boo's niece. We wouldn't want Toadie and the rest of them to know about her, would we?"

The housekeeper's face split into a wide grin. "We sure wouldn't. Go to it, gals. Oh, if you see Weed, tell him to start cleaning that downstairs stove."

The cousins didn't see Weed, but the reek of marijuana was unmistakable. Fortunately, it dissipated as Judith and Renie explored the downstairs corridors. It took them a few minutes to find the telephone. Compact, efficient, and built to resemble a ship's galley, the servants' kitchen undoubtedly had been used for entertaining in a livelier era at Major Manor.

"It smells wonderful," Renie remarked, opening the door to the long, paneled room. "Much better than Weed's joint."

Judith stepped into the saloon. Renie was right. The room smelled of pine, in which it had been finished. The windows were designed to look like portholes; ships' lanterns lined the walls; recessed seats were covered in forest patterns that matched the curtains. The fireplace was huge but empty. It had probably been years since guests had enjoyed the polished dance floor or the well-outfitted bar. The saloon definitely seemed to belong on a luxury liner from long ago, a room where now only ghosts danced in the quiet of the night.

"Lovely." Judith sighed. "Dunlop Major knew how to live. A pity his sons didn't."

"Maybe Rube thought excess wasn't living," Renie suggested as they went into the kitchen around the corner from the swinging doors of the saloon.

"It's not excess so much as comfort," Judith countered. "This house isn't an ode to extravagance. It's just plain . . . livable. But Uncle Boo didn't live. He vegetated."

"True," Renie conceded as Judith used the directory to look up the area code for Phoenix. "Gee, I wonder who will really inherit this place. It would make a wonderful family home."

Judith nodded, then glanced around to make sure they

were alone. From far away came a surprisingly melodious rendition of an old Pete Seeger protest song. It was Weed Wakefield. Judith smiled as she picked up the phone receiver. The model was a modern Trimline, and she was delighted that she could dispense with rotary dialing. The only problem was that there was no response on the line. Judith gave Renie a baffled look. The phone was dead.

Buck Doerflinger had resumed manning his outpost in the dining room. The doors to the kitchen and the hall were closed. Buck's men were busy again in the den. They had already taken photographs and removed any evidence. Judith saw the open door and approached Officer Rigby. She asked if the phone on the desk was working. Rigby picked it up.

"Shucks, it's dead as a doornail," he said. "Maybe the line snapped 'cause of the ice."

That was possible. Judith glanced back into the entry hall. Renie was coming around the corner, shaking her head.

"The alcove phone's out, too," she reported. "We're not only marooned, we're incommunicado."

Judith grimaced. But an opportunity was at hand. Having breached the den's threshold, she strolled into the room.

"Find anything?" she asked in a friendly tone.

Rigby eyed her quizzically. "Such as what?"

Judith shrugged. "A gun, I suppose. It's got to be somewhere, doesn't it?"

"Maybe." Rigby's fair face was impassive, though his eyes were wary. He signaled to his fellow officers. "That's it. Let's go."

The Hispanic policeman was grumbling. "This isn't

140

our kind of work. We're not homicide detectives."

The Asian-American griped, too. "Damned ice. We shouldn't even be here. I had the weekend off."

Rigby smiled feebly. "We'll get overtime. Besides, it's good experience. The Bluff's awful dull. The last call I got before this was about a car that was parked overnight down the street. Big deal. These rich people complain about everything, from stray cats to rubberneckers oglin' their fancy houses. I can use a little excitement on this beat." He paused to remove the crime-scene tape from the door. Judith and Renie took the gesture as an all-clear signal, but didn't move until the policemen were out of sight.

"It looks pretty tame in here," Judith remarked, crossing the threshold and gazing around the room. Nothing much had changed since the previous evening. Except, of course, that Uncle Boo was gone. Permanently.

Mrs. Wakefield, armed with a hand vacuum and a dust-rag, entered the den. She shuddered as she crossed to the desk.

"Creepy, huh? The cops told me I could clean in here, but what's to do? They went over this place with a fine-tooth comb."

Judith was studying the desk. The ashtray had been emptied, but Boo's brandy snifter still stood at the edge of the leather-bound blotter. There was a scant half inch of liquid remaining. A scattering of ashes floated on the surface.

Judith frowned. "What did Boo do, use his glass for an ashtray?"

Mrs. Wakefield leaned over to examine the snifter. "Huh. Crazy old coot." Sadly, she shook her head. "*Poor* old coot. I'll put this in the dishwasher." At the door, she pointed to the big carton that had held the TV. "I'll get Weed to take that outside and put it in the recycling bin with that empty box the Rushes brought."

As soon as the housekeeper left, Judith closed the door. Keeping on guard, she tried the middle desk drawer. To her surprise, it opened easily. To her disappointment, it held nothing more than ballpoint pens, antacid tablets, rubber bands, a box of cigars, matches, a couple of safety pins, a book of postage stamps, and a handful of paper clips.

Judith checked the three side drawers to the left; Renie delved into the two deeper drawers on the right. Stationery, envelopes, and notepads filled one compartment. Another was crammed with magazines featuring UFOs, space aliens, and unexplained phenomena. Renie found the household ledgers, which seemed to be in order. Judith turned up the current bills, neatly filed in a folder. The fifth and final drawer revealed personal correspondence, of which there was almost none, except for a stack of Christmas cards. In desperation, the cousins sorted through them, noting names and return addresses.

"Zip," Renie declared. "Nobody referring to Boo as 'uncle' except the relatives under this very roof, and not a single card from Arizona. Now what?"

Dejectedly, Judith gazed once again around the den. "There's got to be something here that will help us. I keep thinking I've seen it, or that I *should* see it. But I don't know what it is. Crazy as it sounds, if a gun had been found at the scene, I'd vote for suicide. Otherwise, there's no explanation—and no logic, either."

Judith's concentration was interrupted by Vivvie Rush, who fumbled with the door, dithered her way into the den, and broke out with a sob.

142

"Oh! How terrible! The death scene! I feel faint!" She teetered precariously, falling against the big carton.

Dutifully, Judith went to Vivvie and helped her into a chair. "You were . . . uh, fond of Boo?" she asked.

Vivvie snuffled, croaked, and fidgeted. "Well, certainly!" Readjusting her wig, she took a deep breath. "Boo and I were especially close. We had so much in common, especially after Rosie and Mo died. Widowed, both of us the very same year, and lonely." She looked up at Judith, her big blue eyes glistening with unshed tears. "You can imagine, I'm sure."

"I can?" breathed Judith, then suddenly did as she saw the coy expression play over Vivvie's plump face. "Oh . . . I see. You and Boo . . . had *plans?*"

Vivvie simpered. "Well, yes, you could say that. We hadn't set a date, you understand. Boo was the teensiest bit difficult when it came to actually *doing* things. But we were definitely *going together.*"

"Going *where?*" Renie inquired in a baffled voice.

Vivvie looked hurt by the question. "Places. Things. You know, dinners. At my house. Here. I was planning a St. Valentine's getaway as a surprise." The tears began to trickle down her cheeks. "I'd booked the honeymoon suite at the Cascadia Hotel. Oh, my—I still can't believe he's dead! And murdered, too! It's simply not fair!"

Patting Vivvie's shoulder, Judith gazed over the older woman's head to Renie, who was looking ill at ease. "That's very sad," Judith said in consolation. "We had no idea that you and Boo were . . . so close."

Vivvie dried her eyes and sniffed several times. "We kept it to ourselves. You know how Toadie is—she tends to be so critical. And sometimes she meddles. It wouldn't have done to tell her. Not until we were married."

Judith couldn't dispute the statement. She could well imagine Aunt Toadie's reaction to her sister's plans to marry Boo Major. Indeed, an awful thought danced through Judith's mind. What if Toadie *had* known?

"Have you mentioned any of this to Toadie since Boo died?" Judith asked quietly.

Vivvie shook her head, the wig waggling from side to side. "No. I couldn't bear to. Not yet."

"And Derek?" Judith ventured. "Did your son know?"

A trembling smile played on Vivvie's haphazardly made-up lips. "Not exactly. But I think he guessed. He teased me about it. 'Senior Sweethearts,' he called us." Vivvie sighed mournfully, then heaved herself from the chair. She gazed at Judith in gratitude. "You've been so kind. I can't think why Toadie says such awful things about you and your cousin. You must have hurt Trixie's feelings when you were all children. Toadie is very protective, and Trixie can be so sensitive."

"Yeah," Renie murmured, "like a steel girder."

If Vivvie heard the remark, she gave no sign. Suddenly she was a-bustle. "All of this reminds me that I must get the housekeeper to fetch Rosie's jewels. Not that Rosie ever cared much for them, but they belonged to Boo's mother. He felt I should have them, of course, and I would have, once we were married. Excuse me, dear hearts, I must scoot along." Vivvie trudged out of the den, calling for Mrs. Wakefield.

Renie's uneasy expression had turned cynical. "Why am I glad I didn't rush to Mrs. Rush's side and dry her tear-stained cheeks?"

"Don't be so harsh," Judith said, though she was having a few doubts of her own. "Maybe she and Boo

144

did plan to marry. It would fit his mentality. If he was lonely, why not marry another Lott sister? It'd be easier than going out and meeting somebody new."

"True," Renie allowed. "If that's the case, it's a wonder Aunt Toadie didn't do in Uncle Corky and make herself a widow, too."

Renie's remark was intended to be flippant, but Judith was taking her seriously. "That's what doesn't make sense. About this part of the murder," she added quickly. "I mean, if Toadie had somehow found out that her sister was going to marry Boo, why not bump off Vivvie? Unless, of course, Toadie and Trixie are the genuine heirs and they wanted to get rid of Boo before he did something foolish, such as taking a second wife."

Renie gave a faint nod of her head. "That's true. What we need to find is a will. Or if there *is* a will."

"Toadie said Boo kept all his important papers in here." Judith made a sweeping gesture of the den. "I'm beginning to think she said that just to make herself feel important. She told me she had access."

Renie's brown eyes grew wide. "To what? Histories of Little Green Men crawling out of the gazebo? Except for the household ledgers, we didn't find anything important."

Judith had to agree. It was possible that Boo Major had hidden his papers in the bookcases, but except for the shelves behind the desk, the glass fronts were locked.

"I wonder where the key is to those glass doors," Judith mused.

Renie's expression was wry. "On the ring that got misplaced?"

Judith was about to suggest going through the books in the open case when Vivvie Rush and Mrs. Wakefield hurried into the den. Vivvie looked alarmed; Mrs. Wakefield appeared grim. Weed Wakefield, wearing several Band-Aids on his face, sauntered in behind the two women.

"That's a big box," he remarked, gazing at the cardboard carton. "I'll have to break it down to get it in the recycling bin."

"Then do it," his wife snapped. "We got other problems."

Weed wandered off, presumably to get a knife or some other cutting tool. Streaking to the desk, Mrs. Wakefield all but pushed Judith out of the way. The housekeeper began pulling out drawers, riffling through their contents, muttering under her breath. Aunt Vivvie stood in the middle of the room, both hands clasped to her bosom.

Jill Rush leaned against the doorjamb. "Lost something?" she inquired in an amused voice. Unlike the rest of the guests, she was wearing a fresh outfit: a cutaway cardigan, a mock turtleneck, and slim leggings in taupe merino wool.

"Jill, dear," exclaimed her grandmother, "it's dreadful! No one knows the combination to Uncle Boo's safe!"

Jill shrugged. "So hire a safecracker. If you can't get one today, wait until Monday. What's in the safe anyway?"

Aunt Vivvie's eyes veered away from Jill to fixate on one of the twin radiators. "Oh—my dear sister's jewels. We should make sure they're . . . ah . . . intact."

Jill laughed. "Aunt Rosie's jewels? She never wore anything in her life except fake pearls. Didn't Aunt Toadie give everything away to the Salvation Army about two days after Aunt Rosie died? Except, of course, for the stuff she wanted to keep for herself."

Vivvie's soft face had taken on an uncharacteristic edge. "She didn't get her hands on Rosie's jewels. I know that for a fact. Boo showed them to me at Christmastime. You're right, dear, Rosie never cared for them, but they're rather nice. Originally, they belonged to Boo's mother. You'd find them old-fashioned, Jill, dear, but to a woman of my age, they have great charm. Especially the tiara." Her hand strayed to her wig, as if she were feeling how the bauble would fit.

Jill darted her grandmother a curious look. The younger woman's face hardened, but she said nothing and stepped back, as if temporarily withdrawing from the fray.

At the desk, Mrs. Wakefield was glowering in frustration. "You'd think he would have written the combination down someplace," she muttered. "He didn't go out there but once or twice a year. How could he have remembered it?"

"Out where?" Judith inquired, leaning on the opposite side of the desk.

In defeat, Mrs. Wakefield slammed the middle drawer shut. "The garage. The safe's behind that old calendar."

"Ah," said Judith, then fingered her chin thoughtfully. "I don't mean to be pushy, but sometimes I can figure out combinations." Seeing the surprised expression on everybody's face but Renie's, Judith assumed a self-deprecating stance. "When my first husband and I owned a restaurant years ago, he had a safe there. He was always changing the combination and he'd forget to tell me, so when he wasn't around and I had to get at the ready cash, I'd . . . uh . . . fiddle . . . with . . . the . . . lock."

Renie, who knew that Judith had been forced to crack the safe simply to get enough money to pay for a week's worth of groceries, turned away. She also knew that on more than one occasion her cousin had found not cash, but tote tickets from the racetrack. Judith had learned a lot of ways to fix tuna fish.

Aunt Vivvie and Mrs. Wakefield exchanged questioning glances. "Well?" said the housekeeper in her husky voice.

Slowly, Vivvie turned to Judith. "It's a great deal to ask, dear," she said, feigning reluctance. "But it wouldn't hurt to try."

Jill led the way, first stepping aside for Weed Wakefield, who was ambling into the den with a pair of pinking shears. As Judith passed him, he was attempting to cut away one of the cardboard flaps. Buck Doerflinger's voice roared through the entry hall and bounced off the walls of the den:

"Stop! Don't touch that box!" Buck hurtled into the room, pouncing on Weed Wakefield. The detective's white suit was tarnished and rumpled; his pink face was turning plum. "You're destroying evidence, you idiot! I've solved this case and that carton is the biggest clue of all!"

TEN

JUDITH WAS FAR MORE INTERESTED IN HEARING BUCK Doerflinger's solution to the homicide case than she was in working her magic on Uncle Boo's safe. But the detective shooed everyone out of the den—except Weed Wakefield. He not only insisted that Weed remain, but ordered Officer Foster to keep an eye on him. As an afterthought, Buck also insisted that Mrs. Wakefield stay behind.

"Are you nuts?" the housekeeper growled. "Weed isn't exactly the type who plans ahead. What do you want to nail him for?"

Buck glared at Mrs. Wakefield. "Let's start with possession of an illegal substance. We can run right up the scale until we hit Murder One, okay?"

Mrs. Wakefield's horrified gasp followed the cousins out of the den.

"Goodness," moaned Vivvie, "that policeman seems awfully excited! Do you really think he knows who the killer is?"

Unable to believe in Buck Doerflinger, Judith shrugged. "He may," she allowed. "At least he could be on the right track."

Vivvie Rush led the way into the garage. Judith and Renie dutifully followed, with Jill bringing up the rear.

"There," said Vivvie, pointing a stubby finger at the old calendar. "The safe's under that."

Briefly, Judith wished she hadn't offered her safecracking services. It had been quite different to open Dan's safe at the restaurant. She'd known his so-called lucky numbers and had rightly figured he would use them as a combination. The only trick had been to determine the order. That, and a lot of patience. She approached Uncle Boo's safe with considerable trepidation.

"You know," she said in an apologetic tone, "I shouldn't make promises. This might be harder than you'd think. We could start with Uncle Boo's birthday, since we know the date."

"Yes, yes," enthused Vivvie. "What a good idea!"

Judith didn't agree, but was honor-bound to give it a try. Resignedly, she removed the calendar from the rusty nail that held it in place. With her ear to the safe, she touched the dial. The steel door swung free.

The safe was already open, and the Major jewels were gone.

Holly bent over her mother-in-law's inert form and pulled the stopper from a bottle of smelling salts. Vivvie twitched, shuddered, and choked.

"Oh! That's nasty!" she cried, waving away the offending restorative.

"You fainted!" Holly exclaimed, her own hands now shaking and her legs unsteady. "What happened? Jill ran to tell me you passed out from shock!"

Judith and Renie were struggling to get Vivvie on her feet. The older woman had collapsed between the wall and the running board of the Rolls-Royce. Lifting her was like coping with a lead-filled Kewpie doll, but the cousins managed to prop her up against the car. Judith explained what had caused Vivvie to keel over.

A flush crossed Holly's delicate features. "Oh, no! A jewel thief! And a murderer! It's impossible!"

Jill had returned to the garage, too, with her father and Buck Doerflinger in tow. Jill was white around the

150

lips; Buck was trying to disguise his dismay.

Derek Rush, however, showed concern only for his mother. "Are you all right? Should we call a doctor?"

Vivvie shook her head. "It's . . . all so . . . upsetting! First poor Boo! Now the jewels! What next?" With her plump shoulders resting on the Rolls's gleaming exterior, she cast a blue-eyed challenge at Buck. "How could you let a robbery occur while you were in this very house? Someone should write a letter to the Mayor!"

Moving gingerly so as to avoid further blemishes on his white suit, Buck Doerflinger went to examine the safe. A hush fell over the garage as he took his time.

"Picked clean. Anybody touch this?" he asked, jerking a thumb in the direction of the open safe.

Weakly, Judith lifted a hand. "I did. Barely."

Buck faced Judith, feet splayed, fists on hips. His white eyebrows quivered; the barrel chest seemed to vibrate under the now-limp dress shirt. "Why?" The single word echoed off the garage walls.

She offered him her most innocent expression. "I was trying to open it, at Aunt Vivvie's request."

He continued to try to stare her down. "You answer a lot of requests, lady. What are you, a troubleshooter—or just plain trouble?"

Judith's innocence was replaced by impatience. "Look, I had three other people with me. They'll all tell you that the safe was already open. I probably wouldn't have managed it on my own, but I felt an obligation to give it a try."

Buck's sneer wasn't reassuring. He stepped to the inside door of the garage and called to Officer Rigby for reinforcements. "Get out of here," he ordered the onlookers, waving his arms to shoo them away. "We've

151

got work to do. We may have apprehended the murderer, but that doesn't make him a thief, too."

Derek and Holly supported Vivvie between them; an unusually somber Jill followed her family out of the garage. Renie followed Jill, but Judith trailed. She couldn't resist asking Buck Doerflinger a pointed question:

"On what evidence are you arresting Weed Wakefield?"

Buck bristled. "How do you know we're arresting *him?*"

Judith tried not to gnash her teeth. "That's what it sounds like, from what you said in the den a few minutes ago. You also said that the TV carton was evidence. How can that be?"

From deep in his throat, Buck chuckled richly. "Police work is pretty complicated, Mrs. McMonigle. You probably watch a lot of movies and television where detectives go around matching lipstick on cigarette butts and finding pads of paper with impressions of telephone numbers written on a sheet of paper that's been torn off. Let me tell you, in real life it doesn't work that way. We homicide detectives have to take those bits and pieces for what they are, and then use our God-given ingenuity. That's what makes for an airtight conviction and gets cops like me commendations from City Hall."

Judith appeared to be mesmerized by Buck's little speech. "Gosh, that's fascinating!" She stepped aside as Officer Rigby appeared. "You solved this case with a cardboard box! I'm . . . amazed!"

Briefly, Buck looked as though he doubted Judith's sincerity. But his oversized ego finally conquered his common sense, and he bestowed a patronizing smile on her. "It wasn't that hard. You got a locked room, you got a dead body, you got a big box. How did the killer do it? Easy. You ask a lot of questions. You find out who was where when. Which of the suspects was the only one *not* to show up at the door to the den? That Wakefield clown, that's who. So what happened? He locks himself inside the den with the victim, shoots him, and hides in the carton. Nobody thinks to look, and he scoots out while everybody's waiting in the living room for the police to show up. Clever, huh? But not clever enough for Buck Doerflinger!"

The detective seemed to swell before Judith's eyes. He savored the moment of triumph, then scowled. "Now run along, lady. You've had your lesson in detection today from the master!"

With a murmur of appreciation, Judith wandered into the entry hall, looking for Renie, who had disappeared with the others. The door to the den was still closed. Presumably Officer Foster was keeping Weed Wakefield under lock and key. Judith heard voices in the living room, but a quick glance told her Renie had not joined the others.

A hissing sound emanated from the opposite direction. Through the dining room, Judith saw her cousin's head poke around the kitchen door.

"Pssst!" Renie gestured with a finger.

Judith hurried to join her. "What's up?"

"Me, officially." Renie pointed to the teapot-shaped clock above the sink. "It's ten o'clock. I came out to get more coffee."

Judith gave her cousin a sickly smile. Renie hated rising early, and usually her brain didn't function very well before ten. But this morning, at Major Manor, she had come alive as soon as her feet hit the floor. Renie claimed that if the weather was fogged in, her brain was not.

"Ordinarily," she further elucidated, pouring coffee for Judith and herself, "I love fog. It obliterates everything else, and gets my creative juices going. Bill says it's because fog is like an eraser—it wipes the canvas clean, visually and psychologically. He says there are no distractions; thus I'm able to—" Noting Judith's glum expression, Renie broke off. "Hey, what's wrong, coz? You look crappy."

"It's Buck," Judith said flatly. She explained the detective's solution of the case.

Renie gaped. "That's crazy," she said.

Judith arched her eyebrows at Renie. "Is it?" She heaved a gusty sigh. "Sure, it *sounds* crazy. But it is possible. There's even a certain logic to it. The problem is that I can't figure out a better solution. I'm afraid Buck Doerflinger may be right. Damn! Joe will pitch a fit!"

Slowly, inexorably, the fog was beginning to lift. From the third-floor gabled window, the cousins could see patches of sky through the wispy gray morning. They could not, however, see anything of interest in the unfinished attic. Helga Major's sewing equipment, including an old Singer treadle machine, a dressmaker's dummy, and three cabinets of thread, fabric, and patterns, filled up most of the space.

"Boo's mother must have been quite a seamstress," Judith remarked, still sounding disheartened. "I suppose it was her hobby."

"The old girl had to do something," Renie replied, more interested in the emerging view than the attic's contents. "You know, if they finished the attic off, they could see all over the place, just like when the house

154

was built. Look, there's the bay! We may get out of here in an hour or two."

Judith glanced halfheartedly through the mullioned window, then resumed leaning against the tongue-and-groove hemlock paneling. "Maybe. Just because the fog lifts doesn't mean the ice will melt. The outside thermometer still registered under thirty degrees just before we sneaked up here."

"The sun's burning the fog off," Renie countered. "It'll warm up everything. Hey, coz," she went on in a coaxing voice, "cheer up. It's not your fault Buck Doerflinger did his job. Joe can't blame you for being here, either. The murderer is caught, everybody's safe, and we can go home. Relax!"

The attic smelled of camphor and, more faintly, of decay. Treading quietly as well as cautiously, Judith started down the narrow stairs. "Yeah, right, sure," she answered somewhat testily. "But I don't feel right about any of this. Maybe I'm mad at Joe because he didn't take the trouble to fix breakfast for my guests. Maybe I'm mad at Buck because he's more brilliant than I thought. Maybe I'm mad at *me* because I missed . . . the obvious."

The cousins had come out at the far end of the second floor, across the hall from the door to the kitchen back stairs and next to the bedroom that had been occupied by Holly and Derek Rush. Pausing, Judith gently pushed the door open. As she had guessed, the room was empty.

"Isn't Buck famous for taking the obvious route?" Renie inquired as the cousins gazed around the bedroom with its maple-wood furniture and jonquil wallpaper. There was virtually no sign of the Rushes. Apparently the dutiful Holly had made the bed and done whatever

155

tidying up had been required.

Judith nodded. "That's right. And sometimes it backfires on him. He's lucky, though. Joe says Buck often blunders his way to success. I'm afraid this may be one of those times."

Quietly, Judith closed the door. On a whim, she peeked into the opposite room, where Jill Rush had slept. "That's odd," she remarked.

Craning her neck around Judith's shoulder, Renie also peered into the bedroom. The furniture was pine; the walls sported lacy green leaves. "Jill didn't make her bed," Renie noted. "But isn't that Zoe's job?"

"That's not what I mean," Judith responded, moving aside so Renie could get a better look. "Clothes. Didn't you notice that Jill had changed this morning? Oh, Aunt Toadie had brought along her party dress for last night, but none of the rest of us had extra outfits. So why was Jill prepared to spend the night?"

Sure enough, Renie saw Jill's outfit of the previous evening hanging in the closet. So were two pairs of slacks, three blouses, a couple of tailored shirts, a slim wool skirt, and a terry-cloth robe. Judith pointed to the empty box by the side of the bed.

"Isn't that the box Holly carried in last night?"

Renie stared. "Could be. Seen one box, seen 'em all. Unless," she added swiftly, "there's a murderer hiding inside."

Judith gave her cousin a dirty look. "Very funny." Stifling her annoyance, she went to the bed and looked inside the box. Two pairs of shoes lay there, along with a long gold chain. "No wonder that box was so heavy," Judith mused. "Jill brought along enough stuff for a week's stay. I wonder why."

"She's really a meteorologist and knew we'd get

stuck?" Seeing Judith's annoyance resurface, Renie put up her hands. "Okay, okay—I don't know. Let me guess. One, Jill intended to stay, for reasons we can't fathom. Two, Jill was planning to spend the night somewhere else. Or three, Jill expected Trixie to steal the clothes off her back."

Judith shook her head. "Not just the night. She brought enough clothes for several days."

Renie shrugged. "So what? The case is closed. Maybe Jill was going to move in on Uncle Boo and suck up. You know, to keep him from leaving everything to Toadie and Trixie. An end run, as it were."

"That's more like it," Judith replied, her spirits perking up. "Come on, let's talk to Jill."

Renie hurried along behind Judith, outdistanced as usual by her cousin's longer strides. "Hey, wait, coz! I just said this case is closed. Didn't you hear me?"

At the top of the main staircase, Judith turned, a smug expression on her oval face. "I heard you—twice. I also heard Buck Doerflinger. You're both wrong. This case is still wide open."

Judith raced down the stairs. Renie followed, looking baffled. At that moment a helicopter landed on the lawn of Major Manor.

Everyone seemed to have crowded into the kitchen. The back door was open, and the whirr of the helicopter stopped as the cousins joined the others. In answer to Judith's question about what was going on, Jill shrugged.

"It's one of those flying ambulances. Somebody must have called them by mistake." She went over to the sink and poured herself a glass of water.

It was not, however, a mistake. A moment later,

Trixie was heard squealing with pleasure: "Mason! He's here! Oh, how divine!"

Sure enough, Mason Meade was returning to Major Manor. Exercising great care, the attendants lifted Mason's litter out of the helicopter and carried him across the frosty grass to the back porch. Everyone but Trixie stepped aside to allow the patient's passage through the narrow rear entrance. Slipping and sliding on the slick back porch, Trixie greeted Mason effusively. At last the litter was brought into the entry hall. Trixie was still cooing over her beloved, who appeared to be bandaged from head to toe.

"Where do ya want him?" one of the attendants asked.

Trixie tapped her front teeth with her finger. "Oh—the master bedroom, for now." She shot Judith and Renie a swift, faintly malicious look. "You *are* leaving soon, aren't you?"

"You bet we are," Renie retorted, then turned to the attendants. "What's it like out there in the rest of the world?"

"Tricky, at least around here," the other attendant replied. "We lucked out with the fog. It's cleared off at Bayview Hospital, but Heraldsgate Hill and The Bluff are still pretty bad. At first we thought we might have to land over at the playfield, four blocks down."

Derek had moved to block the main staircase. "Just a moment, gentlemen. Why are you here at all?" His cold gaze lighted briefly on Trixie.

On the litter, Mason raised his bandaged head. "I hate hospitals. I insisted on being discharged."

The explanation didn't satisfy Derek Rush. "Then you should have been sent home, not here. This isn't a convalescent center, it's Major Manor, and," he added with a touch of spite, "now that Uncle Boo is dead, it's *mine*."

Aunt Toadie, who had been standing near the coat closet, flew across the entry hall. "That's a lie! You don't own this house, Derek, you miserable egg-sucking leech! *I* do!"

Gazing down at Toadie's irate form, Derek sneered. "You're wrong, Aunt Toadie. Go get Uncle Boo's will."

Toadie, who was practically standing on Derek's shoes, thrust her jaw up at him and snarled. "Go get it yourself! Meanwhile, if my daughter wants to put her fiancé in the master bedroom, that's what she's going to do! Get out of the way before I have the police move you bodily!"

Under the living room arch, Zoe let out a piercing laugh. All eyes turned to the maid, who assumed her typically languid pose.

"If you bunch of crooks want to read the will, why don't you go look for it?" With a feather duster, she gestured around the corner toward the den. "Of course, you'll have to get the cops to release my parents first. They're still holed up in there."

As if on cue, the three Rushes, along with Toadie and Trixie, charged the den. The attendants from the helicopter exchanged glances, then began trundling Mason Meade into the living room.

"To hell with it," the first attendant shouted. "We're getting out of here while there's still a weather window." He and his companion dumped Mason on the sofa. Taking the litter with them, they made their exit. Mason Meade moaned pitiably.

Zoe ignored the patient, but Judith couldn't help but be moved. She went into the living room and asked him if he needed anything.

"I could use a drink," he said in a feeble voice.

Hedging, Judith asked Mason if he was on medication. He asserted that the only medicine that would do him any good was a slug of scotch. Meanwhile, Renie was going through the manila envelope that had been attached to the litter.

"I'm no nurse," she said, "but it looks as if you're on some heavy-duty painkillers. Percodan, for one. I'd skip the booze if I were you."

Mason began to whine, but Renie turned her back on him. "I'll make you a cup of tea," she volunteered.

Since Zoe was still cleaning the living room, Mason wouldn't be totally abandoned if Judith defected, too. Off the entry hall, the family members were stuffed into the little passageway that led to the den, still shouting, still pounding on the door. Officer Foster surrendered just as Judith was about to ask Jill what, if anything, was happening.

Harangued by Aunt Toadie and browbeaten by Derek, Foster finally gave in and agreed to vacate the den with his prisoner. Or, it appeared to Judith, prisoners, since Mrs. Wakefield was under escort along with her husband. While Weed looked unaffected by his detention, his wife took her stand in the entry hall.

"This is all ridiculous!" she declared, her chunky figure and pugnacious expression making her look not unlike an indignant bulldog. "If you people want lunch, you'll have to spring me! And unless you want to freeze to death, Weed has to go check on the furnace."

Wearily, Officer Foster insisted on accompanying Weed Wakefield to the basement. Mrs. Wakefield trotted off to the kitchen, grumbling under her breath. Judith followed the rest of the relatives into the den, but stayed in the doorway. Toadie and Derek assaulted the desk, quarreling over who was going to open which drawer first. Jill was at the open-faced bookshelves, removing the volumes and shaking them out, apparently in the hope of finding the missing will. Using the shears that Weed Wakefield had brought into the den, Trixie was dismantling the big cardboard carton. Meanwhile, Aunt Vivvie and Holly were trying to jiggle the latches on the locked bookcases. They weren't having much luck.

Toadie, who was standing on Derek's foot and wrestling him for one of the file folders, looked up sharply. "Stop that!" she commanded her sister. "You'll break the glass! Nobody's opened those bookcases in years! Who reads that old stuff anyway?"

"All the more reason," Derek shot back, kicking Toadie in the shins, "to hide something there."

Flinching at the family's callous behavior and blatant greed, Judith skirted Trixie and the pinking shears. She joined Jill, who at least wasn't engaged in any sort of violence. Watching the younger woman go through the books, Judith felt a nudge at her brain. Suddenly she remembered: Someone—Derek?—had picked a book up off the floor after Uncle Boo's body had been discovered.

"Here," Judith whispered excitedly to Jill, pointing to Will Rogers's autobiography, "check this one."

With a puzzled glance at Judith, Jill slid the book from the shelf. Dusting it off, she riffled through the pages, then stiffened, and a strange keening sound emitted from her throat. Judith gazed over her shoulder. A legal document was neatly folded in the middle of the Rogers book.

Judith's back was turned on Derek and Toadie, who were still wrangling as they pawed through the desk. Vivvie and Holly, giving in to defeat, had joined them. Jill edged closer to Judith, closing ranks.

"It's the will," she whispered. "Look!"

Judith did. The document stated that this was the last will and testament of Bruno Ragland Major. Scanning the standard printed legal form with its handwritten passages, she saw that the testator's intent was clear: Being a widower and having no issue, he did "give, devise, and bequeath" his entire estate unto his beloved nephew by marriage, Derek Maurice Rush. The date was September 29, three years earlier.

Jill howled with glee. Trixie and Toadie merely howled.

ELEVEN

PANDEMONIUM BROKE OUT IN THE DEN. AUNT TOADIE whirled on Jill, trying to tear the will out of her hands. Derek embraced his daughter, which wasn't easy, since he had to fend off his aunt's clawing fingers. Holly fanned herself with her hand and leaned against one of the radiators. Aunt Vivvie beamed—and fainted again. Judith called for Mrs. Wakefield and the smelling salts.

It was Renie, however, who showed up. "What the hell . . . ?" she muttered, encountering the chaotic scene.

"Derek won," Judith said in her cousin's ear. "Jill found the will."

"Well." Renie stared at Aunt Vivvie, who was lying on the parquet floor and making little mewing noises. "Did you say smelling salts? I think she's coming around."

Renie was right. Vivvie was not only conscious, but also smiling, if in a trembling, anxious manner. "Oh, my!" she gasped out, allowing Judith to prop her into a sitting position. "Oh, my, my! Bless Boo! My son is so deserving!"

"Bunk!" shouted Toadie. "Let me see that will! It must be a phony!"

With an air of victory, Derek waved a hand at his daughter. "Let her read it, Jill. Let everybody read it. I always knew Uncle Boo loved me best." His off-center smile revealed his gold molar, making him look vaguely like a pirate.

Toadie snatched the document from Jill's grasp. She read hurriedly, then sneered. "This thing is three years old! He wrote this just after Rosie died. Do you really

163

think he didn't make another will?" Toadie crumpled the legal-sized paper and hurled it at Derek. "I should make you eat that, you swine!"

Trixie's blond head bobbed up and down like a puppet's. "That's right, Mummy! Uncle Boo promised us his money! And the house! And . . ." Trixie took a deep breath, her cleavage straining at the deep ruffled neckline . . . *everything!* Let's go through those other books!"

Chaos reigned in front of the open bookcase. Shoving, pushing, and otherwise stampeding one another, the four Rushes, including a rejuvenated Aunt Vivvie, vied with the two Grover-Bellews. Books began to fly from the top shelf. Her librarian's sensibilities enflamed, Judith called a halt.

"Wait!" she cried, practically vaulting over the desk. "Stop!" To her amazement, the combatants did, staring at her with varying degrees of curiosity and hostility. Swallowing hard, she made a calming gesture with her hands. "I have an idea. There's a better way to find that will than to tear this place apart. Would all of you agree to a truce and to appointing Renie and me as neutral searchers?"

Aunt Toadie's face turned mulish. "We would *not*. Why should we trust you two?"

Renie had joined Judith by the desk. "You sure don't trust each other," she asserted. "Furthermore, if you don't knock it off, the cops will come in here and throw you out."

Renie's threat didn't strike Judith as a likely possibility, but it sounded good. Toadie and Trixie exchanged perturbed glances; the four Rushes muttered among themselves. Derek was the first to speak up.

"Very well. We'll go out in the living room and wait.

You have precisely ten minutes." He looked at his watch.

The closing of the door was music to the cousins' ears. Peace fell over the den. Judith began replacing the volumes that had been pulled off the top shelf; Renie put back the half dozen that had been yanked from the lower parts of the bookcase.

"Well?" asked Renie. "What's your brainstorm?"

Judith pointed to the Will Rogers autobiography that Renie had just slid into place on the middle shelf. "I don't think the will—or wills, if there's more than one—was hidden at random. Do you remember what happened after we found Uncle Boo's body? I kept trying to recall something I'd seen, but it eluded me until I saw Jill going through the bookcase just now. While we were all gasping and shrieking over poor Boo, Derek picked up a book that had fallen off the shelf. It was the Rogers bio. Now why should it be on the floor? I reasoned that it was because Boo had been looking at it, perhaps while the murderer was with him. What would cause Uncle Boo to take out that particular volume? I couldn't think of any reason—unless there was something hidden among the pages. And there was." Judith gave Renie an eloquent look.

Renie gave Judith the bird. "Stop being obscure, coz. I get the part about the book on the floor and all that, but now where do we find another will—if there is one?"

Turning away, Judith scanned the shelves. Unlike the glassed-in cases, which seemed ordered by chronological publication, the more popular collection wasn't organized. But there were no more than two hundred books. It didn't take Judith long to find what she was looking for.

"Here," she said, a note of excitement rising in her

voice. "Try this one." She handed Renie a copy of *Say Hey,* the autobiography of Willie Mays. "And this," she added, giving her cousin George Will's *Men at Work.*

Still mystified, Renie began flipping through the Mays autobiography. In the middle, she found a folded legal document. Enlightenment struck.

"Aha! It's people named Will—or Willie. Here," she said, hurriedly unfolding the single sheet of paper, "let's see who the next lucky heir is—and hope it isn't Toadie or Trixie."

But it was, both of them. The second will was identical to the first one—except that it left the entire estate of Bruno Ragland Major to Theodora Lott Grover and Trixie Bellew Longrod. It was dated October 4 of the previous year, and revoked ". . . all previous wills and any codicils thereto at any time heretofore made by me."

"Damn," Renie breathed. "Derek's out, Toadie and Trixie are in. Why don't we burn this?"

With a pained expression, Judith shook her head. "We can't. Unlike those creeps in the living room, we're honest." Suddenly she brightened. "Wait—let's see that George Will book."

To the cousins' elation, a third legal document appeared, from the middle section of *Men at Work.* Judith and Renie read frenziedly.

"Yikes!" gasped Judith.

"Egad!" cried Renie.

"Mrs. Wakefield wasn't kidding," Judith said in dismay.

"I guess not," Renie replied in a hollow voice.

The third will was dated January 11 of the current year, and left Boo Major's entire estate to Space Aliens.

The cousins could find no other volumes written by or about men named Will, Willie, or Wills. They tried Ted Williams, William Styron, and even an historical novel about William the Conqueror, but the pages held nothing but words.

Renie sighed. "Now what? How do we face that crew with this?" She waved the most recent will at Judith.

Taking the document, Judith carefully reread the handwritten portion. "He's actually specifying an organization of UFO watchers, so legally this will is probably on solid ground. The American Society for Sighting and Studying Alien Beings Outside Ourselves may or may not be a local group."

"It doesn't matter," Renie said with mixed emotions. "As long as they exist somewhere—which is more than I can say for the Space Aliens—they get the loot. Now, how are we going to tell the would-be heirs that they're cut out of the will? We may be the next victims, coz."

Resignedly, Judith started for the door. She stopped, looking into the cardboard box, which had been partially shredded by Trixie. "I wish Buck Doerflinger's theory didn't actually make some sense. I keep thinking of what Mrs. Wakefield said."

"You mean about Boo not . . ." Renie faltered.

"About Boo not being killed . . ." It was Judith's turn to be stumped. "I'm not exactly sure how she put it, but I think what she meant was that Boo wasn't shot in a locked room. Which may mean," she continued, gathering steam, "he was killed somewhere else and brought in here. But I don't see how." She gazed again at the carton, then shook her head. "No, he couldn't have been transported in here via this box. That's too crazy. Mrs. Wakefield probably doesn't know what she means. The whole thing's so . . . illogical."

167

"But," Renie countered, "if Buck's right, what's Weed Wakefield's motive?"

Judith's wide shoulders slumped. "That's it—I don't know. Unless . . ." Her dark eyes narrowed. "The jewels? Did Weed take them? If so, why kill Boo? I'll bet he didn't go out to that safe once in a blue moon. Except to show the stuff off to Vivvie Rush."

On the other side of the door, a fist pounded so hard that the frame shook. The cousins leaped backward, practically falling over each other. Judith half-expected to see a hand plow through the fine-grained Philippine mahogany.

"Open up!" bellowed Buck Doerflinger.

Judith started for the door again, but Renie held her back. Putting a finger to her lips and her other hand on the knob, she waited for Buck to pound a second time. At the precise moment that his fist made contact, she whisked the door open. Buck careened across the threshold and crashed into the cardboard box.

"Oh, fudge," Renie said in a mild voice. "You just wrecked your evidence! Now what will you do?"

Shooting a malevolent look at her, Buck untangled himself from the cardboard remnants and struggled to his feet. "I ought to haul you in, too," he growled, then began to shout. "Impeding justice! Refusing to cooperate! Sassing an officer!"

Renie assumed her middle-aged ingenue's expression. "Busting a box?" She flinched a bit as Doerflinger loomed over her. "Boxing a bust? Get your paws away from my chest, Doerflinger, or I'll sue you for sexual harassment."

Weary from her efforts at trying to keep the peace, Judith intervened. "Say, Buck—uh, sir—we found some wills. Here." She thrust the two latest editions at him.

"There's another one in the living room."

"There's a goddamned *patient* in the living room," Doerflinger roared. "This isn't no hospital! Who sent that bozo back to Major Manor?"

"Not us," the cousins chorused, then gave each other a bemused look. They waited, however, for Buck to peruse the wills. His face turned red; his voice could have shattered glass.

"Hell! Space nuts! What kind of a deal is this anyway? Does that Wakefield perp think he's from Pluto?"

"His motive does seem obscure," Judith murmured. Seeing Buck's glare, she hastened on: "I mean, nobody in the family or the household appears to benefit from this will. It's very recent, so it must be the latest. Of course, the others probably don't know that . . . yet." Hopefully, she raised her eyes to Buck's crimson face.

"'They'll know it now," he thundered, wheeling out of the den.

Renie made as if to follow, but Judith detained her. "Let's not," she urged. "Do you really want to hear the family's reaction? I'm worn out from all their quarreling."

Renie was easily coerced. "It's going on noon," she noted. "I wonder if Mrs. Wakefield has lunch ready."

There was one way to find out. Judith and Renie left the den, hurrying through the hall. From the living room they could hear the cries of disbelief, followed by shrieks of rage. The cousins traipsed on to the kitchen.

Mrs. Wakefield was taking a pan of rolls out of the oven. "Creamed chicken over noodles with mushrooms, tarragon, and shallots," she announced. "Avocado, shrimp, and asparagus salad. Rolls. Dessert will have to be ice cream, but I got three kinds in the freezer."

Renie was ogling the rolls. "Sounds good," she said.

"You were right," Judith told the housekeeper, then saw her look of mild surprise. "About the Space Aliens. We found the will. Or wills. But the Space Aliens are the most recent heirs."

Mrs. Wakefield smirked. "What did I tell you?" She paused to give her sauce a stir. "But there were other wills? Old Boo must have had those drawn up on the sly."

"He did them himself," Judith replied. "He used those forms you can buy at any big stationery store."

"Really." Mrs. Wakefield seemed intrigued. "Who were the witnesses?"

Judith looked blank. "I don't remember. But there were witnesses to all three of the wills." Her forehead furrowed in concentration. "The last one had simple names—Brown? Jackson?"

Mrs. Wakefield gave a slight nod. "Davey Brown— he's the plumber. And Cal Jackson comes in for electrical stuff. I suppose Boo got them to sign while they were working here. What about the others?"

Judith didn't remember. Neither did Renie, though she thought one of the signatories had a Polish name.

"Andy Wojiechowski," the housekeeper replied easily. "He does the heavy-duty gardening. Makes sense, huh? Boo'd sit there in his den and make out wills and get whoever was hanging around to sign them." She gave a little shrug, then drained the noodles.

Judith eyed her curiously. "Why not any of you?" she asked.

Pouring noodles into a large serving bowl, Mrs. Wakefield arched her eyebrows. "We live here. The others don't." She glanced out through the dining room to the entry hall, and in the direction of the living room

170

beyond. "I hear a commotion. Do you suppose they'll stop fighting long enough to fill their fat, ugly faces?"

"I will," Renie volunteered.

Mrs. Wakefield put the rolls in a covered basket. "Boo had his little secrets. Like I said, I didn't know he made any other wills except for that last one, and I wouldn't have known that if Davey Brown hadn't come out of the den laughing his head off and talking about Martians and money. I sort of guessed what was going on. As far as I'm concerned," she added, gesturing toward the living room with a long metal spoon, "it serves 'em all right. That Toadie's a real piece of work, Trixie's a man-eating tramp, Derek's a stick-in-the mud, his wife's a doormat, their daughter is a conniver, and the old lady—Vivvie—is a dithering idiot. Oh, she had her hooks into Boo, I'll grant you that. And Jill, coming around here and giving Boo rides in her hot little sports car! Could they have been more obvious? I say, let the two-headed monsters from Mars get the lot. It beats having all that money go to the one-headed monsters from the suburbs." With a swish of her well-padded hips, Mrs. Wakefield carried the serving dishes out to the dining room.

Vivvie arrived just as the cousins sat down at the dining room table. She picked up a linen napkin and fanned herself. "I don't think I can eat a thing! All this ridiculous confusion over the wills! And the jewels! Where can they be?"

The question, Judith thought, was interesting. Aunt Vivvie wasn't as curious about who had taken the jewels as she was about where they had gone. Perhaps she had jumped to the conclusion that Weed Wakefield was the thief.

"How do we know they haven't been missing for

171

some time?" Judith asked, taking the roll basket from Renie.

Vivvie's blue eyes grew wider than usual. "Oh! Why, that's so! We don't." Disconsolately, she stared at the noodles on her plate.

"Didn't you say Boo showed them to you at Christmas?" Judith prodded. "Is it possible that he might have sent them out to be cleaned or reset?"

A spark of hope flared in Vivvie's eyes; then she drooped again in her chair. "No. Not Boo. It would never occur to the poor dear."

Even though Renie was stuffing her face with salad, that didn't keep her from speaking up. "Were they insured?"

Fleetingly, the hope rekindled. "I'm sure they were," Vivvie answered, toying with a slice of avocado. "Boo's father would have seen to that. And even though Rosie didn't like to wear them, she tended to business. Rosie was very capable, you know."

It occurred to Judith that Rosalinda Lott Major might have been *too* capable. Perhaps her overwhelming efficiency had stripped Boo of whatever self-reliance he had possessed.

Renie was buttering her second roll. "I assume the corporation would keep paying the premiums, so there'll be insurance money. It'll go to the estate, though," she added with a frown.

Aunt Vivvie grimaced. "The estate! What good is that? Martians! What will they want with my tiara?"

Holly entered the dining room, her delicate features careworn. "This is the most awful weekend I've ever spent," she declared, pulling out a chair next to her mother-in-law.

Vivvie deterred her with a soft, plump hand. "Holly,

172

dear, would you fetch my antacid from my purse? My stomach is so upset."

Dutifully, Holly retreated. Judith used the opportunity to ask Vivvie about Boo's brother, Rube. "I didn't realize he had a brother," Judith said in a conversational tone. "Did you ever meet him and his family?"

Momentarily distracted from her own troubles, Vivvie kneaded the linen napkin and turned reflective. "I must have, at Boo and Rosie's wedding. I know Reuben was there, because no one expected him to come and his arrival was something of a surprise. But my, it's been nearly forty years! And so much strong punch!" She paused, then sadly shook her head. "I honestly can't recall. Perhaps Toadie would remember."

Judith tried a slightly different tack. "He had a wife, I hear. And a . . . daughter?"

Vivvie brightened. "Oh, yes! Ramona—I do remember her now! Quite plain, but she had a way about her. Freckles all across her nose, and the liveliest eyes. Very outgoing." Under the curling fringes of the wig, Vivvie's forehead creased. "That's strange—I can see her so vividly, yet I don't recollect Reuben at all."

"Was she . . . German?" Judith asked.

Vivvie's mouth went round in surprise. "Why, no, she was perfectly normal. An American, I mean, just like you and me."

"And their daughter?" Judith prompted as Holly hurried into the room with a roll of Tums.

Vivvie tapped her lips. "Hm-mmm. Their daughter . . . no, she doesn't spring to mind, either. The punch, you know. So mind-fuddling." She gave a dejected shake of her head and popped a Tums in her mouth.

Judith wasn't quite ready to give up on Vivvie. "Boo didn't speak of his brother much, I take it?"

It was Holly who answered. "Personally, I never heard him mention the brother. But then, I didn't marry into the family until some years after Rube and his wife were killed in that car accident."

Renie was going for seconds on the creamed chicken. "Surely," she said, oblivious to the puddle of cream sauce that had landed on her sweatshirt, "Boo and Rosie must have kept track of their niece?"

Vivvie and Holly exchanged mystified looks. "I don't think so," Vivvie said at last, then made a piteous face for Holly's benefit. "Dear, would you mind getting me a glass of water? That Tums doesn't want to go down by itself."

Holly went out through the door to the kitchen just as Derek and Jill came in from the hall. Derek's long face was still dark with rage; Jill seemed remarkably calm.

"A court of law will decide this matter," he announced, as if his mother and the cousins had been waiting for him to speak. "Uncle Boo, bless him, must have been suffering from hardening of the arteries. He certainly wasn't in sound mind when he made that last will, and he was probably almost as unbalanced when he wrote the other one."

"Ha!" shouted Trixie, who was standing on the threshold. "You wish! Then why not say he was crazy as a bedbug when he made out the will that left everything to you?" With a smirk, she sat down at one end of the table. "Think about it, Derek. I wouldn't count on some senile old judge saying Uncle Boo was . . . senile."

Derek threw Trixie a black look, then stared at his empty plate. "It would be better if he'd never made a will at all," he murmured. "That way, we would simply divide the estate among his natural heirs."

174

Having finished gorging herself, Renie had shifted into her perverse mode. "That could take a while. You'd have to make a search for Boo's niece." Noting Trixie's startled expression, she smiled blandly. "Reuben's daughter. Boo's blood relation. Gee," Renie went on in a musing voice, "since she's on his side of the family, she'd get all of it. What a thrill that would be for her!"

Trixie's face had grown blotchy with high color. Judith wondered if she was verging on apoplexy. Derek, on the other hand, was quite pale. Aunt Vivvie started to twitter, but Jill remained composed.

"Nobody," Trixie began, panting just a bit, "knows . . . anything . . . about her. She may be . . . dead."

Renie wasn't done with taunting Trixie. "Why should she be? From what I can tell, she'd be about your age, Trixie. Early, mid-fifties."

Trixie screeched, then leaped from her chair, leaning in Renie's direction. "I'm nowhere near that old! Why do you and Fatso here always pick on me?"

"*Fatso?*" Judith bristled. "Listen, Trixie, I'll bet I don't outweigh you by more than ten pounds! At least all of me is real!"

"As if you and Bugs Bunny here couldn't use mega-improvements!" Trixie huffed, strutting a little to show off her augmented body. "*Some* of us care about our personal appearance. It's a measure of self-esteem."

Renie wasn't impressed. "I'll say one thing for you, Trixie—getting all those nips and tucks for your sags and bags didn't detract from the character in your face. You've never had any."

Trixie's mouth worked at a frenzied pace, but nothing came out. She whirled away from the table and fled the dining room. Derek's malevolent gaze followed her.

Jill emitted a little snort. "I guess Trixie doesn't like

creamed chicken. I think it's kind of tasty."

Judith gave an absent nod of agreement and rose from the table. "I'm skipping the ice cream," she said, then caught herself. "I'm *not* dieting. I'm just . . . full."

In the entry hall, she encountered Aunt Toadie, heading for lunch. Judith would have preferred passing on without comment, but Toadie stopped her. The older woman's face was stiff with resentment.

"I'll never forgive you for interfering," she said in a harsh voice. "Why couldn't you have left well enough alone? If there's one thing I cannot abide, it's a meddler!"

After the countless squabbles and endless insults of the past eighteen hours, Judith was getting numb. Instead of offering a sharp riposte, she merely sighed. "I wanted to help all of you. It wasn't my fault that Boo made multiple wills." Hoping to extricate herself, she gave Toadie a bleak smile. "It'll all work out. You know what Grandma Grover used to say—it'll all be the same a hundred years from now."

The irony was lost on Toadie. "Your grandmother and her platitudes! Oh, she was a fine one to give advice! Telling me how to cook for Corky and offering her useless old German recipes! And sewing clothes for the children! Did she really think I'd let Trixie and Marty and Cheryl run around in homemade garments looking like hobos?"

Since Grandma Grover's delicious meals and Grandma Grover's homemade dresses and Grandma Grover herself were treasured memories to Judith, Toadie's cutting remarks triggered yet another explosion. "What a wicked thing to say!" Judith fumed. "Grandma had terrible arthritis and it was hard for her to sew clothes for all the grandchildren. But if she made pinafores for Renie and me, she made them for the rest of the girls, too. And overalls for the boys. As for her cooking, you and Uncle Corky would show up for every holiday with your kids and your mother, and not only did you never lift a hand to help, but never once did you bring so much as a jar of peanuts! Rosie and Boo and Vivvie and Mo and the whole damn lot of Lotts would come sometimes, too, and you were all a bunch of freeloaders!" Judith stopped for breath, certain that Toadie would interrupt. But she didn't; she stared at Judith as if she were watching a natural phenomenon, like an erupting volcano. "As for meddling, that's all you ever do! This," Judith went on, her voice rising as she waved a hand around the entry hall, "is a perfect example. You've been trying to run Boo's life ever since Rosie passed away. Why, you were interfering right up until the day he died, firing those masons just so Trixie's shady fiancé could get the contract!"

At last Toadie responded, her eyes narrowed and her jaw jutting. "That's nonsense! I did no such thing! How dare you accuse me of . . . *everything!*" She shook a fist at Judith, setting her charm bracelets a-jangling.

But Judith wasn't finished. "It seems you were the one person who checked on Uncle Boo last night while he was in the den. I presume he was alive and well."

Toadie's rage diminished only a jot. "Of course he was alive and well! But I didn't go in. I merely asked through the door if he needed anything. He didn't. So I left."

"What time was it?" Judith's question was phrased in a sharp tone. She was still incensed by Toadie's slur on Grandma Grover.

"I don't know," Toadie shot back, her temper again rising. "Who do you think you are, asking such

177

questions?" In a fury, she flounced off, not to the dining room, but to the main-floor bathroom. Still fuming, Judith hoped Toadie was going to be sick.

The living room was blessedly empty. Or so Judith thought until she heard Mason Meade moaning on the sofa. Apparently Trixie and Derek were still at loggerheads over who took precedence in the master bedroom. Indeed, it seemed to Judith that the next occupants were likely to be a couple of tourists from Uranus. Unless they made reservations first at the B&B, which wouldn't happen if they heard Hillside Manor's hostess served mush for breakfast.

Still feeling peckish, Judith went to the window to check the weather. The fog was definitely lifting, but as far as she could tell, the ice remained on the walkway and the small patch of street that was visible from inside.

"I can't sleep. I'm in pain." Mason Meade's voice was thin and plaintive.

Judith wandered over to the sofa. "You should have stayed in the hospital. In fact," she said, taking her crankiness out on Mason, "you never should have left this house in the first place. Whatever possessed you to try to get down that horrendous hill?"

Mason averted his eyes, which were about the only exposed parts of his body except for his nose and mouth. "I had an appointment this morning," he replied in a waspish voice. "I didn't want to miss it."

"Well, you certainly didn't miss that lamppost." Judith's tone was prim. She sounded as if she were chiding a raucous library patron. Taking in Mason's obvious misery, she softened her expression. "I'm sorry, I feel edgy. Tell me, Mason, what is your business?"

Trixie's fiancé stopped whimpering. "Concrete.

Foundations, mostly, though we do some paving. We're over on the east side of the lake. My sister and I inherited the company from my father. He started out as a bricklayer."

Judith raised her eyebrows. "You do brickwork, then?"

He offered a feeble smile. "Sometimes. I wanted to change the name to Mason's Masonry, but my sister didn't like it. She thought I was being conceited. So we kept the original name, Eastside Concrete. My first wife owns a third of it now."

Judith perched on the arm of the sofa, careful not to disturb Mason's inert form. "You seem to have quite a bit of family in the suburbs," she said lightly. "Is that where you met Trixie?"

Mason shifted the arm that wasn't in a sling. A cup of tea sat on the floor, seemingly untouched. "I met her at the Lexus dealership right before Christmas. She was buying herself a present." He grew morose. "And now I've totaled the car. I'll bet she hasn't made more than two payments."

Judith wasn't sure what a new Lexus cost, but she guessed it to be in the forty-thousand-dollar category. Such a high-priced automobile was out of her league, even with Joe's salary and the B&B earnings combined. She wondered how much Trixie made selling Wear-House Dressing fashions.

"She must have insurance," Judith pointed out. "It's a state law."

With difficulty, Mason gave a nod of his bandaged head. "Oh, sure, but that car was a custom job. She wanted all the extras and some special features. As I said, it was her Christmas present to herself."

Judith's estimate went up another ten grand. She

179

began to wonder if she was in the wrong business. Being a Wear-House Dressing rep must be more lucrative than she thought.

"Have you and Trixie set a date?" she asked, getting off the unhappy subject of the smashed Lexus.

He gave another laborious nod. "June. Trixie always gets married in June."

"So she does." Dimly, Judith recalled the first wedding, in a fashionable suburban church. Number Two had been held in the ballroom of a lakeside hotel. The third time around, the nuptials had taken place on the stage of Rafe Longrod's downtown movie house. Judith wondered if Trixie and Mason planned to be married inside a concrete mixer, but she had the good taste not to ask.

Zoe reappeared, vacuum cleaner at the ready. Mason caught sight of the appliance and winced. "Oh, no! Do you have to turn that on? I have a concussion!"

The maid gave an indifferent shrug. "Then plug your ears. You've got enough gauze and stuff taped to your head anyway. How can you hear?" Curious, she approached the sofa and inspected Mason more closely. "You should have some of those dressings changed, if you ask me. Where's your ever-loving fiancée? She ought to be taking care of you."

Mason seemed moved by Zoe's show of concern. Or, thought Judith, he was not immune to her considerable charms. The masses of auburn hair were caught up with a pair of copper clips; the blue jeans were snug at the hips and cinched in at the waist; a sea-green shirt set off her eyes, which shone like green gold in the wan winter light.

"I scraped my arm," he said in a pitiful voice. "The one I didn't break, I mean."

Dispassionately, Zoe examined the bandages. Judith noted that the maid was right not only was the gauze loose, but it was soiled with dried blood.

Zoe abandoned the vacuum cleaner. "I'll go downstairs and get the first-aid kit. If your future bride can't bring herself to fix you up, I will. I'm used to it. Dad's always wrecking himself."

She had just left when Jill sauntered into the living room. She nodded at Judith and Mason, then sat down at the piano bench and began to play "Jailhouse Rock." Judith wasn't sure whether or not she imagined that Mason winced again.

"Blast!" Jill exclaimed, breaking off in mid-bar. "This thing is so off-key it drives me nuts!" Getting up from the bench, she stalked to the front window. "When will they all leave?" she muttered, more to herself than to Judith and Mason.

Judith pounced on the cue. "*You're* not leaving?"

Deliberately, Jill turned to look at her. "No. I didn't intend to leave in the first place."

Deserting her perch on the sofa's arm, Judith went over to where Jill was standing. "I didn't think you did." She gestured at Jill's attire. "You brought a change of clothes. Several, in fact."

Indignation was quickly supplanted by defensiveness. "So?" Jill's perfect features hardened. "Why shouldn't I? Boo was all alone here. I'm almost twenty-one. Why should I go on living at home, listening to my father give me orders and having my mother fuss over me all the time? I want to be independent."

Judith kept her response reasonable. "Did Boo like the idea of having you move in?"

"Of course he did!" Jill had raised her voice, all but shouting. "He was lonely, I tell you! He loved having me around! I put new life into this place! It's been a tomb since Aunt Rosie died!"

Surprised by Jill's vehemence, Judith noted that Mason also seemed to be regarding the young woman with a certain amount of puzzlement. At least he had turned his head a jot, and his eyes veered in Jill's direction.

"Actually," Judith said in a measured tone, "it wouldn't have been a bad idea. What did your parents think about it?"

Jill sniffed and tossed her head. "I hadn't told them. We . . . I didn't want to cause a row on Boo's birthday." She had lowered her voice and was looking sulky. Fleetingly, Judith glimpsed the vulnerable young girl she remembered from long-ago family gatherings.

At that moment Zoe returned with a first-aid kit large enough to cure an industrial complex. "It would be better," she asserted, opening the double locks on the steel case, "if we did this upstairs. The living room isn't exactly the place for medical treatment."

"It's just my arm," Mason said with a note of panic. "The rest of me is fine."

"The rest of you is a mess," Zoe declared, sorting antiseptic pads, tape, gauze, cotton, and a pair of small scissors. "If the dressing on your good arm is this bad, I can imagine what the bandages on your body are like." She glanced up at Judith and Jill. "Do I have a volunteer?"

Judith hesitated; Jill floundered. They were rescued by Renie, who bounded into the room glaring at her cousin.

"Where've you been? The ice cream has pecans. I can't eat nuts." She saw Zoe ministering to Mason. "Hey, what's going on? Brain surgery in the privacy of your living room?"

But Mason was rebelling. "Don't touch me! Never mind my arm! Go away, or I'll sue! Help!" His good leg kicked at the afghan someone had thrown over his recumbent form.

Zoe jumped to her feet. "Well, phooey on you! I thought you wanted me to help! Screw it!" She tossed the medical supplies back in the steel case, slammed it shut, and stomped from the room. Mason fainted.

Judith hoped it was from relief.

And then she wondered why.

TWELVE

MRS. WAKEFIELD WAS THREATENING TO QUIT. "OVER twenty years we've worked for Boo Major—and Mrs. Major, too, which wasn't always easy—and now this!" Wildly, she waved her hands, indicating the entire menage that inhabited Major Manor. "Murder, mayhem, robbery, rivalry, wills, and more wills! And worst of all, that big dumb cop who thinks Weed is a killer! If ever there was a man less likely to do somebody in—except by accident, and that would be himself—I can't imagine! It's just plain loony!"

Judith and Renie had pitched in to help Mrs. Wakefield clean up from lunch. It was, they figured, the least they could do, since the housekeeper and her daughter had helped them with the party the previous evening.

"You might want to wait until after the funeral," Judith said mildly. "I mean, I can't blame you, really, but you'll draw your wages and somebody will have to be in charge."

Mrs. Wakefield shook her head in disgust. "The funeral! Who's bothering with *that?* Now that old Boo is dead, none of these creeps care about burying him."

Renie was scouring the sauce kettle. "That's not true," she noted. "I heard Derek and Aunt Toadie arguing at lunch over who would make the arrangements."

If Mrs. Wakefield was at all mollified, she gave no sign. "Argue, argue, argue—that's all they do," she grumbled. "Now we're stuck with a bunged-up medical disaster. And you know what else?" She waved a

184

cooking spoon at the cousins. "Even if the ice melts, none of them will leave. It's like—what do you call it?—squatters' rights. They'll all stay put, waiting for the lawyers to sort it out."

As far as Judith was concerned, the housekeeper had a point. "*We* won't stay," she said, glancing out the window at the thermometer. It seemed stuck at just under thirty degrees. "Say, where is Weed? I haven't seen him since they let him go stoke the furnace or whatever."

Mrs. Wakefield switched on the dishwasher. Over the roar of rushing water, she informed the cousins that her husband was still under house arrest. "He's in the basement with one of those wimpy cops who spend all their time watching for shoplifters at Green Apple Grocery. Zoe just fixed her father some smoked salmon for lunch."

Renie rolled her eyes. "Smoked what?" she murmured.

Even with the dishwasher gushing, Mrs. Wakefield caught Renie's remark. "So what? He's under stress. You'd be, too, if those dopey cops thought you'd shot Boo Major."

Judith decided it was time to change the subject. "Say, Mrs. Wakefield, do you think it's possible those jewels were taken before last night? Did anybody ever check that safe?"

The housekeeper paused in her task of wiping down the counters. "No. I mean, old Boo was the only one who knew the combination. As far as I know, those jewels were all he kept in there. Everything else is in a safety deposit box at the bank."

"Everything else?" Judith arched her dark brows.

The dishwasher went into a quiet mode. The

housekeeper looked momentarily puzzled. "Well . . . insurance policies, deeds to the house and the cars, stocks, bonds, CDs, whatever he had of importance. He never touched the stuff. Whenever something came in the mail—you know, like a dividend or whatever rich people get—he had Weed drive him to the bank."

Judith rubbed at her chin. "Yet he kept his wills here. Odd."

Mrs. Wakefield snorted. "At the rate he was making 'em, Weed'd run out of gas hauling the old boy back and forth. It wouldn't surprise me if two or three more turned up."

The comment didn't strike Judith as incredible. She was about to say as much when Zoe came up from the basement. In one hand she held a luncheon plate; in the other, a key ring.

"Look! I found these in the downstairs stove when I started cleaning up the beets!"

The cousins stared; so did Mrs. Wakefield. "Well, I'll be!" exclaimed the housekeeper. "How'd they get there?"

Zoe shrugged in her languid manner. "Who knows? Dad, maybe. You know how he likes to light up off the stove burners."

Mrs. Wakefield sighed. "At least we got 'em back. Hang 'em on that peg by the back door where they belong."

Zoe complied but almost dropped the ring when Buck Doerflinger burst into the kitchen. "What's going on around here?" he roared. "We used the squad car to report the phones being out of order, and they told us it was an on-site problem. I'll be damned if they're not right—somebody cut the wires!"

Residents of The Bluff didn't have to endure unsightly utility poles. The streets were lined with tasteful lamp-posts but the wires which led into the immaculately maintained homes were buried underground. According to Buck Doerflinger, someone had opened the terminal box, located on the side of the house by the back porch, and cut the phone cable.

"Now, why the hell would anybody do that," Buck demanded, pounding on a cupboard door, "*after* we got here?"

Judith considered the question. "You mean you can see why the killer—let's say that's who cut the wires—might have done it before the police could be called?" She nodded. "Yes, that would make sense. But afterward? I agree, it's baffling."

"Baffling!" Buck paced around the kitchen, his long arms striking a canister here, a teapot there. He seemed not to notice. "I'll say it's baffling! What's the point, especially since we can still communicate on our radios?"

Glancing at her watch, Judith noted that it was almost 1 P.M. "My cousin and I tried to call out around nine-fifteen," she said in an attempt to be helpful. "As far as I know, we were the first ones to notice that the phones weren't working."

Buck paused in his pacing to look at Judith with tepid interest. "That right?" he grunted. "What about the rest of them?"

Mrs. Wakefield rescued a tall glass from his path. "There were some calls from the TV and newspapers real early, but I hung up on 'em. Snoops, as far as I'm concerned." She glanced at Zoe. "You use the phone this morning?"

But Zoe hadn't. Renie, however, had. Finally noticing

187

the cream-sauce stain on her sweatshirt, she was trying to eradicate it with a damp dishrag. "I must have finished with the calls around eight-thirty. My breakfast was cold when I came back." She was still smarting from the interruption.

A sudden flash of recollection struck Judith. "Trixie talked to Bayview Hospital this morning. That might have been a few minutes later. We met her coming downstairs."

Buck scowled. "That narrows it to a thirty-minute time frame, more or less." He turned a glowering face to Mrs. Wakefield. "The evidence against your old man is mounting."

"Are you nuts?" the housekeeper flared. "What're you talking about?"

With a sneer, Doerflinger picked up the coffeepot that was sitting on the stove. He shook it; it was empty. His sneer became menacing. "Who else would know where the terminal box was located? Who else would even know there was a terminal box? Most people have phone poles and lines and all that real utility stuff."

For once, Mrs. Wakefield seemed shaken. Even Zoe had lost her languid air. Renie, however, came to their aid.

"As a matter of fact," she said in a clear but firm voice, "the suburb where the Rushes and Aunt Toadie and Trixie live has underground wiring. It's a newer area, you know, and most of the subdivisions were built with buried cable."

"Well!" Buck turned on her with mock awe. "And how come you know so much about public utilities, lady?"

"Lady *Jones*," Renie shot back, her voice not only clear and firm, but also loud. "I know because I've been there. I also know because I'm a graphic designer and I've worked on a zillion public utility projects—phone, light, gas, the works. They love to rave to their shareowners about how they've beautified the world. Got it?"

The detective smirked and rubbed his hands together. "Then *you'd* know about the terminal box, wouldn't you?"

Renie lost some of her steam. "I should. But I never thought about it. Hunh." She seemed disappointed by the lapse in her powers of observation.

"So you say." Buck's voice was full of sarcasm.

Judith felt that the discussion was going nowhere. She couldn't quite see how the severed wires fitted into the murder case. Arguing over who knew how to cut off the phones seemed unproductive, at least for the time being. She intervened by posing a question:

"Is an autopsy being performed on Mr. Major?" she asked.

"Well, sure!" Buck's expression indicated that he thought Judith was incredibly naive or extremely ignorant. "It's automatic with a homicide. This case calls for a medical-legal autopsy, since we know the guy got shot. What we're looking for here is what kind of weapon, caliber of bullet, distance—all that technical stuff you laypeople don't understand, but think you do because you watch TV. By the time we get done, we'll have plenty more evidence to land a conviction." He gave Mrs. Wakefield an insinuating look.

To save another explosion from the housekeeper, Judith responded quickly. "How soon will you have the report?"

Buck's face wore a patronizing air. "Soon enough. I've got Chao sitting in the squad car, waiting to hear."

Judith's attitude was one of polite inquiry. "And the weapon? Was it ever found?"

The patronizing manner fled. Buck's eyes narrowed at Judith. He brushed impatiently at his rumpled white suit. "No. We're still looking, you can bet your butt on that. But it's a big house, lots of grounds," he rattled on hurriedly, a note of defensiveness showing through. "If we had more manpower . . ."

Officer Chao entered the kitchen, holding his regulation cap in his hands. He addressed his superior. "Sir, you're wanted on the radio."

Buck grabbed the radio from his belt and rushed off to seek some privacy. Renie gave up trying to clean her sweatshirt. "I wonder," she mused, "why Buck doesn't have a cellular phone. Joe has one, doesn't he?"

"He does not," Judith replied pointedly. "If he did, he'd have to pay for it. The city hasn't gotten up to speed on communications technology. It's not in the budget."

Zoe had still not resumed her air of languor. She seemed on edge, which was understandable, given her father's status under house arrest. "Some city employees are on the take. They've got the latest-model cars and everything. Maybe we should offer these cops a bribe and they'll let Dad go."

"Hey," Mrs. Wakefield barked, "knock it off! We got enough trouble already without you getting weird ideas! Your father'll get out of this just fine. That Doerflinger doesn't know his butt from a hole in the ground."

Zoe's gaze was dubious, but she didn't argue. Instead, she removed one of the copper clips from her hair, and gave a languid shrug before heading back to the basement. Having completed their cleanup tasks, Judith and Renie excused themselves and went into the hall.

"Is this a stakeout?" Renie asked in a low voice.

Judith nodded. "I want to hear what Buck has to say about the autopsy."

"Will he tell you?"

"He will if I act dumb enough. And simper a lot. His ego is one of his worst enemies. Alas, Joe is another of them." Judith glanced into the living room. Toadie and Trixie had joined Mason Meade at his bed of pain. The four Rushes were nowhere to be seen. Judith wondered if they'd gone outside to get some fresh air.

Buck burst through the double doors with Officers Chao and Rigby at his heels. Renie whispered that she was discreetly withdrawing in order to give Judith the opportunity to tackle Buck alone.

But the three policemen breezed right past Judith and went into the den. The door was shut firmly behind them. Judith waited a full five minutes, but nobody came out. Just as she was about to give up, Aunt Toadie emerged from the living room.

If Aunt Toadie had any good qualities, among them was numbered the capacity to forget an exchange of harsh words—at least temporarily. Judith's theory was that Toadie's quarreling bordered on addiction. And, like a heavy drinker, Toadie understood that she could go only so far without letting her quarrelsome nature interfere with her life. Being self-serving, she could pretend that the fracas had never occurred, or that if it had, it was over. She was forgiven, if not forgiving. Thus, Judith allowed Toadie to approach her, and was not surprised to see a smile on her lips.

"Trixie's taking such good care of Mason," Toadie declared in her customary gushing manner. "Isn't it wonderful to see two people so much in love?"

Judith refrained from saying that it wasn't wonderful

191

to see one person so much in love so often. "I understand they plan a June wedding," she said noncommittally.

"Yes," Toadie agreed, "in Judge Burbage's chambers. We'll have the reception here, of course."

Judith gaped. "Here?"

Toadie was unfazed by Judith's reaction. "Of course. Boo had already agreed to that, and just because he's dead, there's no reason to change things." She finally took in Judith's astonishment, and her smile tightened. "By June, all this ridiculous inheritance mess will be cleared up. The renovations will be finished, and after the wedding we can put Major Manor on the market. What do you think?" she asked, not so much of Judith as of the house itself. "One-point-six, I should guess."

Judith gasped. Yet she knew Toadie wasn't off by much. The house, the grounds, the neighborhood itself, would command at least a million dollars. And if the kitchen and baths were updated, along with the masonry work and possibly a new roof, another half million could easily be added to the asking price.

Deciding to use the house as the starting point for a bit of probing, Judith explained how she and Renie had come across the shoebox with its collection of family pictures. "We found several shots of the house when it was being built," she said. "We also saw some snapshots of Boo's brother, Rube. Vivvie mentioned that you had met him, maybe at Rosie and Boo's wedding."

The smile on Toadie's face was replaced by a grimace of disapproval. "Oh, yes, I met Rube Major. He's the one who gave Boo his nickname. 'Tass a Boo,' he'd say, instead of 'That is Bruno.' Personally, I never used baby talk with our children. That's why they're all so articulate. Trixie could read before she was three."

Recalling that at twelve, Trixie had trouble making out any word that wasn't "Pow!" "Yikes!" or "Whammo!" in a *Wonder Woman* comic book, Judith dismissed Toadie's little conceit. She preferred to keep to the subject at hand. "But what about Rube Major? What was he like?"

Toadie stopped looking smug and seemed to consider the question. "Corky was fascinated by him. You know how your uncle likes to bore everybody with his adventures in the war." She let her eyes roll up toward the ceiling of the entry hall. "Just because he was in North Africa and at Anzio and Salerno and Monte Cassino and the Battle of the Bulge and all those places, and got shot twice and taken prisoner once, he thinks people ought to fall all over themselves. My goodness, talk about anxiety and suffering! There I was, with a little baby and my worthless first husband and all those ration books—do you know how many coupons you had to save to get a five-pound bag of sugar? And gas! We tried every angle to get an 'A' sticker for our car, but it was impossible. We could hardly go *anywhere* until 1946. Is it any wonder my first marriage fell apart?"

Judith was at a loss for words. She didn't know how to respond to Toadie's callous attitude, nor was she sure if the spate of self-pity was a deliberate diversion from the original topic.

She gave the older woman a bland smile. "So Rube got bored with Uncle Corky?"

"Rube?" Toadie gave a start. "Oh-*Rube*! Well, why wouldn't he? Corky *does* go on."

"And Ramona," Judith said quickly before Toadie could get wound up again. "You met his wife?"

Toadie stared down at her gold-tone flats with their

spattering of rhinestone studs. She was again wearing her black cashmere sweater and slacks. "Ramona . . . Ramona . . . Ramona . . . ? Oh! Rube's wife. Homely woman, very dull, a poet. She looked like she'd come right off the farm. No makeup, no style, no social graces. I can't think why Rube married her. He was quite nice-looking."

Silently, Judith compared images of Ramona Major. Vivvie had called her plain, yet attractive and lively. Toadie's description was harsher. Perhaps Ramona had responded more warmly to Vivvie than to Toadie. Or maybe Toadie never had anything good to say about anybody.

"And their daughter?" Judith coaxed.

Toadie gave a shake of her head. "She was a teenager at Boo and Rosie's wedding. I'm not sure I met her. About sixteen, I think, and you know how adolescents hate to be around their parents at social gatherings. I suppose she was off in a corner, smoking secretly and cadging glasses of punch. It was very strong, and it would have served her right if she'd passed out. I never let my children drink until they were twenty-one."

Since it was well known among the Grover cousins that Trixie had guzzled down everything but Drano before she was fourteen, Judith averted her gaze. "I wonder what happened to—what *was* the daughter's name?"

Toadie was toying with the rivets that decorated her sweater. "It began with an 'R'—like Ramona." She squinted at the entry hall's chandelier. "Rose? Rita? Ruth—I think it was Ruth. Oh, I suppose she married and had a family. Of course, if she kept drinking, she might be dead of some liver disease by now."

Judith also let this farfetched conclusion pass. "The

Majors—the *other* Majors—lived in Arizona, didn't they?"

"They were killed down there. I suppose that's where they lived. I don't really know. Rosie and Boo didn't keep in touch. Boo's father didn't approve of Reuben at all." Toadie's prim expression indicated she agreed with Mr. Major. "I don't imagine old Dunlop was very pleased when Rube and Ramona showed up for the wedding."

Judith took a deep breath and a wild guess. "Was that because of what Rube did in the war?"

Toadie put a hand to her throat. Uncle Corky's pear-shaped engagement ring glittered in the light. "Only in part. Reuben was irresponsible in so many ways. He thought nothing of family. Rosie told me that Rube didn't have a loyal bone in his body."

"He was loyal to something, though," Judith remarked with an edge to her voice. She waited for Toadie's reaction.

"Such as what?" Toadie seemed genuinely perplexed.

"Such as Germany. Uncle Corky must have had a fit when he talked to Rube at the wedding and found out what he'd done."

Toadie dismissed her husband's purported response with a wave of her hand. "I *told* you, Corky was fascinated. He neglected me shamefully at that wedding reception. All he could do was sit there and listen to Reuben talk about his exploits behind the lines. Honestly! Who cares?"

Judith blinked. "Behind the lines?"

Toadie made an impatient gesture, rattling her annoying charm bracelets. "Yes, yes. He was one of those spy types. What do you call it? SOS or OOS?"

"OSS?" Judith suggested.

"That's right. So boring. As I said, *who cares?*"

THIRTEEN

AT THAT CRUCIAL MOMENT, THE DEN DOOR OPENED. Toadie caught sight of the emerging uniformed police officers and scurried away. Judith lingered, waiting for Buck Doerflinger to appear. When he didn't, she tapped on the door to the den. Buck barked an answer that Judith couldn't quite make out.

"It's only me," she said meekly as she opened the door. "I hope you won't mind, but I can't help asking for your expert opinion."

"On what?" he growled.

Judith quietly closed the door behind her and moved to the desk. "It's kind of technical," she said, still wearing her diffident air. "My cousin and I were arguing about how Uncle Boo got killed in a locked room." She saw the surge of anger rise in Buck's face and held up a timorous hand. "I mean, I understand your theory about Weed Wakefield and the carton, but what I don't get is the angle. With that shot through the temple, it looks almost like suicide. Why would Weed get so close? He could have shot Boo from here." She pointed first to herself, then to Buck, who was seated behind the desk in Boo's chair.

The anger dissipated as Buck assumed an avuncular air. "I don't know why citizens have to sit around and try to figure out how crimes are committed. It's bad enough that the criminals do that. But for your information, murderers don't always act in a reasonable way. This Wakefield character's a doper, right? Who knows how his brain—or what's left of it—works? Let's say he just sidles up to the old man, whips out his gun, and—bammo! Blows him away. He takes no chances that he'll miss or only wound him."

"Oh." Judith gave Buck a wide-eyed stare. "I never thought about it like *that*. So you don't think Weed might have wanted to make it look like suicide?"

Buck pretended to consider Judith's theory. "Well, now, he might have thought about it, but he should have left the weapon in here. Of course, there you go again with him being a doper. No rational thinking."

"No logic," Judith murmured, sliding down into one of the two side chairs by the desk. "I wonder where he got the gun."

Buck snorted. "That's no problem in this state. Unless he had a record, of course."

"Does he?" Judith hoped her mask of naïveté was holding up.

"No," Buck answered, sounding disappointed. "At least not in this state. We're not done checking, though. We're running him through the national crime data base even as we speak." He broke into a smile, his big body rocking to and fro in the chair.

Judith uttered a thrilled little sigh. "This is so . . . interesting! I mean, I'm sorry Uncle Boo is dead, but watching you bring his murderer to justice is terribly impressive. It makes me realize how well the system works—when it's in the hands of a master." Judith felt like choking.

Buck beamed. "You bet, sweetie. When we're allowed to do our stuff and not get all hung up in a bunch of legal mumbo jumbo, we can catch our perps. And get a conviction. It's these damned lawyers and civil liberties lamebrains who make it tough on us cops. You'd be surprised what we have to put up with."

Judith, of course, would not. To her sorrow, she'd often heard Joe express the same opinion, though in a more modified tone. It seemed that Buck Doerflinger and Joe Flynn had more in common than just hating each other.

"Now," she said, giving the detective a shy glance, "if you could only find the gun. But, of course, you can't know what kind of gun you're looking for, can you?"

The chuckle that came out of Buck's mouth bounced off the paneled walls. "Oh, we can figure that out eventually. We already dug the slug out of the victim's skull. It was pretty damned disfigured, but we can tell it was a 9-millimeter hollow point. Hey, what do you care about that ballistics stuff?"

Judith laughed, a trifle weakly. "Nothing, that's for sure!"

Buck started to get up. "Got to check the weather. The fog's just about gone, so maybe the ice is starting to melt. I want to get out of here before spring." He chuckled some more.

Reluctantly, Judith also rose. She put a hand to her mouth and closed her eyes. "It's so awful when you think about it. That someone could go right up to an elderly man and stick a gun against his head and . . ." She winced.

"Hey, I didn't say that, did I? Look." Buck stood next to Uncle Boo's chair. "This won't mean anything to you, sweetie, but there was no smudging on the victim. There was tattooing, though—from the gunpowder. So that means this Major guy was shot from a distance of not more than three feet and no less than one. I figure Wakefield stood right here"—Buck shifted his bulk to the end of the desk—"and maybe the victim never saw it coming. Wakefield was off to the side, see."

Judith's brain was whirling. There was something not quite right with Buck's assessment of the case. She visualized Boo Major slumped over the desk, his unseeing eyes staring at the wall. She looked at the window to the left of the open bookcase. If it had not been latched from the inside, the murder would make more sense. But both windows had been shut tight when the body was discovered.

"What about the casing?" Judith asked as Buck started for the door.

He stopped, stiffened, and turned to stare. Judith flushed. In her absorption with the murder scene, she had dropped her guileless manner.

"Casement?" She giggled nervously and pointed to the window. "What do you call them in mansions like this? I was wondering if anybody could have seen Weed through the window."

To Judith's relief, Buck seemed appeased. "It was getting foggy. Besides, nobody goes out at night around here. They all stay home and count their money." With a final, quizzical look, he exited the den.

Judith felt an urgent need to talk to Renie. Buck's revelations about the autopsy results must provide evidence as to how the murder was committed. Unless, Judith thought with a wince, he was right. The Butler-in-a-Box theory was beginning to look more plausible by the minute.

Peeking out into the entry hall, Judith saw only the Hispanic police officer, whose name she now knew was Gallardo. He was standing at attention by the double front doors. Judith wondered if Buck and Company were about to make their exit. If so, she realized she would miss her chance to speak with Weed Wakefield. Giving Officer Gallardo a friendly smile, she headed, not for the kitchen entrance to the servants' quarters, but upstairs. She didn't want to take a chance on running into Buck Doerflinger again.

The second floor seemed empty. Judith hurried down the hallway, then used the back stairs. She came out in the kitchen, where Renie was talking to Mrs. Wakefield. The housekeeper's back was turned to her. Judith signaled for Renie to be quiet, then slipped through the door to the basement. Passing the coatrack, she noticed that the reek of marijuana wasn't as strong. In fact, the downstairs area smelled very odd, no doubt a combination of pot, beets, and whatever else Weed Wakefield might have introduced into the servants' quarters.

Officer Foster was on duty in the basement. Weed was nowhere to be seen. Judith already had her story on the tip of her tongue.

She smiled diffidently at Foster. "Could I see Mr. Wakefield, please? I lost my Miraculous Medal and I'm afraid it might have gone into the trash." She patted her chest where the medal rested safely under her navy-and-maroon Rugby shirt.

Foster's round face clouded over. "The accused is in the galley. He shouldn't really be talking to anybody, unless you're his attorney."

"But he hasn't been charged yet," Judith pointed out, figuring that guile would be lost on Foster. "Anyway, I just want to find out where he put the garbage."

Foster's expression was ironic. "How about the garbage can?"

Judith gave an impatient shake of her head. "It's not that simple. Mrs. Wakefield has some complicated method of separating everything. All this recycling, you see. I doubt if they even use those old recessed cans by the porch. You know how it is these days—everything has to be wheeled up to the curb or it doesn't get collected."

Foster relented. He pointed down the hall. "The galley is that kitchen right there, off the big rec room."

Amazingly, Weed Wakefield was actually working. He had the stove pulled out from the wall and appeared to be rewiring it. He heard Judith before he saw her.

"You'll have to wait to haul me off until I get this freaking thing hooked up again. It'd be easier if the wires went into an outer wall, not inside like this one, next to the saloon. I got all the damned insulation in the way. I ought to call the electrician, he'll charge—" He poked his head around the side of the stove. "Oh, you're not the fuzz." For once, his eyes were in focus, but apparently his memory was cloudy. "Who are you?"

"Half of the catering team," Judith replied. "The birthday party? Uncle Boo? Last night?"

Wakefield unfolded his gangling frame and stood up, brushing off cobwebs and dust. "Oh, right, murder and mayhem and all that stuff. Exploding beets, too." He gestured at the stove. "That's why this thing got all screwed up. When Zoe tried to clean up the mess, she moved the stove and yanked out some of the wires. What can I do for you?"

Anxiously, Judith glanced over her shoulder. She was sure that Officer Foster was lurking outside the open entrance to the galley. Swiftly she explained about the allegedly lost medal. Weed informed her which of the outdoor bins would be the most likely receptacle for anything that had gotten swept up by mistake.

"I'll go look," Judith fibbed. "By the way, Mr. Wakefield, did you hear the shot last night?"

A strange smile spread over Weed's face. "Are you kidding? *I* fired the shot, remember?" Noting Judith's startled expression, the smile became a grin. "You don't think I did it? Want to be a character witness, or whatever they call them?"

Judith's response was uncertain. If Buck was right, she was face-to-face with a cold-blooded killer. "I think it's a farfetched hypothesis. But if you didn't shoot Boo Major, you were the only one present in another part of the house. Whatever you heard might sound different from your vantage point. I'm curious, that's all."

But Weed wasn't much help, either to Judith or to himself. "I heard the freaking pressure cooker blow up, all right," he said, gingerly touching one of the Band-Aids that still clung to his face. "There could've been some other noises, but I was kind of out of it. In pain, you know," he added quickly, lest Judith get the wrong idea—which, in Weed's case, was also the right idea.

Disappointed, Judith gave a slight nod. "Of course. Some of us remembered a couple of other odd noises. I thought maybe you heard something that nobody else did. But you probably spent the rest of the time in your room at the rear of the house."

Weed considered. Off his marijuana high, he revealed a certain native intelligence in his brown eyes. For the first time, Judith noticed that there was a serious, even earnest cast to his features.

"I'd *like* to remember," he declared. "I'm no great believer that justice is always served. When I think of all the protest marches and sit-ins . . ." His voice trailed off; then he gave Judith a proud, almost radiant look. "You know, I was at Dr. Martin Luther King's speech in D.C. in 1963. Man, was that powerful!" He pounded his fist into his palm.

"Wow!" Judith replied in sincere appreciation. Around the corner, she heard Officer Foster's shoes squeak. She imagined it was the African-American policeman's seal of approval. Maybe Weed had inadvertently bought her a few minutes of grace. "You were active in the civil rights movement?"

"From the start," Weed replied with verve. "I got in on some of the anti-Vietnam action, too, but by the time that heated up, I was married and had a kid. Making a living can screw up your ideals. Then you start to feel like a failure. Things get to you, the world comes down around your ears, and . . ." Weed stared at the floor, which was strewn with various tools. "Thirty years later, you wonder if any of it mattered. Everything's changed, but it's still a mess."

"It matters," Judith said firmly. "If nothing else, it matters to *you*. If you really believe in something, you have to act on it."

Weed didn't look convinced. "So I spend over twenty years working in this big old barn for a freaking capitalist who doesn't give a rat's ass about anything—and what have I got to show for it? Or him, either. He gets himself shot, and I get the blame. Whatever happened to truth? And justice? See what I mean?"

"Boo was a victim in more ways than one," Judith said quietly. "His father's success made him a prisoner. He didn't have to work, so he just sat. It's really very sad."

"A leech," Weed declared fervently. "He never gave anything back, either. Not even money. Talk about a crime!" The servingman was beginning to work himself into a self-righteous frenzy.

Judith didn't want to hear Weed Wakefield deliver a polemic about the injustices of capitalism. Indeed, it occurred to her for the first time that perhaps Weed had a motive after all. Perhaps his personal failures and his rage at the system had driven him to kill Boo Major.

Buck Doerflinger's theory was growing more and more believable. Judith hated the idea, but its credibility made her eager to get away from Weed Wakefield.

"I'd better go look for my medal," she said with a feeble smile. "Thanks for your help."

Weed made a self-deprecating gesture. "What help? Your miracle thing might have fallen off into the sink and gone down the drain. You'll need a miracle to find it."

She was turning around when he spoke again. "When's a shot not a shot?" he asked abruptly.

"What?" she swiveled, frowning at him.

"You asked me about hearing a shot," he said, his tone reasonable. "I've heard plenty of them, like the pigs firing over my head at rallies and stuff. I didn't hear a shot last night. But now that I think about it, I did hear a couple of weird noises. They were more like pops or thuds. I mentioned the first one to the wife after she came back to tuck me in, but she didn't pay any attention. She's always telling me I imagine stuff anyway." Weed looked wounded, yet a trifle naughty.

"You're right," Judith said thoughtfully. "There *were* two odd noises after the pressure cooker blew up. And they didn't sound like shots to me, either. Not exactly. They also didn't sound the same."

Weed shrugged. "I wonder if it's quiet in the slammer."

Judith doubted it, but didn't say so. She gave Weed another weak smile, nodded politely to a bemused Officer Foster, and went back upstairs.

In the kitchen, Renie was gleeful. "Look!" she cried, pointing to the thermometer outside the window. "It's up to thirty-three! The fog's all gone! The sun's trying to come out! We may be able to get out of here pretty quick!"

Judith beamed at her cousin. The housekeeper chuckled. "Isn't it great? I'll get rid of all of you, and my old man'll go to jail! Talk about mixed emotions!" She shook her head as she hauled a load of garbage out through the back door.

"Garbage!" Judith gasped, suddenly putting her hands to her face.

Renie stared. "Huh?"

But Judith shook her head, then spoke rapidly in a whisper. "I'm supposed to be looking for my lost Miraculous Medal. Never mind why, but I just had a brainstorm about where the missing jewels might be. Let's wait for Mrs. Wakefield to come back inside."

A moment later, the housekeeper reappeared, shivering. "It may be getting warmer, but it's still colder than an Eskimo's nose out there. The steps have thawed, though, and the walk, too, at least close to the house."

Judith grabbed her green jacket from the peg by the back door. "I could do with some fresh air. Renie and I haven't seen the gardens in daylight."

"Not much to see this time of year," Mrs. Wakefield remarked, but she didn't try to stop the cousins from leaving.

"What's up?" Renie asked as they crossed the frosty grass to the gazebo.

Judith filled her cousin in on the autopsy report, Weed Wakefield, and the revelation from Aunt Toadie that Rube Major had been in the OSS. Renie was astounded.

"So Rube was a spy for the Office of Strategic Services," Renie mused as they poked their heads into the latticed gazebo. Despite the new roof, it had a forlorn air, with tendrils of ivy growing over the

205

wooden seats. "Disguised himself as a German soldier and went behind the lines. That's really dangerous. He's lucky he got out alive."

"That's for sure," Judith agreed as they wandered over to the small orchard, which seemed to have two each of pear, apple, cherry, and plum trees. "But we know he spoke German, probably like a native. We also know that he was an adventurer and no doubt relished taking risks. You'd think Dunlop Major would have been proud of his son."

The cousins paused by the huge stone birdbath. The ice was beginning to break up. On a whim, Judith poked her finger into the chilling water.

Renie regarded Judith curiously. "You thought the jewels were in the birdbath?"

"Not really. But it doesn't hurt to check. That thing's big enough for a buzzard." In a seemingly aimless manner, Judith meandered under a rose trellis and down a narrow path that led between tall trees and leafy shrubs. The ground was frozen solid, but the footing was decent. "As long as we have the chance, we might as well check out this whole place. I suspect we'll never come back here."

"Ha! What about Trixie's wedding reception?"

Judith wrinkled her aquiline nose. "I'm skipping this one. Next time, maybe."

The path ended at the entrance to the rose garden. It was small but beautifully laid out, with arbors at each end and a stone fountain in the middle. The central path led past a sundial on one side and a statue of a dancing nymph on the other. The rose bushes looked limp with cold, but Judith knew from her own gardening experience that they would recover in time for their March pruning.

"Nice," she commented, bending over to read one of the metal tags on the nearest bush. "Abraham Lincoln. The ones on each side are Peggy Lee and Bing Crosby. And there's Tropicana and Peace and Brandy and Sterling Silver and—"

"Frozen Cousin on your immediate right," Renie cut in. "Don't get me wrong, I love roses as much as you do, but my teeth are chattering. I thought we came out here to find the loot."

"We did," Judith replied, a bit shame-faced. "But you've got to admit, this is a wonderful property. I think I like the lily pond best."

"It's great," Renie agreed as they wound their way back along the dirt path. "By the time the lawyers get through fighting, it'll probably have fallen down."

They reached the back porch, where Judith gazed around to make sure no one was watching them. The outer steps to the basement, the driveway to the three-car garage, and the grounds appeared to be uninhabited. On the other side of the porch, about a foot above the ground, Judith noticed a metal box with the phone company's bell. Anyone could have gotten at it and clipped the wires, even someone who wasn't familiar with the house. The terminal box was in plain sight, and despite the fog, the porch light would have illuminated it.

Cautiously, Judith approached the nearer of the two recessed garbage cans. The lid stuck. She realized that it probably hadn't been used in fifteen years, or however long it had been since the city had issued new regulations about curbside collection. She tried the second can. The lid all but sprang up in her grasp. She peered inside.

"Well?" Renie demanded, trying in vain to peer over

her cousin's shoulder.

Judith didn't answer at first. Instead, she knelt down on the concrete that surrounded the cans. "Hang onto my jacket," she urged Renie. "I don't want to fall in."

"Are your eyes bedazzled by the pile of gems?" Renie inquired, getting a firm grip on Judith's collar.

"They are not," Judith replied in a strained voice. To Renie's amazement, her cousin had pulled the sleeve of her Rugby shirt down over her right hand. Judith made a final lunge and grunted. "But my eyes are opened. Sort of."

In triumph, she sat back on her heels and waved her trophy in her covered hand.

It was a gun.

FOURTEEN

JUDITH AND RENIE WERE ARGUING, NOT IN THE MULISH, self-absorbed way of their childhood, but on a higher, less personal plane. They weren't angry, though an eavesdropper might have mistaken their fervor for antagonism. No one, however, could listen in, for the cousins had shielded themselves from the house by going down to the lily pond. They were seated on one of the stone benches, safely hidden from prying eyes.

"You could get arrested for suppressing evidence," Renie pointed out for the third time. "You've got to turn that gun over to Buck right away."

Judith's expression was dogged. "He—or his men—should have found the damned thing by now. They didn't do much of a search, if you ask me. Face it, coz; except for Doerflinger and maybe Foster, these aren't homicide detectives. They're straight off the beat. They don't know the drill."

"That's no excuse for you," Renie countered, huddling inside her black hooded jacket. "You know better than anybody how wrong it is to keep something from the cops."

Judith swung her head from side to side. "I told you, I'm not doing that. As soon as I can, I'm giving it to a cop. My cop. Joe."

"It's not his case," Renie protested. "How will he explain it to his superior? Buck will have Joe's rear end in a sling, and you know it."

"He won't dare," Judith responded. "How will Buck explain why he didn't find the gun in the first place? Besides, the police will be leaving any minute. The ice is breaking up on the pond. We'll say we found the gun after they took off. What difference does fifteen or twenty minutes make?"

The climbing temperature and the skittish sun might have been melting the ice, but Renie was still cold. With regret, she gave in. "I wish you hadn't put the damned thing in your pocket. If it's still loaded, you'll shoot your butt off."

Judith smiled, both at her cousin's fears and at her own apparent victory. "The safety's on. It's okay. In fact, I'll put it in the trunk of the car. Let's go."

As Judith and Renie were about to cross the street, a tow truck slowly turned the corner. The studded snow tires crunched on the pavement, but the vehicle showed no signs of slipping. Judith was further cheered by the realization that freedom was at hand.

"Half an hour, tops," she said after the tow truck had passed by and they'd crossed over to her blue compact. "Think of it—we'll have a change of clothes, the use of a telephone, the comfort of our own little beds, the company of people who aren't Aunt Toadie and the rest of this wretched crew! Whoopee!"

"I thought you were mad at Joe," Renie reminded her. "And at your mother."

Judith made a face. "Well, I am. But no matter how annoying Joe and Mother can be, they don't begin to be as annoying as this bunch." She lifted the lid of her trunk. "Some of them are better than others, but I don't care if I never see any of them again."

"They're pretty odious, all right," Renie agreed, nervously watching Judith extract the gun from her pocket and carefully put it inside the box that held the leftover wine. "What kind of gun did you say that was?"

Judith had memorized the engraved barrel. "Walther

P-38. It looks old to me. Joe will know all about it." She closed the trunk and gave Renie a dazzling smile. "In case there are fingerprints, notice I didn't touch it in any way, though I suspect the weapon was wiped—"

"*Touch* it?" Renie snapped. "You *stole* it. Now I'll have to testify that you're nuts."

Renie's criticisms couldn't dampen Judith's spirits. She genuinely could see no difference between handing the automatic over to Joe and giving it to Buck. Both were homicide detectives, and she had a lot more confidence in her husband than in his rival.

Judith all but clicked her heels when they entered the house and found the police contingent gathered in the entry hall. Weed Wakefield stood among them, his lanky frame draped in a black raincoat. Along with the collapsible rain hat, he looked not unlike a scarecrow. His wife and daughter were on the fringes of the group. They both had on warm jackets and appeared to be going downtown, too. Mrs. Wakefield looked angry; Zoe was near tears.

"We'll post bail, no matter what we have to do to get it," the housekeeper vowed. "This is all so damned dumb!"

Buck Doerflinger gave her a nasty look. "Murder is dumb," he thundered. "You'll be lucky if the judge allows bail."

Zoe turned a stricken face to Judith. "Is that true? Can they deny bail?"

Sobered by the little scene, Judith bit her lip. "Yes, they can. But it's usually only when the crime has been particularly brutal." She thought of the gun in her trunk, of Uncle Boo slumped over the desk, of the gaping hole in his temple. How did you define brutal? How violent did death have to be? How many corpses? Wasn't one enough? Judith shuddered.

Zoe wiped at her cheek with a gloved hand. Huddled in her dark green quilted jacket, she looked very young and vulnerable. "My dad's got his faults, but he's no killer," she insisted. "What proof have they got? It doesn't make sense! They didn't even let him finish wiring the downstairs stove."

Buck and his subordinates were ready to go. Weed's long raincoat flapped around his ankles as he made a detour to hug his wife and daughter.

"I'll see you downtown," he said. "You be careful driving. Take the Rolls." He planted a kiss on Mrs. Wakefield's forehead.

"I've never driven that thing," she replied. "We'll use the Cadillac. At least it's an American car."

Zoe was now sobbing in earnest. Weed ignored Buck's prodding and embraced his daughter. "I told you, don't get yourself upset. They can't convict an innocent man."

Zoe pulled away from her father and gazed up into his long, seamed face. "You don't believe that," she said, the anger showing through her tears. "You've always taught me that it's the little guy who gets screwed!"

Weed was being bodily pulled away by Buck and Officer Rigby. "I also taught you that iron bars can't imprison the spirit. Don't let the bastards get you down. And always root for the underdog! See you in court . . ." He disappeared through the double doors, his feet bumping over the threshold.

Zoe lifted her chin. "He's right." She grabbed her mother by the sleeve of her red wool jacket. "Let's go. We're the voice of the people. We have the power; we can do anything. I can even finish that stove. I'm not helpless. I'm like you, Mom, an independent female. It's a red wire, a black wire, and a white one. I watched you do it upstairs once . . ." The Wakefield women disappeared through the door to the triple garage.

Trixie had been watching from the arched entrance to the living room. *"Finally!"* she said with a huge sigh of relief. "Now we can all go home."

Renie looked askance. "Mason, too? How are you going to get him out of here?"

Trixie smirked. "A cabulance, how else? I'm calling one right now." She started for the phone in the alcove.

Judith put out an arm. "It's broken, remember? Somebody cut the wires." She saw Trixie's face flood with confusion. "Say," she went on, taking advantage of the other woman's temporary befuddlement, "who did you really call last night, Trixie? It wasn't Marty. He said he never left the phone after nine o'clock."

Trixie's eyes flashed as she shook off Judith's hand. "It's none of your beeswax!" she snapped. "I'm going across the street to use the neighbor's phone."

Aunt Vivvie had materialized from the dining room. "I wouldn't bother if I were you, Trixie, dear. They're snowbirds. In fact, most of the people around here are. They much prefer spending their winters in the sun. You know—Palm Springs, Tucson, Hawaii."

Briefly, Trixie looked stumped. Then she went to the closet and got out her trench coat. "Somebody's got to be home. I'll just march up and down the street ringing doorbells as if I were a—" Her heavily made-up face brightened. "A Wear-House Dressing rep! And I am! How funny!" She took off through the double doors.

Holly and Derek came down the main staircase together. Derek nodded at his mother. "There's no reason we have to stay on. Let's get our things and go.

Where's Jill?"

Jill was in the living room, glaring at the piano keys. "I'm getting this thing tuned," she announced to no one in particular. "It's a crime to neglect a wonderful instrument like this."

In the wing-back chair, Toadie coiled like a snake. "If you do, pay for it yourself. I'll sell it along with the rest of the furniture before I put the house on the market."

Derek's thin face was a mask of impatience. "Never mind the piano, Jill. Let's take our leave. The streets are almost clear."

Jill played a series of minor chords. "I'm not going," she said without looking at her father.

Running a hand through his dark hair, Derek uttered a choked laugh. "Now, Jill, I understand your desire to watch over our inheritance, but right now I think it would be better if you came along—"

Jill played one final, emphatic chord. She gazed up at him and offered a cool smile. Judith waited for her explosive announcement.

"I'm staying here," she repeated. "I'm moving in." She closed the lid on the keyboard and stood up. Judith saw Derek's face contort and Holly's shoulders slump. There would be a big argument, no doubt, and Judith preferred not to hear it. Along with Renie, she started to slip out of the living room.

"See here, Jill," Derek began, straining to keep the rage out of his voice, "we're going to resolve all of this in a legal, orderly—"

"You don't understand," Jill broke in calmly. "I'm not staying to make sure nobody else takes over. That's not a problem. I'm living here because it's where I belong. I'm Mrs. Bruno Major. Boo and I were married two weeks ago."

214

Judith and Renie raced back into the living room.

Vivvie had collapsed on the sofa, unfortunately on top of Mason Meade, who howled with pain. Toadie had sprung from the chair like a boa constrictor, wrapping herself around Jill and shaking her. Derek reeled, leaning on the piano for support. Holly burst into tears, then sank into the sea-green armchair.

Jill struggled with Toadie, while the cousins watched with a mixture of horror and fascination. Stunned by Jill's announcement, Judith finally took action, attempting to separate the two women. Renie joined in, obviously taking particular pleasure in putting a hammerlock on Aunt Toadie.

"Knock it off," Renie panted, dragging Toadie across the Oriental carpet and heaving her into the wing chair. "Can't any of you act like civilized human beings?"

"They can't define 'human being,' " Judith muttered, letting go of Jill and hurrying over to lift Aunt Vivvie off the groaning Mason Meade.

Vivvie staggered to a chair, holding her backside. "That hurt me, too," she declared in an aggrieved tone. "I feel as if I've been stabbed."

"Good," Toadie snapped, though she, too, was breathing hard. Her narrowed, angry eyes darted to Jill. "Now, what's all this nonsense about marrying Boo?"

Derek, who was torn between comforting his wife, interrogating his daughter, and succoring his mother, made a series of faltering steps in various directions before deciding to stay put. "Yes, by all means, Jill, what are you talking about?"

Jill uttered a weary sigh. "Exactly what I said. Boo and I were married two weeks ago, on January twenty-fourth. We went to City Hall—in my Mazda Miata.

215

Don't you recall when I took him for a ride?"

"You certainly did!" Toadie shouted, her breath restored. "In more ways than one!"

Vivvie was clutching at her bosom, eyes closed. "Oh! Oh! I can't believe it! Boo and I were promised to each other! Oh!"

Jill's expression was half disdainful, half pitying. "Grandmother, I'm sorry. Boo didn't intend to marry you. I'm afraid you were misled."

Vivvie's blue eyes opened wide. "Misled! He led me on, the scoundrel! And all the while two-timing me with my own granddaughter! Thank goodness I never permitted him liberties! Oh! To think of it! Oh!"

Toadie was back on her feet, though a warning look from Renie kept her from advancing on any of the others. "Vivvie, you're an old fool, even if you are my sister."

"Maybe that's why," Renie murmured.

Toadie either didn't hear Renie or chose to ignore her. "And, Jill, you're a young fool. Or the biggest opportunist I've ever met."

"That'd take some doing with this crew," Renie remarked.

"The marriage will have to be annulled," Toadie went on doggedly. "It's obvious that Boo wasn't of sound mind when he married you, Jill."

Jill stared at Toadie, then broke into laughter. "How can you annul a marriage to a man who's dead? And if he was crazy, doesn't that ruin your chances of proving the will he made out in your favor? That one was dated last October, which isn't all that long ago."

Holly had stopped crying and was tentatively approaching her daughter. "That's true," she said, blowing her nose in a Kleenex. "The most recent will,

216

which left everything to the little men from Mars, was written last month. It seems to me that the only real will is the one he made just after Aunt Rosie died—leaving everything to Derek." She gave her husband a tremulous smile, then put a delicate hand on Jill's arm. "So you see," Holly continued between sniffles, "it comes out the same. Even if Boo was unbalanced in the last year, we get the estate."

Jill moved away just enough to break free of her mother. "Not quite," she said in a wry voice. "Whether he was sane or insane, all those wills aren't worth the paper they're written on. This is a community property state. As Boo's widow, I get everything he had. It's no contest, folks. Shall I see you all out?"

Judith and Renie didn't mind leaving in the least. Indeed, they practically sprinted out the back door. Holly, however, called after them. She wanted to apologize for her daughter's behavior.

"I'm sure Jill didn't mean the two of you," she explained, twisting a fresh Kleenex in her dainty hands. "We all appreciate what you did for Uncle Boo's party. And your other . . . efforts. You've been so kind."

Judith patted Holly's arm. "No problem. It's been a very eventful—and upsetting—twenty-four hours. As for Jill, it's easy to excuse her. She was carrying around a big secret, and that's a burden. It must have been terrible for her to become a widow and not be able to let anyone know." Judith watched Holly's reaction carefully. Mother and daughter had had the opportunity for confidences when they'd left the living room in tears the previous evening.

But Holly seemed quite natural. "Jill should have said something earlier. I, of all people, know what it's like to lose a spouse and have no one to turn to. When Andy, my first husband, was shot down in Vietnam, I was utterly alone. No parents, no brothers or sisters—just the baby to console me. It was a nightmare."

"What about Andy's folks?" Renie asked, with one foot on the threshold and the other in the passageway.

Holly's fine brow furrowed. "They were from the South. I never really knew them. Once Andy was dead, they showed no interest in me—or in Jill. At least they didn't cause any problems when I married Derek and he wanted to adopt her." With that remark, Holly seemed to fade away, literally and figuratively. The cousins made their farewells and were out of the house.

The walk was clear of ice; only patches remained on the street. To elevate their sense of relief, a Federal Express truck passed by effortlessly. So did a new Volvo, going in the opposite direction. By coincidence, the tow truck they had seen earlier was now hauling away its prey, a late-model compact which bore the city's official seal.

"Too bad it's not a police car with Buck Doerflinger in it," chortled Judith as they reached her Nissan Stanza.

Renie settled into the passenger seat, fastening her safety belt. "Do you mind if we stop at Falstaff's Market? I have a need for a half-rack of Pepsi. They've got a special this weekend."

Judith didn't mind. She was too pleased at the prospect of escaping Major Manor. Her determination to flee had all but put the murder case out of her mind. She didn't care that Jill had secretly married Uncle Boo; she was immune to the ongoing war of the wills; she was even willing to concede that Buck Doerfinger was right and that Weed Wakefield was the killer. Nothing mattered except being reunited with Joe, making peace with her mother, and getting back to Hillside Manor in time to greet her next round of guests.

The car wouldn't start. Judith turned the key, but nothing happened. She tried again. And again. She swore.

"Cars! It's always some damned thing!" She waited a few moments, then made another try, this time tromping on the accelerator. There was still no response.

"Battery?" suggested Renie, looking worried.

"Probably," Judith replied testily. "My car's used to being in the garage. It probably got too cold sitting out here since yesterday afternoon. Drat, I should have tried to start it this morning. It's after two now." She drummed her fingers on the steering wheel. "I wonder if Derek has jumper cables."

But Derek's black Ford Taurus was reversing out of the driveway. The cousins had been too absorbed in starting their own car to notice that the Rushes—minus Jill—had loaded up and were leaving.

"Toadie's car is still there," Renie noted, pointing to the Buick Park Avenue.

"I hate to ask her for help," Judith said in a dismal voice. But as she spoke, Trixie came hurrying down the street. "Oh—I forgot she'd gone to borrow a phone." Judith couldn't help but break into a wry smile. "She doesn't know about Jill and Boo. Shall we tell her?"

Renie scowled at Judith. "I thought you wanted to get out of here."

"I do. I can't." Judith made a desperate gesture with her hands. "I've got to get a jump-start first." She opened the door and swung out of the driver's seat just as Trixie was stepping off the curb.

Trixie looked startled to see Judith. "You're leaving?" she asked in a hopeful voice.

"We were, but my battery's dead. Does your mother have jumper cables?"

Trixie frowned in the effort of concentration. "I don't think so. I do, but they were in the Lexus." Her face turned wistful. "I had *everything* in that car. It's really a shame Mason wrecked it. I'll have to wait weeks to get a customized replacement."

Judith knew she should stick to the crisis at hand, but Trixie had given her an opening she couldn't resist. "I'm impressed by how well you've done as a Wear-House Dressing rep, Trixie. Maybe I'm in the wrong business."

An elderly couple drove slowly past in a large, aging Chrysler Imperial, testimony to the safety of the streets. Trixie gave Judith a self-satisfied smile.

"It's all on commission, and if I do say so myself, I'm a very persuasive salesperson. Some months I net as much as a thousand dollars!"

Judith tried not to let her jaw drop. Trixie wasn't making a living wage. Maybe she'd reamed her first three husbands. The family rumor mill had said as much. But Vaughn C. Vaughn had been a junior-high-school teacher. Hamlin McBride was a repairman for the gas company. And Rafe Longrod, with his scattering of X-rated movie houses, had usually been one stumble away from bankruptcy. None of the three ex-mates had had much, though Judith was sure they'd ended up with even less by the time Trixie got through with them.

"My, my!" Judith exclaimed after she had collected herself. "I guess I *am* in the wrong business! I sure couldn't afford a fancy car like a Lexus on what I make with the B&B! You must be a smart money manager."

Trixie made a futile attempt at looking modest. "Mummy taught me everything I know." She gave

Judith a sly glance. "It's not always what you have, but what you're going to get. And I believe in making the most of what's coming to me."

"So do I," said Renie, who had finally gotten tired of waiting in the car. "What *have* you got coming to you, Trixie?"

Trixie turned a malevolent eye on her. "You know what it is," she asserted. "My inheritance. I've used my expectations to help me get by."

The cousins exchanged swift, vaguely startled glances. "You mean . . ." Judith began, then stopped for fear of jumping to the wrong conclusion.

"You know what I mean," Trixie said in a querulous tone. "Uncle Boo was always an angel about co-signing loans with me. He knew I'd never default, because I wasn't paying back with my money. It was his. Which was going to be mine anyway. And Mummy's," she added as an afterthought.

Judith's brain was spinning. "You mean . . . ?" This time she was overcome by Trixie's sheer audacity. "You had Boo take out loans for you? Like to buy your car?" She couldn't keep the shock out of her voice.

Trixie, however, was undaunted. "Of course. He was so sweet about it. We'd have a few drinks and visit and laugh, and the next thing you knew, he'd sign those old papers as if he were doing Christmas cards. What a sweetie! I'll miss him, though." Her effort at sorrow failed.

"You'll miss his signature," Renie said, not bothering to disguise her venom.

Exasperated, Trixie made a face at Renie. "Now, now! Sour grapes and all that! After all I've done for Uncle Boo! Why, he couldn't have gotten along these last few years without me. And Mummy."

Renie leaned against the roof of Judith's car. Her brown eyes danced with mischief. "He got along, all right. To the justice of the peace. Gee, Trixie, didn't you know Boo and Jill tied the knot last month?"

Trixie's reaction was to laugh, a merry sound that seemed to linger on the cold winter air. "Very funny, dearest cousin! You always were the family joker! Or," she continued, the smile swept from her face, "are you just a joke?"

"The joke's on you, Trixie." Renie nodded toward the big house. "Go ask Mrs. Major. She's still in there, playing the piano—and playing her cards just right."

For the first time, Trixie seemed shaken. "I'll just do that," she declared with an attempt at dignity. "Jill! She's a mere child! What does she know about getting married?" Trixie stamped off across the street.

"Not as much as you do," Renie called after her.

"Coz." Judith's tone was mildly reproachful. "If I didn't know better, I'd think you enjoyed trading barbs with this bunch."

"I do," Renie answered promptly. "The only problem is that in a duel of wits, they're all unarmed."

Judith gave a faint shake of her head. "Now, we'd better not ask Aunt Toadie about the jumper cables. I'll have to call the AAA. I wonder if Trixie found a phone. I forgot to ask her."

The cousins resorted to the same method that Trixie had used, walking down the street until they found someone at home. No one responded until they got to the end of the block. The square-jawed, middle-aged woman who came to the door of the Roman brick rambler acted suspicious.

"How many of you are going to bother us?" she demanded. "Isn't it enough that there's a crime spree

222

going on around here? On The Bluff!" She tossed her head, almost but not quite loosening the tightly wound chignon at her neck.

After a brief lecture on why modern society was going to hell in a handbasket, the woman offered to call the AAA for Judith. Obviously, she was not going to permit strangers into her impeccably maintained home.

The cousins waited on the porch, which was decorated with planters containing fading winter cabbages. Renie paced, from the covered lawn swing to the red, white, and blue mailbox; Judith silently tried to identify the shrubs that lined the graceful walk.

It was more than ten minutes before the woman reappeared. "That was very tiresome," she complained. "I was on hold forever. The AAA tow truck will be here in about two hours. They're all backed up because of the weather. And accidents, of course." She slammed the door in the cousins' faces.

"I guess I won't ask her if she has jumper cables," Judith muttered as they returned to the street level. "Two hours! Damn! What do we do now?"

"The neighbors aren't exactly what I'd call warm," Renie noted. "That's the trouble with rich people—they're always afraid you're after their money."

Judith uttered a short, dry laugh. "Sometimes they're right. Look at Trixie, getting Uncle Boo swizzled and then having him sign those loans."

"How did she get him to make the payments?" Renie mused. "Even Trixie wouldn't go through all that every time she had to send a check."

They had reached Judith's car. "Automatic deductions, I'll bet. Trixie probably had Boo's bank account number, gave it to whoever she was borrowing money from, and then the payments would come out as

223

regular as rain. Boo would have to sign only once."

"She's not smart, but she sure is cunning," Renie allowed. She paused with her hand on the car door. "Well? Do we sit here and wait for the AAA?"

Judith's shoulders slumped as her gaze traveled across the street to the house. "Not for two hours. Still, I hate to go back in. Trixie and Jill must be going at it by now."

But they weren't. At least not anymore. Toadie came flying out from around the side of the house, with Trixie bringing up the rear. A second later, Jill appeared, waving a fireplace poker.

"And never come back!" she yelled as Toadie and Trixie scrambled to get into the Buick.

The cousins waited for mother and daughter to depart. Ironically, Toadie's car didn't start on the first two tries, either. But the third time, just as Jill began to lunge with the poker, the engine turned over. Toadie and Trixie fled the scene of the crime. Literally.

Judith set her jaw. "We might as well go back inside. I could use a drink, I guess."

"I could use a ham sandwich," Renie said. "Creamed chicken is never very filling."

"You ate all the ham," Judith reminded her cousin.

Renie looked mildly surprised. "I did? Well, I'll have to finish the Havarti, then."

Jill was still standing on the lawn outside the den. Her satisfied expression changed to curiosity as she saw the cousins return to the house.

Judith explained about the dead battery and the delayed arrival of the tow truck. Jill's reaction was resigned, but not entirely cold.

"You can keep me company until that cabulance hauls Mason off," she said, leading the way back around the house to the front entrance. She paused at the end of the house with its plastic-draped scaffolding. "I wonder if there are jumper cables in the garage. Do you know how to use them?"

Judith did, having had the opportunity to learn when her old Mercury went through its last winter and died shortly before Dan did. Her most memorable disaster had occurred after the 2 A.M. closing at the Meat & Mingle. She had shut the bar down, taken the money from the till to put in the bank's overnight drop, and discovered that the car wouldn't start. The Thurlow neighborhood was tough, rough and ready for any innocent person who wasn't as armed and dangerous as most of its inhabitants. Judith couldn't afford the AAA membership in those days. She had considered spending the night in the car but had known she'd be afraid to sleep for fear someone would come along and rob her. Or worse. At last a gang of teenagers had pulled in behind the restaurant, stereo blaring, speakers pounding, bass throbbing. Judith had hidden under the dashboard. But one of the youths had sauntered over to the Mercury. He'd seen her and called her by name. She had recognized him from her day job at the branch library. In gratitude for her help with a history paper the previous semester, he had shown her how to use jumper cables. It was only after he had got the car started for her that she learned he'd flunked the paper and dropped out of school.

But a search of the Major Manor garage revealed no jumper cables. Judith figured that if they existed, they were probably in the Cadillac Mrs. Wakefield had driven downtown. The three women returned to the house through the door off the entry hall. Judith and Renie were taking off their jackets when the cabulance

225

arrived.

"Thank God." Jill sighed. "I'm sick of listening to that guy moan and groan."

"Where are they taking him?" Judith inquired.

Jill gave a little snort of contempt. "Who cares? Actually, he's going to stay with Trixie, who, I gather, lives with Toadie. Or has since her last divorce." She opened the double doors for the cabulance attendants. "Come and get him," she urged, stepping aside for the stretcher and its bearers.

Moments later, Mason Meade was being rolled out of the house, down the walk, and to the waiting vehicle. His pleas for caution fell on deaf ears. Wheels squeaking, the litter bumped, thumped, and almost dumped him onto the ground. Jill went as far as the brick steps which led to the sidewalk, apparently to make sure the patient was really gone. Keeping their jackets on, the cousins followed her.

"Whew!" Jill exclaimed as the cabulance drove away. "Now I can have a little peace!" She turned, gazing up at the front of the house. The fitful sun was now out, casting its pale rays on the brick facade. Above the dining area, the half-timbered overhang was the color of rich cream. The windows with their small panes of leaded glass winked in the afternoon's western light. "It's so beautiful," she murmured. "I suppose I should be grateful to Aunt Toadie for having the masonry work done. The house was beginning to show serious neglect."

Judith regarded Jill carefully. In some ways, she seemed older than her twenty years, and it dawned on Judith that she had been genuinely affected by Boo's death.

"You must have cared for Boo quite deeply," Judith

said in what she hoped was a concerned tone.

With her foot, Jill nudged at an errant pebble in the border next to the walk. "I did. I loved him. Oh, not madly, but as a friend. My father . . ." She frowned. "I never knew my *real* father. He was killed in 'Nam soon after I was born. Derek adopted me, but he's an aloof sort of man. He played the role of father fairly well, but I always sensed something was missing. Maybe that's what I was looking for in Boo."

Jill's reaction was understandable. Though Boo had never had children of his own, his easygoing manner would strike a responsive chord in a child. Boo Major had been like a father to Derek; it seemed he had held a special place in Jill's heart as well.

"Boo was lonely after Aunt Rosie died," Jill went on, leading the way back to the house. "He told me that he thought my grandmother wanted to marry him. At first, it sounded like a good idea. But Grandmother is such a ditz—she'd have driven him crazy. I told Boo that if he wanted to marry a Rush, why not me? I thought I was kidding." She opened the double inner doors for the cousins and gave them a rueful smile. "He took me seriously. And it dawned on me that it could work. I'm not ambitious. I dropped out of college after two years. I couldn't decide on a major. The only thing I really like to do is play the piano, but I'm not good enough to perform. So I asked myself, why not make Boo happy and be his companion? I'd have some purpose."

"But you hadn't told your parents," Judith remarked as Jill took them into the breakfast room.

Sitting down at the round table with its gay flowered cloth, Jill nodded. "We were going to surprise everybody just before they left last night. I think Boo went off to the den to steel his nerve. He hated scenes;

he hated being involved in any kind of controversy. And you know how they'd react. You saw how they *did* react when I told them this afternoon, even with Boo dead."

Someone, presumably Mrs. Wakefield, had left a plate of oatmeal cookies on the table. Renie took two. "Why didn't you tell them sooner? After Boo was killed, I mean?"

Jill rolled her eyes toward the ceiling. "And make myself the prime suspect? Can't you see the headlines? 'Young Bride Shoots Elderly Groom—Estate Valued in Billions.'"

Judith gave a start. "Billions? Really?"

Jill's response was nonchalant. "I suppose. Major Mush is a huge international conglomerate now. They make more than cereal. Pet food, breakfast meats, baked goods—I don't know what all. They went public shortly after Dunlop Major died, but Boo retained the majority share, which must be enormous in terms of actual money. And Dunlop wasn't only a shrewd businessman, but a sharp investor. We're talking about a man who weathered the Depression and prospered by it. If nothing else, people could afford Major Mush."

Recalling the determined cast to Dunlop Major's face in the family photographs, Judith had to agree with Jill's assessment. "Do the police know?" she asked as Renie gobbled up another cookie.

Jill toyed with a stray tendril of hair. "Not yet, but they will. That's another thing. I'd like to see a lawyer before I find myself in too deep."

It occurred to Judith that Jill was already in up to her neck, and possibly in over her head. Tactfully avoiding the issue, she asked a more innocuous question instead: "Will you live here?"

"I'd like to," Jill said, but her forehead creased. "It's

228

not practical for one person, though. I know Uncle Boo was all by himself, but that was different. He had the Wakefields. If Weed killed Boo, I couldn't possibly let the family stay on. And I'm not sure I'd want live-in servants. There's no privacy."

Renie had slipped off to the kitchen. "Milk, anybody?" she called.

Judith and Jill declined. "There's still quite a bit of work to be done on the house," Judith noted. "You'll have to hire some more masons, and it looks as if you could use a new roof."

Jill nodded. "The brickwork can be finished right away. I'll wait until the weather gets better before I have the roof done. In fact, that silly Toadie should have held off on the masonry until summer. It's so cold in here."

Judith was about to concur when something peculiar dawned on her. It was a stray comment, seemingly without relevance. And yet, with Jill's remark about the chill feeling inside Major Manor, Judith's brain began to follow its customary pattern of logic.

But before she could pose a question to Jill, the front doorbell chimed. Jill went off to answer it just as Renie returned with a tall glass of milk. Judith hurried over to the window. She saw a KINE-TV van pulled up at the curb.

"Drat! The media have landed," she said to Renie.

Renie shrugged. "They were bound to, eventually. I suppose they couldn't get up the hill until now. You want to be on television?"

"I sure don't," Judith replied. "I'd have to identify myself, and then Buck Doerflinger would know who I am. Let's go upstairs. Or better yet, out the back and hide in the garden."

Renie bolted her milk, grabbed three more cookies, and followed Judith out through the kitchen. Shrugging back into their jackets, the cousins headed for the lily pond. They descended the steps furtively, looking over their shoulders to make sure that the TV reporters on the front porch couldn't see them. A glimpse told them that Jill must be fending them off: The quartet of three men and one woman hadn't yet penetrated Major Manor.

"She can't stop them from filming the house," Renie noted. "They can go around in back and get an exterior of the den. That ought to satisfy them."

The cousins were now out of sight, in the sunken garden next to the pond. Judith shielded her eyes from the afternoon sun, which had grown uncommonly bright for February. She started to sit down on one of the stone benches, but the ripples on the thawed pond caught her eye.

So did the body which had floated to the surface. Judith stifled a scream. Renie choked on her last cookie.

FIFTEEN

WITH A SHAKING HAND, JUDITH HIT RENIE ON THE back. The cousins' eyes were riveted on the corpse. It was a man of medium build, perhaps middle-aged, facedown among the lily pads. He was wearing dark slacks and a deep green ski parka. Renie sputtered and turned away. Judith gritted her teeth and edged closer. The body bobbed peacefully as the winter wind ruffled the waters of the pond.

"What do we do?" Renie asked falteringly.

Judith craned her neck, trying to see over the terraced bank that led up from the sunken garden. Despite her height, she couldn't manage it. "We wait. The last thing I want to do is alert the media and get myself plastered all over KINE-TV. Or KWIP, or any of the nightly newscasts."

"Great," Renie said, her tone morbid. "We get to sit down here in this hole with a stiff. Is there another way out?" Trying to avoid looking at the dead body, Renie scanned the terraces that surrounded the pond. "We might climb up the other side and escape through the rose garden."

Dubiously, Judith regarded the landscaping. The spaces between the terraced plots were fairly steep.

"We'd still have to hide out until the TV people leave," she said.

"We'd have better company," Renie pointed out. But she didn't press her cousin. It wouldn't do to sprain an ankle or break a leg trying to climb out of the sunken garden.

Judith went over to stand on the bottom flagstone

step. She saw no sign of Jill, but after cautiously ascending to the second step, she could observe the TV crew opening the van and removing their equipment.

"They're going to film something," she told Renie. "Let's make for the gazebo while they're busy with the cameras and stuff."

Renie was only too glad to follow orders. Once away from the sunken garden and the lily pond with its gruesome burden, the cousins dashed from shrub to shrub to ensure not being spotted. Moments later, they were in the gazebo, brushing away cobwebs, dried leaves, and dust.

The hexagonal structure gave them the opportunity to see out while staying hidden. They had just settled in when the KINE crew hauled their equipment onto the front lawn. Judith figured they had Jill's permission to go that far and no farther.

"They shouldn't take too long," she said. "We don't want to call the police until after they leave."

"And how do we do that?" Renie asked wryly.

Judith's face fell. "Damn! I forgot. Maybe we can go back to the neighbor up on the corner." She sounded dubious.

Renie was peering through an opening in the latticework. "The woman must be the reporter. They're hooking her up with a mike."

Judith glanced outside, but since she'd overcome the initial shock of finding yet another body, her mind was racing ahead. "Who can it be? There's nobody from the household or family unaccounted for."

It was clear from Renie's blank expression that she hadn't given the man's identity much thought. "The jewel thief?" she said off the top of her head. "Making his getaway and slipping on the ice? Maybe he drowned."

Judith was silent for a moment. "I've heard worse theories—like Buck and the big box." She snuggled into her jacket and gave Renie a half smile. "This is nice. Peaceful, I mean."

Renie looked aghast. "Coz, you *are* nuts. There's a corpse floating around with the lily pads, a murderer may or may not be on the loose, somebody's made off with a fortune in jewels, your husband let you down, and your mother's acting like . . . your mother."

Taken aback, Judith stared at Renie, then lowered her eyes, along with her voice. "You know me—I always try to look on the bright side. I've had to. For years there was so little of it."

Renie's expression softened. She knew that the only thing that had seen Judith through the dark decades of her marriage to Dan had been her buoyancy. And her courage and her patience and her inner strength, which were all the same when it came right down to it. As ever, Renie could overlook almost any of Judith's flaws.

"So what's your idea?" Renie inquired as the TV crew marched around the south side of Major Manor, presumably to get the den on film.

Judith looked a bit startled at Renie's change of subject. "About the body? I don't know. I can't imagine who it could be. As a wild guess, I'd say it was one of the masons. Maybe Toadie fired them because they drank. Nothing people do is ever too outlandish. That's where logic sometimes fails me. Often, people don't act at all logically. Let's say this guy got drunk, got fired, went down to the pond to sulk, passed out, and fell in. It's no weirder than your jewel-thief scenario."

"True," Renie agreed. She jumped as a spider crawled out of a crack and headed for her wrinkled pants. "But

233

he isn't dressed like a workman. It looked as if he was wearing slacks. And that parka is too snazzy to wear for laying bricks."

There was no argument from Judith, only a craning of her neck as she tried to see where the TV crew was now. The garage jutted out from the house, blocking the view of the den and the surrounding lawn.

"Weed Wakefield said something interesting—a couple of things, actually," Judith told Renie. "He asked me when a shot didn't sound like a shot. Now, it's possible that the pressure-cooker explosion, which was very loud, might have masked the noise of the gun, but I doubt it. The coincidence would be too great."

"Unless it was planned." Renie arched her eyebrows.

Judith reflected briefly. "That would mean collusion, probably on the part of the Wakefields. And that's impossible, because Mrs. Wakefield and Zoe were both helping us serve at the time."

Renie cocked her head inside the hood of her jacket. "Okay, scratch the pressure cooker. So what about the other noises?"

"Two fairly loud thuds—for want of a better word, but not exactly the same. And, as Weed asked, when doesn't a shot sound like a shot? When a silencer is used, that's when." Judith gave Renie a self-satisfied look.

"So where's the silencer? It wasn't attached to the gun you found in the garbage can."

Judith deflated. "I know. But it could have been removed. You're right, though—it has to be somewhere, which leads me to the other remark Weed made."

"Which was?" coaxed Renie.

But Judith put a finger to her lips. The crew from KINE was coming around the north end of the house.

234

They stopped by the back porch, a mere ten yards away. One of the men went over to the terminal box and bent down to examine it. The cousins sat motionless while the camera recorded the cable cutting. They could hear the clear, professional voice of the female reporter speaking to her would-be viewers:

". . . and to add to the mystery of Major Manor, someone severed the outside telephone wires, thus cutting the inhabitants of the house off from the rest of the world. This is Sheila Resnik, reporting from the murder site on The Bluff, a neighborhood where violence is not only a stranger, but in very poor taste."

Judith winced. She winced twice more, since Sheila apparently wasn't satisfied with her first two versions. At last the television crew headed back to the van. The cousins waited until the vehicle was out of sight.

"As you were saying," Renie urged as they went back to the house. "Weed?"

"One thing at a time," Judith replied. "I'm still wondering about that other sound. What was it? More to the point, *why* was it?"

Jill was in the kitchen, pouring herself a glass of wine. "Thank God they're gone. What pests! I could only get rid of them by promising not to call the police and have them thrown off the lawn, and then I let it slip that I *couldn't* call because the phone wires were cut! I'm not very good at handling crises, I guess."

"This isn't your usual crisis," Judith said in consolation. "By the way, what's going on with the phones?"

Jill took a sip of her wine, then offered some to the cousins, who declined. "My parents were going to report the problem to the phone company when they got home. I bet nobody will come until Monday, though."

Judith waited for Jill to take another drink. "Uh . . . there's something you should know, Jill. I hate to mention it, but . . . ah . . . there's somebody out in the lily pond."

Jill's reaction was one of annoyance. "Kids? They should be in school. Oh, no—it's Saturday . . ."

"Not kids," Judith said gently. "A man. A dead man. We've got to call the police. Again."

Jill went pale. The wineglass trembled in her hand. "Oh, no! I can't believe it! This house is cursed!"

Alarmed by her reaction, Judith led the younger woman into the breakfast nook and sat her down at the table. "It might have been an accident," Judith said quietly. She described the man as best she could. "We can't tell what happened to him just from looking. Do you have any idea who he might be?"

Except for the possibility of the masons, Jill didn't. Her color began to return, though she drank her wine with haste. "Somebody walking in the fog last night . . . Maybe he wandered onto the grounds and fell in the pond . . . ?" She gave Judith a hopeful look.

"It's possible." Judith tried to sound encouraging. "The main thing is that we have to call the police." She explained about the chilly reception from the neighbor on the corner. "I hate to bother her again, but we didn't find anyone else at home. Of course, we could try the street across from the front of the house."

Jill, however, was eager to volunteer. "I belong here now, so the neighbors better not treat me like an intruder. I'll tell this stuck-up shrew that I'm Mrs. Major. She'd better kneel and kiss my feet."

The cousins wished Jill luck. After she had left, Judith checked her watch. It was a few minutes after three. "An hour or so until the tow truck gets here," she murmured. "Say, won't Bill be wondering what's

236

happened to you?"

Renie gave Judith a wide-eyed stare. "Bill? My husband, Bill, on a Saturday in February? Even now, he's watching the final one hundred and twenty-eight college basketball teams dribble their way to the Final Four. The kids all had plans, so he's home alone, and loving it. You know Bill, the Neville Chamberlain of family life—peace at any price."

Judith acknowledged Renie's wifely appraisal. Joe was probably still at work. Her six guests could be checking in at any time, though officially they shouldn't show up until after four o'clock. "I wonder if Mother will think to be in the house so that she can let the new guests in. I should have gone with Jill and asked to use the phone, too."

"What makes you think your mother will open the door?" Renie asked, her eyes dancing.

Judith made a face. "What makes me think she'll answer the phone? She doesn't always. Honestly, the one time I get in a bind, my nearest and dearest treat me as if I were a big germ." She glanced at her watch again, seeking reassurance that the minute hand hadn't spun ahead and eaten away her hour of grace. "I can wait, I suppose, and see if the tow truck gets here a few minutes early." Without another word, she headed for the entry hall. Renie tagged along.

"The noises," Judith said doggedly as they went into the den. "Think about them. Skip the pressure cooker, and concentrate on the other two. When did we hear them? Who was where?"

Renie sat down in one of the two side chairs. Judith seated herself behind the desk. "We were getting ready to leave," Renie recalled in a measured voice. "I'd estimate it was around nine-twenty or a couple of

237

minutes earlier. Zoe was helping us, Mrs. Wakefield was with Weed, Aunt Toadie came from the living room to ask about the noise—"

"No," Judith broke in, emphatically shaking her head. "Toadie came out after the pressure cooker blew up. She didn't return again. How long before we heard the second of the two unaccounted-for sounds?" Judith was relying on Renie's keen sense of time.

"Five minutes? No more. Mrs. Wakefield and Zoe helped us cart the stuff out to the car, remember? Then I realized I had forgotten my purse." Renie looked chagrined. "If only I hadn't—"

"Never mind," Judith interrupted briskly. "We might have skidded down the hill and killed ourselves. Jill said it was nine-thirty-seven when the rest of them decided to go. We came back in the house just as they were trying to say good-bye to Uncle Boo." She paused, opening a desk drawer and taking out a ruled tablet and a ballpoint pen. She made out a time schedule, based on Renie's and Jill's estimations.

> 9:01—Boo goes into den
> 9:06—Guests move to living room
> 9:08—Beets blow up
> 9:20—First unidentified noise
> 9:25—Second unidentified noise
> 9:35—Cousins leave
> 9:37—Guests start leaving
> 9:39—Cousins return

"One of those two sounds must have been the shot with a silencer affixed to the gun," Judith declared. "Why two? What was the other one and which was which?" She tore off the paper on which she'd been writing and passed it to Renie.

"What," Renie mused, staring at the sequence of events, "if the man in the pond was also shot? I know the sounds weren't exactly alike, but if they were fired in two different places, couldn't that account for the discrepancy?"

"Maybe." Judith chewed on her lower lip. "But why? Neighbor strolling through sleet storm just happens to see murder most foul and killer runs out and shoots him on the spot, then throws his body in the lily pond? It's possible, I suppose, but . . . Ah!"

Renie saw Judith's face light up. "What?"

Excited, Judith jumped around in Uncle Boo's swivel chair. "I just had an idea which we will check out shortly. But first, let's take another look at these times. When were Jill and Mason out in the entry hall?"

Renie wasn't sure. Neither was Judith, but after some intensive concentration, they agreed that Mrs. Wakefield had spotted the pair before the pressure-cooker explosion.

"Which," Judith noted, "would have been between nine-oh-one and nine-oh-eight. But we don't know when either of them came back to the living room. And we don't know exactly when Holly and Vivvie made their separate trips to the bathroom."

"If Derek went out to the garage to smoke, why didn't he see Mason coming or going?" Renie queried. "Had Mason already returned to the living room? He would have had to come in that way or go through the kitchen if he really went outside to the car."

Judith nodded. "Unless Mason went somewhere else. Or Derek did. And Toadie—she checked on Uncle Boo but says she didn't go in the den." She tapped the timetable. "My, but there was a lot of activity in and out of the entry hall during this thirty-six-minute period."

Renie looked rueful. "There sure was. Along with the Wakefields, we were about the only ones who weren't there."

"Zoe could have been there," Judith pointed out, "while she was cleaning up in the dining room. Her mother, too."

Renie quibbled. "I doubt it. Both of them were back and forth at a pretty good clip. Then the pressure cooker blew and Mrs. Wakefield went downstairs to tend to Weed."

"True." Judith had to concede the point. For a long moment the cousins were silent. Renie appeared to be admiring the rich mahogany paneling. Judith was studying the room itself, as if it might reveal something she'd overlooked. "What's missing?" she asked at last, her gaze fixed on the desk.

"You mean besides Boo?" Renie considered. "The brandy snifter. Mrs. Wakefield took it away. The key. Ditto. Or was it the police?"

Judith tipped her head to one side. "And?"

Renie frowned. "The blotter's still there; so's the ashtray. I don't remember anything else."

Judith leaned forward and grinned at Renie. "The cigar. Where is Boo's cigar?"

Renie scoffed at the question. "Boo dropped it, I suppose. It probably fell on the floor and the police picked it up."

But Judith had pushed the chair back from the desk and was leaning down to examine the intricate parquetry. "Then why isn't there a burn mark? The cigar would have smoldered for some time before the police arrived. There's no sign of it."

"So? Maybe it fell in Boo's lap and the medics

carried it off with him. Maybe he'd finished it. Maybe you're wacky."

But Judith was still looking pleased with herself. "None of the above, coz—I'm willing to bet on it. Boo had come in here to smoke his cigar, which means he didn't light up until after nine-oh-one. How long does it take to smoke one of those big long things? Forever, it seems to me, and I ought to know, because Joe likes to make Hillside Manor smell like a saloon every weekend. Remember all those ashes? They were on the floor, on the desk, even in Uncle Boo's brandy snifter. Why?" She sat back in the chair and gave Renie a knowing look. "Because the cigar blew up, that's why. And now we know what made the other noise."

Still smarting from Judith's theory about the exploding cigar, Renie impatiently jiggled her foot as she waited for the outcome of her cousin's latest experiment. Judith was miming a fall forward on the desk. First she fell headlong, facedown on the blotter. Then she turned slightly in the chair and landed on her cheek.

"What do you think?" she asked Renie.

"I think," Renie said, glancing at her watch, "it's almost three-thirty. Oatmeal cookies don't fill me up and I'm starved."

"Nothing fills you up," Judith replied, her enthusiasm dampened by Renie's skepticism. "This is important. If I were shot in the back of the head, I'd collapse face-forward. But if I turned, I'd land on the side of my head, like Uncle Boo did. Now why would I move in the chair?"

"Gosh, I don't know," Renie responded in mock stupidity. "As far as I could tell, Uncle Boo didn't move, ever. Maybe somebody put a bomb under him.

Or an exploding cigar."

"Coz, you're being a dork," Judith said, her exasperation mounting. "First my husband, then my mother, now you. Stop bugging me. I'm trying to be logical about this, and I think I've finally hit on the answer."

Heedless of the desk's well-kept finish, Renie put her feet up. "Fine, okay, let's have it." Her round face was resigned.

Judith pretended Renie wasn't being a pill. "Something made Boo turn his head. Otherwise he wouldn't have fallen on the desk the way he did. That's bothered me all along. I kept picturing him as we found him, then I listened to how Buck Doerflinger described the alleged shooting by Weed Wakefield, and it didn't quite jell. The angle was all wrong. Why would Weed come around to the side of the desk and shoot Boo? Why not straight on, standing across from the desk? And even if Weed did do what Buck said, Boo would have turned to look at a man with a gun in his hand."

Judith stopped and swiveled around in the chair. "We got misled by that Will Rogers book. Yes, it contained one of the wills, but that wasn't why it was on the floor." She paused to remove the volume from the middle shelf. "It fell on the floor because it was pushed there by the killer."

Renie was still wearing a leery expression. "Pushed, or tossed?"

"Pushed." Judith was very firm. Renie's face showed a trifle more interest, especially when Judith got out of the chair and began to pull out more books. Seconds later, she uttered a cry of glee: "I thought so! There's a hole in the back of the bookcase!"

At last Renie succumbed to her cousin's excitement.

Swinging her legs onto the floor, she jumped out of the chair and raced around the desk to join Judith. "You mean . . ." Shoulder to shoulder, the cousins peered into the four-inch hole. Judith reached through the wall, touching brick a foot or more away.

"You see?" she breathed, her black eyes sparkling with the thrill of logical deduction. "There's no inner wall. It's been removed for the masonry work. I realized that after the fact. Weed had complained about rewiring the downstairs stove. He said it was hard to do because of the insulation in the wall between the galley and the saloon. I forget exactly how he put it, but the implication dawned on me later. The inner wall was a problem compared to—what? The outer wall, of course."

Having bought into Judith's mental machinations, Renie tried to make sense out of them. "The walls between the exterior brick and the actual rooms had to be pulled for the masonry work, right?" She saw Judith give an eager nod. "The insulation goes, too, which explains why this house is so blasted cold."

"Right," Judith replied. "I finally stumbled onto that when Jill mentioned the present brickwork and the future roof repair. She said she'd wait on the roof—the house was cold enough already because the insulation had been removed for the masonry work on the outer walls." Judith's excitement was mounting. "If we go outside, we'll find that there are a few bricks which can be removed, too. That's how Uncle Boo was killed in a locked room. He was shot from outside, not inside. Oh, coz, isn't that better than a box?"

"Not for Uncle Boo," Renie replied dryly. But she clapped Judith on the arm. "Forgive me. I've been a fool." Her face was wreathed in mock chagrin.

"Come on," said Judith, still exhilarated by her discovery. "Let's go check those bricks."

But in the hallway, they were both suddenly aware of how empty the house felt. "Where's Jill?" asked Judith. "She's been gone a long time. She should be back by now."

They called for Jill all over the main floor; they ran upstairs and looked for her there; they went to the servants' quarters, but found the basement deserted. Judith and Renie both felt uneasy. Too much had happened at Major Manor to take Jill's tardy return lightly.

"Maybe," Renie suggested, "that old crone up the street refused to let her use the phone. She might have gone searching for another neighbor."

Judith had already checked her watch. It was almost a quarter to four. Jill had been gone for at least forty minutes. Nor was there any sign of the police.

"Let's go look for her," Judith urged. "We'd better get the keys. I don't want to leave this place unlocked."

Taking the ring from the peg in the kitchen, the cousins hurried out the back door. They practically ran across the street and up the block to the brick rambler. The severe-faced woman who answered the door looked as if the cousins had brought plague to her threshold.

"I've lived here for thirty-two years," she declared. "I've never had a bit of trouble until today. If I have one more of you troublesome people ring my bell, I'm getting a restraining order. It's harassment, and that's not allowed on The Bluff."

Judith had intended to try tact, but Renie didn't give her the opportunity. "Look, kiddo," she said, putting a foot in the door, "we're dealing with life and death here, and we've already had two of the latter and not much fun out of the former. Have you seen Mrs. Major in the last half hour?"

Briefly, the woman looked startled, then resumed her formidable air. "She called herself that, but I knew Mrs. Major and she's been dead for three years. I don't know who that young trollop is, but I did the right thing and called the police for her, and then I summoned a taxi, too. She's been gone for at least a quarter of an hour. I say good riddance, and the same to you!" Giving Renie a firm shove, she slammed the door.

Staggering against Judith, Renie swore. "Butt-face! She could have broken my toe!"

"Well, she didn't," Judith replied absently. "Damn! Now Jill's run out on us! Not that I blame her—she's still a kid in a lot of ways."

"She's a kid with a billion bucks," Renie muttered, examining her shoes. "She can afford taxis and changes of clothes and medical care. I've got a dent in my Dexters."

Judith glanced at Renie's feet. "They look okay to me. Come on, let's go."

"Right," said Renie. "The tow truck should be along in a few minutes."

"We'll just have time to check that outer wall," Judith noted as they started back down the street. "Am I dreaming, or do we have a reason for the masons getting fired?"

Renie almost stumbled in her reaction to Judith's query. "You mean . . . Toadie? That's too good to be true. Besides, didn't we figure she was trying to finagle a contract for Trixie's fiancé?"

"Toadie denies it. But since when did she always tell the truth?" Judith arched her eyebrows.

Renie's smile was almost blissful. "That would be

perfect. Aunt Toadie in the dock. Aunt Toadie in chains. Aunt Toadie doing life while breaking up large concrete boulders." Renie's smile evaporated. "Poor Uncle Corky! Poor family! Poor *us!* I keep forgetting we're related."

Judith didn't seem perturbed. "Uncle Corky might like it. He'd only have to see her on visiting days. It'd be cheaper than having to go off on safari or sign up for Arctic explorations or fly to the moon. Too bad we can't figure out a way to nail Trixie, too. If she's not in prison, she might still show up for Christmas Eve."

They had reached Judith's car. Across the street, Major Manor looked lonely in the late afternoon sun. Above the crenellations of the triple garage, the leaded-glass bedroom windows on the second story wore a forsaken air.

"If Jill remarried and had a family," Judith remarked, "this place could—"

The sound of a siren interrupted her speculations. The cousins hurried across the street to the front of the house. A patrol car was pulling up. Judith and Renie waited until the officer emerged.

Githa Lagerquist was very large, very tall, and very blond. She swaggered up the brick stairs, eyeing the cousins with suspicion.

"Which one of you is Mrs. Major?" she demanded in a husky voice.

"Neither," answered Judith in a strange squeak. "Mrs. Major left."

Officer Lagerquist first scrutinized Judith and Renie, then surveyed the house. "Where's the body?" she demanded.

Wordlessly, the cousins led her to the lily pond. The corpse still bobbed among the greenery. The policewoman stood at the edge of the pond for a full minute, studying the scene.

"You know him?" she asked.

Judith and Renie said they didn't. Lagerquist nodded abruptly, then marched up the flagstone steps. At the top, she whirled on the cousins. "I think I do. You two go in the house. This is a job for Homicide. I'm calling Detective Joe Flynn."

SIXTEEN

THE COUSINS FOUND THE LIQUOR. JUDITH POURED herself a scotch and handed a Canadian whiskey to Renie. By the time Githa Lagerquist returned from her patrol car, they were seated in the living room, looking decorous and feeling awful.

"I should explain—" Judith began, but Lagerquist cut her short.

"Later. I'll wait outside for Flynn and the ambulance. I just wanted to make sure you two weren't going anywhere."

"But—" Judith started anew.

"Later, I said." Lagerquist gazed around the long living room. "Nice place. Rich people. Trouble. Flynn'll like this. He knows how to handle your kind." The policewoman swaggered from the living room and, presumably, out of the house.

Judith leaned back against the sofa pillows. "Drat! I'm about to be interrogated by my own husband! What next, they hire Bill as their consulting psychologist to see if we're crazy?"

Renie brightened. "Not a bad idea. He could use the retainer fee. When all this is over, we'll talk."

Judith checked the time. "It is over. It's five after four, and my guests will be arriving at any minute—if they aren't there already. Mother won't let them in, but if she does, she'll frisk them for drugs and weapons. She'll serve them green baloney for hors d'oeuvres and Milk of Magnesia cocktails. Sweetums will puke on their luggage. I'll lose my rating in the guidebooks. Hillside Manor will be closed by the Health Department

248

or the bed-and-breakfast state association or the CIA, whichever catches on to me first. I'll end up selling the furniture in a garage sale where people come and haggle over whether or not they want to pay four dollars for Grandma Grover's handmade comforters. And Aunt Toadie will show up and say that Grandma used the pink elephant motif on the kids' quilts because she was a dipso and that's all she ever saw—"

"Stop!" yelled Renie. "When Joe gets here, have him call back to headquarters to alert the Porters or the Steins or the Ericsons. They can get the key from your mother and let the guests in. Heck, Corinne Dooley might be back from the ski trip by now. Stop *fussing*."

But Judith couldn't help it. Her earlier triumph of figuring out how the murder had been committed was obliterated by her concern for Hillside Manor. Unlike her husband, Judith wasn't a detective. She was in the hostelry business, and her dereliction from duty plagued her.

To divert Judith, Renie asked a simple question: "How come Joe's been called in?"

Judith, who had been taking a long pull on her scotch, eyed Renie quizzically. "How come? Well, he works Homicide."

"But we don't know this *is* a homicide," Renie answered in a reasonable tone. "Haven't we—Jill included—tossed around the idea of an accident connected with the lousy weather?"

Judith set her glass down on the uncluttered ebony coffee table. Unlike the cherry-wood model which sat between the matching sofas in the living room of Hillside Manor, it held no stacks of magazines, newspapers, travel brochures, ashtrays, or candy dishes. The sole adornment was a polar bear carved from cream-colored ivory. Judith figured it had come from Alaska, courtesy of Dunlop Major.

"You're right," she said in wonder. "Why Joe? Why Homicide? Hmmmm."

Renie affected an innocent air. "Joe's on a special assignment, right? Why haul him over here? I mean, doesn't it seem sort of strange?"

Judith's mouth widened into a smile of sorts. "Oh, coz, I think you're onto something! Now I'm the one who's being dense!" She leaped up from the sofa and began to pace. "That car! The one we saw being towed away earlier this afternoon—it belonged to the city! And the Mayor's missing cousin was a building inspector! It all makes perfect sense!" She stopped smiling and turned grim. "Ugh, that means that the guy in the pond is . . . well, maybe not."

"Does it mean you know who did it?" asked Renie hopefully.

Judith flopped back down on the sofa. "I never claimed I did. At the time, it seemed enough to know how it was done. I still haven't any idea who . . ." Her voice trailed off as Githa Lagerquist came into the living room with Joe Flynn and a half-dozen other people.

"We've got to stop meeting like this," said Joe, coming over to the sofa and giving Judith a perfunctory kiss on the cheek. No gold flecks danced in his green eyes.

"Mush," said Judith, ignoring the warning signs in Joe's manner. "Mother served them mush and it's all your fault."

"What's wrong with mush?" he asked, stung by her reception.

"What next, milk toast?" She sounded testy.

"Mother's idea of hors d'oeuvres is a bowl of gummy bears. As for you, lending a hand is a big burden."

"So I tell the Mayor I can't come to work because my little pigs aren't sizzling yet?" He was keeping a tight rein on his temper, but the effort was causing him to hiss. "You married a barkeep the first time. Why didn't you try for a chef on this go-around? Better yet, a bellboy who could run around Hillside Manor in one of those little caps and funny suits with all the brass buttons!"

Judith crossed her arms over her chest and stuck out her chin. "Sounds good. I could put one of those suits on Sweetums. He'd be about as much help as you and Mother."

Githa Lagerquist was aghast, but she tried not to show it. "Sir," she said in her husky voice, "do you know the suspect?"

Joe gave Lagerquist an enigmatic smile. "Only in the biblical sense. Otherwise she's a mystery to me."

Judith bridled at the comment, then flushed. "Actually, Officer, Detective Flynn is my—"

But Githa Lagerquist raised a large, well-manicured hand. "Please. Spare me the seamy details. Sir," she went on, addressing Joe, "the body is in the lily pond. I merely wanted to make sure the suspects hadn't left the premises."

Glancing at the highball glasses, Joe chuckled, a curiously mirthless sound. "Don't worry, they won't leave until they've finished their drinks. If you feed the little one, she'll follow you anywhere." Dutifully, he let Lagerquist lead him and the others outside.

Renie sulked into her highball glass. "Joe makes me sound like a hog. I'll bet he ate more than creamed chicken for lunch."

Judith only half-heard her cousin's comment. "He's being a selfish jerk," she asserted, then tried to put aside her pique. "Do you remember how long that building inspector's been missing?"

Renie didn't. "You're the one who talked to Joe about his assignment. How would I know?"

"I thought he might have mentioned it this morning when you spoke to him on the phone." Judith frowned, trying to recall Joe's account of the Mayor's missing cousin. "I think he must have disappeared Thursday. I seem to remember Joe saying something about usually waiting forty-eight hours to start looking for a missing person, but they started the search sooner because he was related to the Mayor."

"We don't know for sure that it's the Mayor's cousin out in the pond. Aren't you getting ahead of yourself?" Renie asked.

Judith wasn't inclined to argue. "Maybe. You got any better ideas?"

Having already exhausted other possibilities, Renie didn't. The cousins sat in silence for several minutes until Judith grew impatient. She got up and went to the long window that looked out over the front lawn. From that angle she could see nothing of the sunken garden or the lily pond. Nor was there any sign of Joe, Githa Lagerquist, or the other emergency personnel.

With a determined step, Judith crossed the room to the smaller window next to the marble fireplace. The AAA tow truck hadn't arrived yet. It was almost four-twenty.

"Damn!" she cried. "Now I'm really screwed! I wish I'd never let Aunt Toadie talk me into doing this job in the first place! It's been one disaster after another!"

Renie glanced at her with mild reproof. "You haven't

gotten shot yet, which is more than I can say for some. Count your blessings."

Judith wasn't appeased. "Such as what? Going out of business? I mean it, coz, every time our side of the family has anything to do with Toadie and her crew, there's trouble. Remember when she took her bridge club to the family cabin and they set fire to the outhouse? If it hadn't been raining, the whole place would have gone up. Then there was the Labor Day picnic at Grandma and Grandpa Grover's, and Marty brought along a baby alligator that got loose and ate all the hot dogs. Auntie Vance sat on it by mistake and swore it bit her in the backside, so your father shot it with his .22."

"The alligator was better looking than most of Marty's dates," Renie noted. "Yes, yes, I know you're vexed and all that, so am I, but there's not much we can do about it. Two hours ago we could have called a cab and come back later for your car. Now we're stuck waiting for . . ."

Joe, Githa Lagerquist, and a young plainclothes policeman Judith didn't recognize returned to the living room. Joe wore a grim expression.

"It's the Mayor's cousin, all right. Poor devil," he added, smoothing his red hair and straightening his tie. "The I.D. was intact. Fortunately, most of it was encased in plastic, so it didn't get ruined in the pond."

"What happened to him?" Judith asked, not overly anxious to hear the reply.

Joe gazed longingly at Judith's almost empty scotch glass. "It appears he was shot through the chest. I'm not making any guesses about when. The pond was frozen over last night, right?"

Judith nodded, unsettled by her husband's reserved

253

manner. "Was that his car we saw being towed a couple of hours ago?"

"Right." Joe turned to Lagerquist. "Call for a couple of officers to secure this place. Althaus is staying, but I'm going downtown with the body. I'd better give the Mayor the bad news in person." He nodded at his subordinate. "Jack, you're in charge. I'll see you later." As ever, Joe's step was light; he headed for the entry hall.

"Now wait a minute," Judith called, running after him. She caught up with her husband at the stained-glass double doors. "*I'm* the one who's supposed to be mad. You put me on the spot with this overtime. Renie and I are coming with you. You can drop us off at the B&B on your way downtown."

Joe's mouth twitched, not with his usual amusement, but in exasperation. "No way am I running you and Renie over to Heraldsgate Hill. That's at least fifteen minutes out of our way. I've got the Mayor's cousin in a body bag and Buck Doerflinger as the detective of record on what is turning out to be my case. I'll have everybody—the Mayor included—on my case if I don't get my ass in gear. The least you can do is sit here like a good girl and wait for . . ." Joe paused, his annoyed expression turning quizzical. "What *are* you waiting for? I thought you'd be home a couple of hours ago, but when I called, your mother said you hadn't shown up yet."

"The Stanza won't start," Judith said, her own anger rising. "We're waiting for the AAA. Listen, Joe, you can call Hillside Manor and make sure Mother welcomes the guests. Did you say she was in the house?"

Joe made an impatient gesture with his hand. "I told

254

you, I don't have time for this crap. I'm out of here. See you." He started through the double doors, but Judith grabbed the tail of his tweed sport coat.

"Don't you dare call my work crap! I make as much money off the B&B as you do playing cop! Why the hell are you so mad anyway?"

Joe, who had been trying to tug free of Judith's grasp, suddenly pivoted on one heel. His face had turned very florid and his green eyes snapped. "You didn't tell me about Boo's murder. I had to find out when I went to work this morning. On top of it, that jackass Doerflinger got assigned to the investigation. I come in wearing my best babe-in-the-woods expression, and before I can look at the case list, half the force is giving me a hard time about the murder at Major Manor. Not," he went on, the ire rising in his voice, "because of you, since nobody—thank God—seems to know you're here, but because of Buck. Here's a corpse worth billions, a member of a family whose name is synonymous with breakfast around the globe, an investigation that will make news from downtown to Delhi, and the man of the hour is none other than my all-time favorite meathead, Buck Doerflinger! But does my dear wife tell me?" He lowered his voice and leaned down, so that his nose was almost touching Judith's forehead. "No. She keeps it all to herself. Now she can play amateur sleuth and help Buck-the-Wonder-Cop come up wearing roses on his big fat butt. As I said, see you." Joe slammed the double doors and the outer door, almost simultaneously.

Seething, Judith stomped back into the living room. Renie had just made herself another drink. "You're driving," she said lightly, then noticed Judith's angry face. "Oops. What's wrong?"

"Joe's what's wrong," Judith replied angrily. "Here I

was, trying to spare him some worry, and now *he's* mad at *me!* Men!" She stormed past a bewildered Jack Althaus and collapsed onto the sofa.

Knowing it was futile to try to placate Judith in her present mood, Renie poured her cousin a dollop of scotch. "Bill's mad, too," she said in a small voice. "I'll probably get home too late to put the beef ribs on."

"We're never getting home," Judith grumbled, accepting the drink and glaring at the unfortunate Althaus. "Well? Are you securing the crime scene or studying us for aberrations?"

Althaus cleared his throat. He was not yet thirty, with fair hair already thinning on top and pointed features that gave him a fey look. His gray eyes were sharp, however, and though his frame was spare, his hands were long and sinewy.

"I need to ask you two some questions." He remained standing at the end of the sofa. His tone was diffident, but Judith sensed authority in his manner.

"Like what? Why I married Joe Flynn?" she blurted out. "It seemed like a good idea at the time, but now I'm not so sure. I enjoyed being a widow. Maybe I'll try it again." She took a deep pull on her scotch.

Althaus appeared jarred by her comment. "I'd like to leave personalities out of this," he said, concentrating on removing a notebook from the inner pocket of his jacket. "Let's start with names."

"How about jerk, creep, and insensitive boob?" Judith shot back. "When we get through with Joe, we can move on to Bill."

"Bill?" the young detective echoed in a faint voice.

Judith sighed. "Never mind. I'm Judith McMonigle Flynn. Mrs.—excuse the expression—Joseph." She went on to give her address, phone number, and occupation as a B&B hostess and a caterer. "Or so I was, until today. Now, because of my husband and my mother, I'm going on food stamps and will have to get into a work-study program at a community college so that I can reeducate myself and—"

Renie did her best to jab Judith in the ribs without spilling her drink. She failed. Scotch splashed onto the sofa. Renie winced, then smiled at Jack Althaus.

"You'll have to forgive my cousin. She hasn't been married as long as I have. At least not to the same man." Renie frowned, aware that her explanation hadn't come out exactly right.

Eventually, Althaus extracted the information he needed, which involved the discovery of the body in the lily pond and any knowledge of the victim's presence at Major Manor.

"We didn't get here until late yesterday afternoon," Renie explained, taking over for the still-fuming Judith. "Nobody mentioned anything to us about a building inspector. You might try contacting the masons who were working on the house."

"Which firm is it?" he asked, grateful for Renie's cooperation.

She had no idea. "They were fired Friday by Mrs. Grover. Mrs. *Theodora* Grover," she added, to avoid any confusion with the rest of the family. "The housekeeper would know, too, but she's not here because her husband . . ." Renie made a vague gesture with her hands.

"Is that Wakefield?" Althaus asked.

Renie nodded. "It's probably a mistake. Weed's arrest, I mean. Since Buck Doerflinger hauled him away, we've found—"

"The liquor cabinet," Judith interrupted, suddenly

back on an even keel. Noting the plainclothesman's puzzled reaction, she gave him her most engaging smile. "We needed a stiff drink. Two bodies in two days, you know. Very stressful."

"I see," responded Althaus, though his uncertain tone indicated he didn't. Flipping through his notebook, he asked if there was anyone else in the house. The cousins said there wasn't, though the housekeeper and the maid should be returning shortly.

Satisfied, he left the living room, presumably to make a search of Major Manor and have a last look at the sunken garden.

"Well?" Renie arched her eyebrows at Judith.

"It was best to quit while we were ahead," Judith replied with a sheepish expression.

"How come? Don't you want to help Joe?" Recalling her cousin's anger with her husband, Renie bit her tongue.

But Judith didn't jump on the remark. "Of course, though he doesn't deserve it. The problem is, I forgot to give him the gun."

"Oh!" Renie slapped a hand over her mouth.

Judith nodded. "That's right, it's still in the trunk of my car. I was so mad at him that it slipped my mind."

Renie let the blunder slide. The door chimes rang, signaling the arrival of Althaus's backup. Judith and Renie saw them go through the entry hall. Althaus apparently was leading them out via the back door.

Judith sprang off the sofa. "Let's go check on that exterior wall of the den. We can watch for the tow truck from there, too."

The cousins slipped out through the garage. The sun was going down, and the air had again grown chilly. Clouds were gathering, coming in from the north.

Anxiously, Judith scanned the street in both directions. There was no sign of the AAA.

A flower bed about three feet wide separated the lawn from the house. It was empty, except for a few low-lying evergreens and an azalea. Judith stood on the grass, searching for footprints. There were plenty of them, no doubt from the workmen, and probably from the murderer as well.

"I hate to walk on the dirt, just in case the police might get a print," Judith fussed. "What do you think, coz?"

Renie stared at the ground. "It looks pretty chewed up to me. And what would it prove? Anybody could have come out here and stomped around by the den."

"Anybody could, but I don't think everybody did, except the bricklayers—and the killer. You're right, though—the impressions are too muddled." She plunged into the flower bed, then began to gauge the level of the bookcase inside.

"We should have turned the lights on in the den," Judith said, vexed with herself for not thinking of it beforehand. "What little sun is left is on the western side of the house."

But to her surprise, the first brick she touched felt loose. She jiggled it repeatedly. At last she freed it enough to be able to pull it away from the wall of the house. The surrounding bricks, four in all, also came out without much effort. Judith peered through the opening. She couldn't see a thing.

"I'll have to feel my way," she murmured, reaching through the wall.

She only had to go as far as her elbow. Her fingers touched the spine of a book, which moved easily. She pushed. The volume fell off the shelf and, presumably,

259

onto the floor behind Uncle Boo's chair. The light from the den allowed Judith to see the opening in the den's wall and the bookcase itself.

"Look, coz," she said excitedly as she stood aside to make room for Renie. "Somebody's cut a hole about four inches in diameter. It must be at eye level with Boo's head. Can you see the chair?"

"No," Renie answered, straightening up. "All I see is the door to the den. But that would figure, wouldn't it? If we could see the chair, it would've blocked the killer's view." She shivered as she stepped back onto the grass. "Ugh, it's awful thinking about somebody going to all this trouble to shoot poor old Uncle Boo."

Judith, however, wore a calculating expression. "It's not so much work. The inner wall and insulation had been removed already. It was just a matter of taking out a few bricks and cutting a hole in the den and the bookcase. The only problem would be making sure the shot was in line with Boo's head." Abruptly, she shook herself. "You're right, it is awful. But it's pretty darned clever."

To Renie's surprise, Judith went back to inspecting the opening in the wall. "We need a flashlight," she said, then changed her mind. "Nix. We need a mason. I don't think we can use a flashlight at that angle." She patted the remaining bricks. "The bottom part of this wall is going to have to come out."

"Why?" asked Renie, looking puzzled.

"Because that's where the casing is. Maybe the silencer, too." Judith started back for the garage. "Let's check the den and see where that book landed."

The Rolls and the Ford looked lonely without the Cadillac to keep them company. On the opposite wall, the safe still stood open, like a naked wound. Judith paused in mid-step, causing Renie to stumble.

"What now?" Renie inquired in a resigned voice.

Judith continued to stare at the safe. "I'm not sure," she replied slowly. "But I think I may have figured out who took the jewels and where they're hidden."

"Oh, jeez!" Renie exclaimed. "Dare I ask how?"

Judith was smiling, albeit a bit tensely. "It's a guess, you understand."

"Sure, sure." Renie followed her cousin into the house. "My only consolation is that sometime your guesses are a crock of bull."

In the entry hall, Judith glanced at Renie over her shoulder. Her black eyes danced. "Not a crock—a gator. Think about it, coz. And remember Auntie Vance."

SEVENTEEN

THE WILL ROGERS BIOGRAPHY HAD FALLEN DIRECTLY behind Uncle Boo's chair. The cousins couldn't be sure, but they seemed to recall Derek picking it up from approximately the same place.

"Now," said Judith, dusting off her hands, which had become grimy from working with the wall, "we need to distinguish the gunshot with the silencer from the exploding cigar."

"We've been over all that," Renie said, growing impatient. "I want to hear more about Auntie Vance and the alligator."

But Judith waved a hand. "In a minute. This part is really important. Think, coz. It could tell us who killed Uncle Boo. And the Mayor's cousin."

"I'll tell you one thing," Renie said, moving restlessly around the den. "If the building inspector disappeared on Thursday, that limits the suspects. Were any of them here that day?"

Judith sat on the edge of the desk. "I've thought about that. I really don't know, but I'd guess Toadie came by to get things ready for the party. Maybe Trixie, too. Jill was in and out quite a bit, as we now know. Vivvie was keeping her hooks into Boo. Derek might have stopped by to arrange for the delivery of the big TV set. And if there were errands to run, Holly would have been sent to fetch and carry. The only unlikely suspect is Mason Meade. I can't see any reason for him being here— unless he came with Trixie."

"We can check on all of that with Mrs. Wakefield," Renie said, beginning to relax a little. "She must have seen the building inspector, too."

"Yes," Judith said thoughtfully. "So she must. I wonder when she'll be back."

Voices could be heard in the entry hall. Judith dashed to the door. Jack Althaus and the other two policemen were about to leave. Wearing her most appealing expression, Judith approached Althaus.

"If you'd do me a big favor, I'll show you something interesting." She almost gagged at the coy sound of her own voice.

He looked puzzled. "Like what, Mrs. Flynn?"

She explained about the necessity of reaching Hillside Manor. To her amazement, he readily agreed to contact the B&B and relay her urgent message. Encouraged by his response, she also asked if he'd check in with the AAA and find out what was causing the delay in the arrival of the tow truck. Again the young detective said he'd be glad to comply.

Keeping up her end of the bargain, Judith led Althaus and the others outside to her car. She opened the trunk and presented the Walther P-38. Althaus was amazed.

"That's excellent," he enthused, then gave orders to one of the other men to get an evidence bag. "Where did you find it?"

She explained about searching in the recessed garbage cans. "I intended to hand it over to my husband, but he . . . ah . . . left in such a hurry that I forgot."

He gave her a dubious look, but made no comment. The evidence bag arrived and the handgun was duly placed inside. Judith was about to reveal her most recent discovery in the wall of the house when Althaus uttered another command to his subordinates:

"Make sure Detective Doerflinger gets the weapon as soon as possible. In fact, call in and tell him you're on

263

the way."

"But," Judith began in confusion, "what about Detective Flynn?"

Althaus frowned. "Flynn? But this isn't his case. Not officially. He's on the missing-persons investigation."

"But the missing-person isn't missing—he's dead and probably shot with that gun," she protested.

The plainclothesman shrugged and offered her a lame smile. "Let's talk turf, Mrs. Flynn. Originally, this was Doerflinger's case. It still is. It's just a really strange coincidence that both investigations dovetailed. Oh, we'll get it sorted out down at headquarters. Meantime, I'll make those calls for you. So long."

Althaus and the others left. Angrily, Judith slammed the trunk of her car. "Damn! Now Joe will really be furious! But it's his own fault, for being such a pill!" She marched back across the street, going straight to the wall of the den. "I'm putting these damned bricks back until we get somebody to go inside and find the rest of the evidence."

"The silencer and the casing? Or a stray alligator?" Renie inquired, watching Judith replace the missing bricks. Her tone indicated she thought her cousin might be taking things for granted.

"Not just that," Judith replied, again brushing off her hands. "Trace evidence. You know, hair, fiber, anything that can identify the killer. There should be some residue on the bricks and maybe the holes in the wall and the bookcase. Everybody wore long sleeves last night, right?"

Renie allowed that that was so. The cousins trooped back into the house, and as before, Judith went straight to the den. From her pocket she removed the key ring that they had borrowed to get back into the house.

"I think I know which sound came first," she said, sorting through at least two dozen keys of various sizes and styles. "It was the gun. It had to be. The killer put a load in Uncle Boo's cigar to confuse the time of the real shot and to provide an alibi. It takes a while for a cigar to burn down, especially if the smoker isn't puffing on it. Boo puts the cigar in the ashtray, gets shot, and a few minutes later, the cigar explodes. Two noises, right? If the cigar had blown up first, even Uncle Boo wouldn't sit there like a stuffed duck. He'd have yelled in surprise or maybe even come out of the den. Thus, he must have been dead when the thing exploded."

Renie acknowledged her cousin's logic with a grin. "I like it. Now all we have to do is try to figure out who was where when that first noise sounded."

Judith was trying keys in the locked bookcase on their left. "No easy task, either. Except for Jill's fairly accurate account of time, you and I have no idea of who went where when. And you can bet the rest of them won't remember—or won't tell."

"Not even Derek?" asked Renie, then finally gave in to her curiosity. "What are you doing? Are the jewels in that bookcase?"

"No," Judith answered, finally making a match of key and lock. "The jewels are in Mason Meade's bandages. The bookcase is sheer guesswork. Here, coz," she said, handing a large volume to a startled Renie, "brush up your Shakespeare."

The familiar printed-will form was found at the beginning of *The Merchant of Venice*. "Will," Judith said as Renie unfolded the legal-sized document. "The one Will we overlooked was Shakespeare, because he was in the classics section. I should have thought of it

265

sooner, since Shakespeare's own will has been a subject of controversy for centuries."

"Ever the librarian," murmured Renie, scanning the first of two pages. "Who did Shakespeare leave everything to?"

Judith grinned as she looked over Renie's shoulder. "Mainly his daughter, Judith. That's how I remember it so well."

In this version, the formal passage that identified family members did not include any in-laws. According to the handwritten portion, Bruno Major's family consisted of his late brother's daughter, Ruth Helga Major, and any heirs of her body. It also included Jill Andrea Rush Major, his lawful wife. Under disposition of the estate, Boo did give, devise and bequeath unto Jill Andrea Rush Major the sum of one million dollars. The remainder of the estate was left to Ruth Helga Major. The document was dated February 6. It was witnessed by Arthur L. Peterson and Patrick J. O'Brien.

"Wow!" breathed Renie. "This was made the day before yesterday! Who do you suppose these witnesses are?"

Judith was still frowning at the document. "The masons?" She stared at the addresses, which were handwritten below the signatures. "If only we had a phone, we could call and ask them about this."

"Now they'll have to find Ruth Major," Renie said, a note of excitement in her voice. "Imagine inheriting all this money from out of nowhere! Won't she be thrilled?"

Judith, however, wasn't joining in her cousin's excitement. "I wonder," she muttered under her breath.

"What do you mean?" asked Renie.

Judith gave an impatient shake of her head. "I don't

know what I mean. This final will—and it has to be final unless Boo came into the den last night to make out yet another—bothers me. Why leave everything to the niece and a measly million to Jill?"

"A million isn't measly to me," Renie remarked.

"You know what I'm saying." Judith glanced out the small window next to the open bookcase. The street was quiet. Shadows were inching across the lawn, as the sun disappeared behind dark clouds. "This strikes me as odd," she declared, slapping the will with her hand. Disconsolately, she sank into one of the side chairs.

Renie sat down in its mate. "Well, odd or not, there it is. Why not tell me about the stolen jewels instead?"

Judith didn't seem very interested in the theft. "It had to be Mason Meade. Vivvie probably had blabbed to the rest of the family and Trixie told him about the jewels. Who else would bother to steal them? The family members all thought they were going to get everything anyway. But Mason was an outsider. How would you like to count on Trixie for your bread and butter?"

"So he's a crook?" Renie grimaced. "I thought he was into concrete."

"He is," Judith replied, gathering momentum. "But maybe his business is in a hole. It was started by his father, but he died, and now Mason and his sister have taken over. I don't know about the sister, but does Mason strike you as bright?"

Briefly, Renie considered. "Not really. But he could still count on Trixie and her expectations."

"Maybe," Judith allowed. "But Trixie isn't exactly a work in fidelity. She says she was making a phone call last night, supposedly to Marty. But we know she wasn't. Now, who do you suppose she was trying to reach?"

"Oh, good heavens," cried Renie in exasperation, "I have no idea! Her cosmetic surgeon?"

Judith smiled feebly. "Not a bad guess. But I'm voting for that offensive lineman, Biff Kowoski. He was tall, dark and dumbsome, which is how Trixie likes them. Never mind his wife, Myra—Biff probably doesn't mind her, either. We know all about Trixie's track record, which reads like a handicap sheet for Sluts R Us."

Renie chortled. "So Trixie was making a late date. Or something. Maybe Mason wasn't too stupid to figure it out."

"Could be. In any event, he managed to crack the safe, the combination of which I'll bet was indeed Uncle Boo's birth date. Mason would know that, of course, because of the party. It's what I was going to try first. He grabs the jewels and takes off in Trixie's Lexus. Unfortunately, along the way he meets a lamppost."

Renie was looking bemused. "So how do you figure he managed to hide the loot in his bandages?"

Judith gave a shake of her head. "I don't know how he did it, but when Aunt Vivvie accidentally sat down on him, she felt something poke her in the rear end. 'Stabbed,' was the word she used. It went right by me at the time, but then we got to talking about Auntie Vance and Marty's alligator. I was reminded of Vivvie. Bandages shouldn't 'stab' anybody. So what was under them? A tiara?"

"No wonder Mason didn't want to stay in the hospital." Renie chuckled. "And he didn't want Zoe changing his dressings."

"Right." Judith got up and went to the window again. "Drat. Still no sign of that damned tow truck. They must be hauling cars all over town. I suppose a lot of people got stuck on the freeway last night. I sure hope Althaus called the B&B. It's past five o'clock." Judith rubbed anxiously at her forehead, then tensed. "Here comes the Cadillac."

Renie got out of the chair to join Judith at the window. "There's only one person in it. Can you see who it is?"

"No," Judith answered. "But we'll find out soon enough."

The big car stopped briefly in the drive to wait for the automatic garage door to open. Then the Cadillac slipped inside. The middle door closed. Judith turned to Renie, an odd expression on her face.

"Think back on your love life, coz. Who was the girl in the Cascadia Hotel elevator with Cousin Denny?"

The cousins had moved into the living room. They were freshening their drinks when Zoe Wakefield walked through the arched doorway. Her auburn hair had come undone from its copper clips and her skin was pale. She seemed surprised to see Judith and Renie sitting side by side on the long sofa.

"Hi," Judith said with forced cheer. "We're still waiting for a start. Or a tow."

"You can borrow the Cadillac," Zoe said, taking off her jacket. "I don't need three cars."

"That's okay," Judith answered in an agreeable voice. "We've waited this long. Another few minutes won't hurt."

Noting the cousins' highball glasses, Zoe uttered a mirthless laugh. "I could use a drink. Maybe I'll get myself some wine." She headed out for the kitchen.

Renie poked Judith. "All I remember is that she had freckles," Renie whispered. "Curves, too. Egad, it's been nearly forty years! I'll bet Denny doesn't remember!"

Judith didn't respond. She sat on the sofa, rocking slightly and waiting expectantly. Zoe reappeared, a glass of white wine in one slim hand.

"Where are your parents?" Judith asked in a conversational voice.

Zoe sat down in the sea-green armchair. "They released Dad on a five-hundred-thousand-dollar bond. It took forever to raise the ten percent. My mother must have spent an hour on the phone, but she did it." Zoe took a deep sip from her glass.

Judith had stopped rocking and had edged forward on the sofa. "Where are they now?"

Zoe's expression was wary. "Dad wanted to chill out. But not here. I dropped them off uptown. Maybe they'll check into a hotel for the night."

"They can't go far," Judith said, a note of warning in her voice. "Your father is under arrest. Surely you must know where they'll be staying. The police will have to be notified."

Zoe's eyes, which looked amber in the lamplight, grew very wide. "But I don't know. They didn't tell me."

"Maybe we'd better find out," Judith said briskly. "We'll borrow that Cadillac after all and go use a pay phone."

Zoe shrugged. "Go ahead. The keys are in the garage. You can't miss them—they've got the Cadillac emblem. I'm going downstairs to bed. I'm beat."

Judith frowned. Something was wrong. She remained seated on the sofa, with a puzzled Renie at her side. "Zoe, wait. I've got a question for you. It's really important."

But Zoe wasn't about to wait. Her languid air had long ago deserted her. She struggled to her feet in an almost clumsy manner. *"Please.* Don't harass me. I've had all I can take."

Judith also stood up. "Hold on, Zoe, this is absolutely essential."

Zoe's eyes glinted oddly. "You mustn't try to stop me." Doggedly, she headed for the entry hall.

"What are your parents' first names?" Judith's question cut like a cleaver.

Zoe not only didn't turn around, but kept on going. "Dad's real first name is Clark," she called out in a toneless voice. " 'Weed' is just a nickname."

Judith and Renie exchanged quick glances. "And your mother?" Judith shouted.

But Zoe had disappeared into the dining room.

"Now what do we do?" Judith asked anxiously.

Renie was also on her feet, gazing through the window next to the fireplace. "Go home?" She gestured toward the street.

The AAA tow truck had just pulled up at the curb.

It took less than five minutes to start Judith's blue compact. As the engine hummed, Judith waved her thanks to the AAA emergency crew and put the car into reverse. Moments later, the cousins were going down the steep hill that had held them prisoner at Major Manor. Near the bottom, they saw the damaged lamppost, bent at a forty-five-degree angle.

"You think Zoe did it?" Renie finally asked as they drove through The Bluff's tasteful shopping area.

At the four-way stop, Judith looked ruefully at Renie. "Everything points that way." Abruptly, she pulled into the parking lot of a large drugstore. "There's a pay

271

phone. I'm calling the cops."

Renie dutifully waited in the car. Judith was inside the phone booth for almost five minutes. When she emerged, her face was grim.

"Well?" said Renie.

"They put me through to Buck Doerflinger. Damn all." Judith turned the keys in the ignition, reversed out of the parking lot, and headed, not for Heraldsgate Hill, but back toward The Bluff.

"Now what?" demanded Renie.

"Joe's about to go off duty. I told Buck to have Detective Flynn meet me at Major Manor. It took some doing, but I convinced him I knew something more about the Mayor's cousin. Buck still doesn't realize I'm Mrs. Flynn."

Renie gave Judith a sidelong look. "And are you?"

Judith snorted. "I said as much, before God and man. I'm stuck with the jerk, aren't I?"

"I guess." Renie noticed that her cousin didn't seem unduly alarmed at the prospect.

Judith expected the worst. Guilt washed over her as she stood in the outside stairwell next to the back porch of Major Manor. No one responded to her loud knock on the basement door to the servants' quarters. She regarded Renie bleakly.

"We never should have left. Whatever Zoe intended to do, she must have done it." Judith put a hand to her forehead and swore softly.

"The key ring," Renie said suddenly. "Haven't you still got it?"

"Oh!" Judith felt in the pocket of her jacket. "How could I not have noticed!" She held up the collection of keys, then hurriedly tried to find the one that fit the basement door.

Judith called Zoe's name as they made their way down the narrow hall. The house seemed to echo. Except for the loden coat, the brass hooks were naked, mute testimony to the departure of the Wakefields. Even the marijuana odor had faded away. The basement smelled damp, and vaguely like a sheep.

Judith checked the rooms on the left side of the passageway; Renie looked into the ones on the right. Neither cousin showed much enthusiasm for the task.

They peeked into the furnace room and the coal bin, then moved on to the galley, where the stove was still pulled out from the wall. Next door, the guest bathroom was also empty. At last they reached the saloon. But Zoe wasn't there, either.

Judith uttered a sigh that was half relief, half frustration. "I don't get it," she said under her breath, then sank down into one of the saloon's recessed alcoves. As before, the scent of pine hung on the air. "I had it all figured out—logically. Somehow, Zoe slipped out of the house while she was cleaning up from dinner. Probably she went through the door to the garage that goes from the hall. Otherwise we'd have seen her go out via the back way, or down through the basement, or into the garage by the door from the kitchen. She shot Boo and then raced back inside. But everything backfired on her. Weed was suspected of killing Boo, and while Zoe may be a killer, she's obviously very fond of her father. More so, I'd guess, than she is of her mother. Weed's ideals have made a deep impression on the girl."

Renie was gazing up through one of the small windows which looked out onto a concrete wall. The leaded panes offered light, but no view. Like the rest of the basement, the saloon was set deep in the ground.

"I'm not following you," Renie admitted. "Weed's ideals are typical of his age and era. His type isn't much interested in money, only in the equal distribution of it."

Judith gave an abrupt jerk of her head. "I know, I know. That's why I figured Zoe was overcome with remorse. Not only had she betrayed her father's principles, she'd gotten him arrested. Gruesome as it sounds, I expected to find her dangling from a rope or succumbing to an overdose of sleeping pills. But she's gone."

"We haven't looked upstairs," Renie pointed out with a grimace.

"True," Judith agreed, getting up. "Let's search the rest of the house. I don't think we'll find her, though. Zoe would do herself in down here, where she lived. Maybe," she added without much spirit, "we should check the garage, too."

The cousins headed for the basement stairs. Judith suddenly stopped, staring at the loden coat. She felt the fabric, then sniffed.

"This thing's damp. It also smells like a sheep." Judith clapped a hand to her head. "Oh, my God! I've been an idiot!"

"At times," Renie replied in a calm voice, though her eyes narrowed at Judith. "Now what?"

Judith was already running up the stairs. "The garage! I'll bet the grocery money that Zoe's gone!"

The Ford certainly was. The Rolls and the Cadillac stood side by side, looking smug, like two beauties at a party who've finally managed to ditch the Ugly Duckling.

"Okay," said Renie, "now give me your revised edition of this sorry story."

"It's simple," Judith responded eagerly. "All along,

274

I've tried to equate the kind of murder with the murderer's personality. This was carefully planned, though there was a surprise element, namely the—"

Outside, a horn honked impatiently. Judith and Renie hurried to the garage doors. "It must be Joe," Judith said, trying to figure out how to open the doors from the inside. "Shoot, I wonder what trips the automatic locks."

The horn sounded again. Unable to find the mechanism that opened the doors, the cousins hurried through the garage, into the kitchen, and out the back door. Judith expected to see Joe's battered but beloved MG at the curb, but instead, they found a big blue Chevrolet.

"Bill!" Renie shouted. She waved in a frantic gesture, started across the lawn, then stopped. "Coz! What shall I do? It's nearly six o'clock! Bill must be hungry!"

"Then feed him." Judith shrugged, well aware of the ulcer-prone Bill Jones's need to eat promptly. "Joe will be along any minute." In the gathering darkness, she, too, waved at Bill. He saluted stiffly.

Renie, however, was hesitating. "I don't know . . . maybe we should wait until Joe gets here."

Judith was adamant. "Get going. Nobody's here but me. If it makes you feel any better, I'll go sit in my car."

"Do that," urged Renie as Bill gave one long toot of the horn. "And call me. I can't wait to hear the rest of the story." She jumped into the Chevy, barely getting the door closed before Bill tromped on the gas.

Judith started for her Stanza, then realized she still had the key ring in her pocket. Going around to the back porch, she let herself in. *Maybe I should leave a couple of lights on*, she thought. Moving to the entry hall, Judith switched on the ship's lantern over the front

275

porch. She decided to keep the chandelier in the living room burning, too.

On her way out, she placed the key ring on the peg by the back door. From force of habit, she checked the stove to make sure it was off. A noise which seemed to come from the entry hall made her pause with her hand on the kitchen light switch. Someone must have entered the house through the front door.

Judith knew she should leave at once. Her brain told her to take the two steps to the back porch, but her feet wouldn't obey. Whoever had come in wasn't necessarily the killer. Indeed, it flashed through Judith's mind that she had already been wrong once about the murderer's identity. Could she have made two mistakes? As if frozen to the spot, she craned her neck, to watch a furtive figure cross the entry hall.

"Trixie!" Judith gasped. "What are you doing here?"

Trixie seemed equally surprised. Her face was haggard and she carried a grocery bag in her left hand. "I . . . I forgot something. We left in such a hurry," she added lamely. "Why are you still here? Where's Serena?"

"She's gone," Judith replied, edging away from the back door. "Joe's coming. He should be here any minute."

Trixie looked blank. "Joe? Joe who?"

"My husband," Judith snapped. "You seem to have ignored our wedding invitation."

"Oh. When was it?" Trixie's eyes were darting around the kitchen; the knuckles on the hand that clutched the grocery bag turned white.

"A year ago last June," Judith answered, her mind racing along other, more frightening lines.

"June?" Trixie's eyes grew wide. "I think I got

276

married around that time, too. Rafe, you know."

Judith remembered that the Rafe Longrod nuptials had taken place the year before her own wedding, but she could hardly expect Trixie to keep track. "How did you get in?"

"Mother has a key to the front door." Trixie saw Judith's curious reaction and hastened to explain: "In case something happened to Uncle Boo and one of us needed to rescue him. The Wakefields might be gone. You never know. But she only had the *house key*. I mean, why would she need anything else?"

"Why indeed," Judith echoed. "So what did you forget?" she inquired in what she hoped was a casual tone.

Trixie frowned. "A bracelet? My mother's bracelet," she said, suddenly smiling. "Yes, the silver charm bracelet. You know how much she likes it. I'll go hunt for it now." Her smile widened, but it never went past her nose.

Trixie all but ran from the kitchen. Judith watched her go through the dining room and into the entry hall. But Trixie didn't head for the living room or upstairs. Instead, she turned into the passage which led to the garage. Judith's expression grew thoughtful.

She almost didn't hear the footsteps on the basement stairs. It was the husky voice that caused her to turn around. Unlike Trixie, Mrs. Wakefield didn't seem surprised to see Judith.

"What's up?" the housekeeper asked, running a comb through her graying red hair. Except for a few lines of fatigue on her face, the arduous day hadn't seemed to affect Mrs. Wakefield's spirits. "I noticed your car had been moved. I saw it parked on this side of the street when I pulled into the garage."

Judith laughed lightly. "It's a long story. Where's Weed? Where's Zoe?"

Mrs. Wakefield was at the refrigerator. "Weed's in search of grass," she replied in a disgruntled voice. "I tried to stop him, but it's never any use. Zoe knew where he'd be, so she came looking for him. That girl's wasting her time trying to change her dad. She told me to take the Ford and go home. I figured I might as well. They may be gone until tomorrow."

"You're staying on?" asked Judith.

The housekeeper had taken a roll of turkey breast from the refrigerator. She used a sharp knife to cut paper-thin slices. "Nobody's fired us yet. We don't know who really owns this place, do we?" She gave Judith a sly smile. "This will, that will—I say it's not over yet." Mrs. Wakefield chewed lustily on a piece of turkey.

"It's certainly not," Judith replied evenly. She glanced through the kitchen window. It was now dark, and a pair of headlights had cruised up to the curb in front of the house. Judith was sure she recognized Joe's MG. "In fact," she went on, feeling a sense of relief as well as elation overcome her, "it's far from over. Isn't that right, Ruth?"

Mrs. Wakefield's reaction was delayed. She was complacently devouring another mouthful of turkey when her eyes narrowed. "Ruth? Where do you get off calling me Ruth?"

Judith shrugged. "It's your name, isn't it? After all we've been through in the past twenty-four hours, you don't mind if I call you that, do you? Go ahead, I'm Judith."

The housekeeper's chunky hand tightened around the handle of the butcher knife. "Who told you my name was Ruth?"

Discreetly, Judith tried to determine if Joe was approaching Major Manor from the front or the back. He had parked halfway between the main entrance and the back porch. She hoped he would choose to come in through the kitchen. But, of course, he wasn't as familiar with the floor plan as she was.

"You're Reuben Major's daughter," she said in a quiet tone. "I'm guessing that Boo—and Rosie—hired you and Weed as a favor to Rube. Old Dunlop had cut Rube out of his will, not because he was a German sympathizer—far from it; he was an American hero— but simply out of sheer pigheadedness. Dunlop might have understood your father's wanderlust—he should have, since he had some of it himself—but he couldn't forgive him for cueing loose from the family. Dunlop dies, so does Rube, and somewhere in there, you show up on Boo's doorstep with a small child. Say what you will about both him and Aunt Rosie, they were good-hearted. No doubt you were down on your luck due to Weed's politics and pot, which, given the late sixties, were often one and the same. Boo and Rosie take you in, give you jobs and a home. The debt is paid. Which," Judith continued, straining to hear any sound that would signal Joe's arrival, "is why that last will is all wrong."

Mrs. Wakefield blinked, but her eyes didn't leave Judith's face. "What will?"

Judith was growing uneasy. How long did it take to cover the distance from the street to the house? "The one in the Shakespeare book. The forged will, with the masons' signatures. What did you tell them they were signing—a time sheet for their severance pay?" Noting the startled expression on Ruth Wakefield's face, Judith knew she'd guessed right. "For once, Toadie told the

279

truth. She really didn't fire the masons—*you* did. And you shot that poor building inspector, too."

The housekeeper took two steps forward, brandishing the knife. "Aren't you the clever one! It's a good thing the cops hire dopes like that Doerflinger instead of people like you! But if you think you're going to blab all this and get me arrested, you're as crazy as the rest of them!"

The knock sounded at the kitchen door. Judith's eyes darted in that direction. Joe Flynn's outline could be seen through the frosted glass.

"It's the police," Judith said through taut lips. "You'd better let him—them—in."

The slip proved costly. Mrs. Wakefield grabbed Judith, twisting an arm behind her. "March! I can handle one cop just fine! Open that door, and if you do anything stupid, I'll slice you like that turkey roll!"

Starting to tremble, Judith obeyed. She flung open the door. Joe Flynn was smoothing his red hair and his round face was smiling. His hand dropped and his smile died when he saw the knife against Judith's throat.

"Get in here," ordered Mrs. Wakefield. "Close the door."

Wordlessly, Joe did as he was bidden. His green eyes flashed as he quickly surveyed the kitchen. Judith knew he was assessing their chances. She wondered if he'd called for backup. Probably not, since he couldn't be sure why Judith had summoned him to Major Manor.

"Interesting," he said at last, leaning lightly against the kitchen counter. "One knife, two victims. How does that work?"

Judith couldn't see Mrs. Wakefield's face, but she could hear the grim humor in her voice. "Easy. I've got another gun stashed in the drawer next to the flour bin.

280

Mrs. Flynn and I are going to mosey over there and get it. Any false moves from you and she gets blood all over my nice, clean floor."

"I don't suppose," Joe said, his mellow voice deceptively lazy, "anyone would care to tell me what's going on here. I understood an arrest had already been made."

It wasn't easy for Judith to talk with the knife pressed against her throat. She was sure that if she moved at all, the blade would cut into her flesh. "Buck," she said in a strangled voice. "He was wrong."

"What else is new?" Joe's eyes were now riveted on the hand that held the knife. "Who are you? It's always nice to know your local homicidal maniac."

"Funny man," Mrs. Wakefield sneered, nudging Judith in the direction of the cupboards. "If you're a cop, you can figure it out. *She* did." The housekeeper gave Judith's arm a little twist; then she let go to reach for the drawer handle.

If Judith had thought the moment's distraction would give Joe his chance, she was wrong. The housekeeper didn't miss a beat. The knife never wavered. Deftly, Mrs. Wakefield pulled the gun out from under a pile of twine, aluminum foil, and used paper bags.

"It's loaded, in case you're wondering," she said, flipping the knife into the sink. "Move it!" Giving Judith a sharp shove, she propelled her toward Joe. "You City Hall types sure are a pain," she said with a nasty chuckle. "All my plans almost undone by that snooping building inspector! I couldn't believe it when he told me there were loose bricks in the den wall. As if I didn't know! He insisted it was shoddy workmanship. I was tempted to let him go on thinking that, until he started filling out a stupid report."

Judith was rubbing her sore arm. "You must have had to act fast," she said, her voice breathless. "How did you manage to shoot him and not have somebody see or hear it?"

Mrs. Wakefield snorted. "I asked him to come have a look at the bricks down by the pond to see if they could be used on the house. Quality control, I called it. Meantime, I'd gotten the Walther out. Weed was puffing away, Zoe was running the vacuum, and old Boo—what else? He was asleep. The masons were on their lunch break. I shot the guy and pushed him in the pond; then I took his keys and drove the city car down the street a couple of blocks. In this neighborhood nobody ever comes outside this time of year, and the rest of 'em are out of town, chasing the sun. I figured I'd get rid of the guy later, after everything quieted down."

"Everything, including the surprise revelation about the latest will?" Judith asked, amazed that her voice didn't come out in a squeak.

Mrs. Wakefield nodded, a cunning smile playing at her lips. "As will happen, excuse the pun. It could take weeks, even months—what difference does it make? I'll still get it all, except for that measly million that goes to Jill."

"And you'd let your husband pay for your crimes?" Joe's career in law enforcement had made him cynical, but nonetheless, Mrs. Wakefield violated his basic concept of justice.

Mrs. Wakefield sneered. "That dope of a Doerflinger couldn't have made his case stick. The charges would've been dismissed. I said so all along."

Judith dared to ask one more question. "How did you know about the marriage?" She wondered if she dared try to edge closer to Joe.

"That was a lucky stroke," the housekeeper replied. "The building inspector insisted on meeting old Boo first. He was already half asleep, but I introduced them. Afterward, the guy tells me he recognized him—saw Boo down at City Hall taking out a marriage license with some young trick. I called down there and found out he'd gotten hitched to Jill. That's why there had to be a new will. The Space Alien version wouldn't have been any good as long as Boo had a wife."

Momentarily, Judith lost her fear. "You forged that one, too?"

Mrs. Wakefield shook her head. "Oh, no. I didn't have to. I talked Boo into it. No sweat; he liked the idea of leaving the money to himself."

It was Joe's turn to be startled. "Himself?"

Mrs. Wakefield's laugh was gusty, but her gaze never moved from Joe and Judith. "The American Society for Sighting and Studying Alien Beings Outside Ourselves? The first letters spell out TASSABOO! 'Tass a Boo'—that was my father's nickname for his brother!"

"Wait a minute!" Joe didn't seem fazed by Mrs. Wakefield's sudden two-handed grip on the gun. "I don't get it. Who is this woman?" His question was directed at Judith.

"Ruth Major Wakefield," Judith responded, swallowing hard as she saw the housekeeper take aim. "Rube Major's daughter. Rube and Boo were brothers. Rube and his wife are dead, so Ruth and her daughter, Zoe, are Boo's only blood relations." Beyond Mrs. Wakefield, Judith saw Trixie tiptoeing across the main hall. Judith had forgotten that the other woman was still in the house. Whatever Trixie had been doing in the past several minutes, she'd exercised the greatest of stealth.

Knees weak and chin trembling, Judith tried to say something, anything, to make Trixie understand what was going on. The housekeeper's back was turned; Trixie couldn't see the gun.

"Once I knew that a Ruth Major existed," Judith blurted out, her voice uneven, "I knew somebody had a serious motive for killing Boo. Toadie and Vivvie might have seen you at Boo and Rosie's wedding, but you were just a kid. As with most of us, thirty or forty years can make a big difference. Anyway, Vivvie is muddleheaded and Toadie is self-absorbed. You could count on them not to recognize you." She faltered briefly as panic seemed to overtake her. "But Renie remembered a freckle-faced teenager at the reception." Now frantic, Judith forced herself to all but shout: "I knew the killer must have red hair!"

Halfway through the dining room, Trixie froze. Mrs. Wakefield's keen ears heard the soft footsteps behind her; she turned ever so slightly. Trixie had already crouched and started to spring. With a snarling yelp, she leaped across the floor—and dove straight at Joe Flynn.

EIGHTEEN

THE GUN WENT OFF, NARROWLY MISSING JUDITH. THE bullet lodged in one of the cupboards. Mrs. Wakefield took aim again, but Judith had thrown herself at the housekeeper. Off-balance, the second shot hit the floor. So did Joe and Trixie. Fighting for her life, Judith grabbed the arm that held the gun, fingernails clawing into flesh.

"Let go!" Joe shouted at Trixie, finally delivering an openhanded slap to her cheek. "I'm a cop!"

Trixie stumbled backward, holding her face. "But . . . you've got red hair!"

Joe had pulled his own weapon. "Hit the deck!" he ordered Judith.

Judith, however, wasn't inclined to let go. She could feel the housekeeper weakening. The gun went off a third time, striking the ceiling. Bits of plaster fell over the combatants. Judith used her knee to knock the wind out of Mrs. Wakefield. The other woman sagged, groaned, and collapsed on the floor. The gun rolled harmlessly from her hand to lie on the linoleum next to Trixie's foot.

"You're right," Trixie said in wonder, still rubbing her cheek. "She does have red hair. But it's going gray. She ought to touch it up."

Joe removed a pair of handcuffs from his belt. Expertly, he locked them on Mrs. Wakefield, who was making small, whimpering noises. "I need backup," he said, yanking his radiophone off his belt. He spoke rapidly into the unit, then flipped it off and turned to Trixie. "Do I know you? Should I?"

"Maybe at Christmas . . ." Judith began, panting a little.

Trixie gave Joe a coquettish look. "If we met, I can't believe I wouldn't remember. I'm Trixie Bellew, and you're a real tiger." She wasn't wearing her false eyelashes, but that didn't stop her from fluttering away at him.

He searched in vain for a notebook. "Damn! I must have dropped it in the car! Find one for me, will you, please?" he asked a bit curtly of Trixie.

Trixie, however, was inclined to linger. She put a hand on Joe's shoulder and purred provocatively. "You play kind of rough, Mr. Policeman. I like that. How's your rubber hose?"

Judith marched over to Trixie and slugged her on the other cheek.

Zoe Wakefield was crying. No amount of white wine or words of consolation could comfort her. Joe stood in front of the marble fireplace; Judith sat with Zoe on the sofa. A miffed Trixie had departed half an hour earlier, swearing she would never speak to Judith—or Joe— again. Mrs. Wakefield had been taken into custody a few minutes later. Zoe had shown up in a cab just as the squad car pulled away.

"Dad's going to take this very hard," Zoe sniffed. "Once he comes down from . . . wherever he is."

"I feel terrible," Judith confessed, trying to console Zoe. "There were so few suspects who were . . . uh . . . qualified to commit this kind of crime. It was very clever and well thought out. Trixie is cunning, but totally disorganized. Toadie was a definite possibility, yet she'd have blown it somewhere along the way. Vivvie is too addled. Jill lacks the courage and Holly hasn't got any nerve. Derek seemed the most likely of the family members, but his grief was genuine. He's no actor. In fact, he has trouble showing emotions of any kind."

Zoe blew her nose. "I knew about Rube Major, but I never guessed we were related. Dad has his pride—he's probably ashamed that we had to accept charity in the form of working for his wife's uncle. Imagine! All along, Mom should have had half of this! But would it have made us happy?" One of Zoe's hands fluttered like a dying bird. Judith started to interject a comment, but Zoe continued speaking. "I never dreamed Mom was related to Boo. Oh, I knew her first name was Ruth, but that didn't mean anything. I had no reason to learn her maiden name. Dad didn't believe in the capitalist-based principles of public education, so he home-schooled me. And I didn't ever have to fill out a job application, because after I grew up, I worked here as the maid."

Judith nodded. "That was the problem—there didn't seem to be any motive for you or your parents. It was only when I learned that Rube had a daughter that I began to wonder about Ruth Major's identity. As a teenager, she had attended Boo and Rosie's wedding reception. Aunt Toadie said Ruth didn't spend much time with the grownups. My cousin Renie had glimpsed your mother in the hotel elevator. All she could remember was freckles."

Zoe's amber eyes were wistful. "Mom's freckles faded as she got older. It's strange, you know," she mused. "I wonder now if Mr. Major—Dunlop—might have relented about his own will if Mom hadn't married a hippie."

The theory struck Judith as possible. "Your mother didn't seem interested in politics. She wanted justice, though. Eventually, after the homicide investigation had petered out, she'd have trotted out the forged will. Until then, she had to keep her family ties a secret. That's why she cut the phone wires—so we couldn't do any checking on what had happened to Ruth Major after her parents were killed. An obituary would have given her married name."

Joe had found one of Boo's cigars and was puffing away. "We'll still need proof that Ruth Wakefield is Ruth Major. We need evidence, too. Otherwise we might be forever accusing the wrong Wakefields." His tone was ironic.

Judith made a rueful face. "It was an honest mistake on my part. You're bright, Zoe. It could have been you. But your mother is smart, too, plus she admitted that she could do just about anything around the house. She had to, because Weed was such a washout. When it came to removing bricks, drilling holes, cutting phone wires, and all the rest, Mrs. Wakefield overcame every obstacle." Judith turned back to Zoe. "You might have as well, if you knew you had a motive. But I realized you had something else—an alibi. It was so hard to keep track of who was where when, and, I have to admit, I got mixed up. Finally I remembered that you were with my cousin and me in the kitchen when the gun was fired. Your mother wasn't there—she was in the basement, tending to your father's burns."

Zoe's flushed face was puzzled. "But . . . then how could she have done it?"

"It all began with the pressure cooker," Judith said, ignoring Joe's incredulous expression. "Your mother set all of us up—especially your father. She put those beets on the upstairs stove, knowing the catering team would object. Which we did. So she took them downstairs and

288

told your father how to tend them. But, of course, her directions were incorrect. She wanted them to explode, not only to make a misleading loud noise, but to give herself an excuse to go downstairs. Your dad was instructed to lift the lid and check the beets. He did, which is a definite no-no with a pressure cooker. Ka-blooey!" Judith folded her hands in her lap. "That started the series of noises that were intended to confuse us and mask the actual gunshot. To provide an alibi, she had to make it impossible to pinpoint the actual time of death."

Zoe was shocked. "Dad might have been badly burned. How could she?"

Judith avoided Zoe's pitiful gaze. "Your mother was single-minded. She saw only her goal and ran over any obstacles along the way. Even your dad, though I don't think she ever intended him serious harm."

Zoe's face crumpled again, then regained some of its composure. "Mom was cunning," she said in a bitter voice, "but Dad has the real brains. Compassion and wisdom, too."

"That may be. I should have listened more closely to what your father said." Judith spoke with regret. "He told me that he'd asked your mother about one of the muffled sounds *after she'd come back* to tuck him in—which should have made me realize that for a brief period, she was out of your father's sight. She didn't come back upstairs, so where was she? She'd gone outside through the basement door by the back porch. And then your father said that your mother had ignored him. That didn't strike me as strange until I smelled a sheep in the basement."

Joe expelled a big puff of smoke and started for the arched entrance to the living room. "We're leaving now.

289

I have to get down to headquarters, and my wife has to see her nut doctor. She's gone over the edge, I'm afraid."

But Judith waved a peremptory hand. "Now wait just a minute! It wasn't a real sheep, it was wet wool. It was raining like mad at the time of Boo's murder, and Mrs. Wakefield had to put a coat on over her uniform or else everyone would have known she was outside. She grabbed the loden coat, which would cover her completely and not show up in the dark. The coat was still damp this afternoon. I could smell it when Renie and I were in the servants' quarters." Judith redirected her remarks to Zoe. "There was no way you could have gone from the dining room to the basement without being seen. So the coat had to have been worn by someone who had been downstairs. That, and the fact that when your mother came back up to the kitchen, she didn't seem to hear too well. Ordinarily, her hearing was very keen. But even with the silencer, the gun must have made a very loud noise inside the open wall of the den. She was temporarily deafened by the shot, which is why she ignored your father's question about the noise. She simply didn't hear him."

Sniffing and nodding, Zoe tried to smile. "I knew Dad wouldn't kill anyone. He always wanted to turn the world upside down, but he wouldn't hurt people in the process. Dad's so gentle. That's why he does pot. It keeps him from seeing the ugly side of life."

Judith refrained from making the obvious rejoinder, that a man who married a murderess faces ugliness personified. Instead, she patted Zoe's arm. "It wasn't really a selfish crime. Oh, your mother isn't as indifferent to money as your father. I suspect she always resented Uncle Boo's inheriting everything. But I

290

honestly think she did it for you, Zoe. You'd been cheated of your inheritance as well as your future. Ruth Major Wakefield might have killed two people, but her goal was to make you happy."

The young woman's reddened eyes stared helplessly at Judith. "Then why am I so miserable? I don't want money! I never did! Why do other people always think they know what's best for you? It's wrong! I don't give a damn about a billion dollars! I'd rather be a maid!"

Which was a good thing, thought Judith, since Zoe Wakefield probably wouldn't inherit one thin dime.

Hillside Manor was dark. There was no sign of a guest, a neighbor, or Gertrude. Frantically, Judith searched the front porch for notes left by disappointed B&B visitors. She scanned the street for cars she didn't recognize, but at the corner, the Steins were giving a party. There was no way of knowing which cars belonged where.

At last she let herself in through the front door. A strange, wavering light beamed from the living room into the dining room. Drawing nearer, she heard Gertrude's rasping voice:

"Watch, now . . . she'll trip, just as she gets her diploma . . . There she goes! Whump! . . . Here's the wedding to Lunkhead Number One. Looks don't count, folks. A year later, my little girl is living with Mr. Blimp. It gets worse . . . there he is, all four hundred pounds of him. Now, that's Mike, my grandson. Cute, huh? Ignore the drooping diapers—my daughter was working two jobs to support Blubber-o. That's their house on Thurlow Street—see the hookers standing down at the corner? Lousy neighborhood, but they kept getting evicted from—"

Judith flipped on the lights. At the far end of the long

living room, the movie screen faded into a jumble of pastels. The eight startled faces that blinked at Judith belonged to strangers. In the middle of the room, Gertrude sat behind the projector with Sweetums curled up at her feet.

"What's going on?" Judith demanded, sounding almost as raspy as her mother.

Gertrude flinched, then drew herself up straight in the armless rocking chair. "Well, finally! Out gallivanting all day and all night! I've been entertaining your guests with home movies."

Fury and humiliation warred within Judith's breast. She flew across the living room, scaring Sweetums and alarming Gertrude.

"Delightful," breathed a woman with steel-gray hair and several strands of pearls.

"Gritty," declared a roly-poly, middle-aged man wearing a gold cardigan.

"Fascinating," commented a younger woman with the dewy air of a new bride. She held her husband's hand and gazed into his face. "Just think of the memories we'll have if we always use our camcorder."

Judith was about to grab Gertrude by the collar of her jungle-print housecoat. She hesitated as her mother smiled innocently. "Homey stuff. Real life. I skipped the appetizer thingamabobs and made dinner. Pig hocks, sauerkraut, and neflë. They loved it." She pointed to the projector. "Want to see the part at your second wedding where Uncle Corky serenades you on the swinette?"

The reference to Uncle Corky caused Judith to think of Aunt Toadie. Recalling Aunt Toadie made Judith take a long, hard look at Gertrude. She threw her arms around her mother.

"Sure, I'll get the lights." Judith scampered to the

switch, Sweetums at her heels. "Roll 'em!"

The room went dark again. "Okay," said Gertrude, "now there's my sister-in-law Deb, in the wheelchair. You can recognize her because her mouth moves faster than her brain. On the right, in the tan sport coat, is my brother-in-law Al. Watch his right hand—he's stealing that skinny guy's wallet. Lightest fingers in town . . . Now there's Mike, all grown up and wearing a *tie*—can you believe it?"

Judith could. After more than twenty-four hours at Major Manor, she could believe anything. She could even believe that her mother had done her a favor. With Sweetums on her lap, Judith settled into Grandpa Grover's favorite armchair and let Gertrude go on with the show.

Joe didn't get home until almost midnight. By that time, Judith was fast asleep. If he hadn't dropped his .38 Smith & Wesson, she would never have known he was there.

"What was that?" she asked foggily.

"My gun," Joe muttered. "It's okay. The safety's on."

Judith rolled over in bed. Joe was undressing without turning on the light. "Everything all right?" she asked.

"Oh, sure," he grumbled. "Terrific."

Judith fumbled for the switch on the lamp next to the bed. Joe was wearing an uncharacteristically glum face. "What's wrong?" she asked, forcing her eyes into focus.

"Nothing. You're a star. Go back to sleep."

"Joe . . ."

"You didn't have to tell the Mayor his cousin was wearing lily pads on his head," Joe said in his disgruntled voice. "You didn't have to watch Buck Doerflinger try to talk his way out of making a wrongful arrest and still take credit for bringing in the real murderer. On Monday, you'll probably see me directing traffic around the city's latest street improvement. Which," he went on, his tone growing more forsaken, "will be the route where Buck's parade will pass when they make him Public Safety Officer of the Year."

"Oh, Joe!" Judith held her arms out to her husband. "Buck's a bungler! He can't take credit for solving this case!"

Ignoring Judith's embrace, Joe sat down on the bed. "He's pretending it was a trick to get the wife to confess to save the husband. Buck says he didn't have any evidence against her, so he was using psychology."

"But there's tons of evidence," Judith protested. "The loden coat, the timing of the real shot, our own knowledge of what Mrs. Wakefield said she did, especially to the Mayor's cousin!"

"Hearsay," Joe declared. "In a court of law, it won't mean a thing."

"And Trixie," Judith went on, undaunted by Joe's attitude. "She saw Mrs. Wakefield trying to kill us!"

"Trixie!" Joe snorted. "What kind of a witness will she make?"

Judith had to concede that point to Joe. "But the guns—what was the one she tried to use on us?"

"A Luger." Joe finally swung into bed.

"Exactly," Judith said, her excitement mounting. "A Luger and a Walther. German guns, from World War Two. I'll bet they belonged to Rube Major, souvenirs he brought back from his OSS assignment behind the lines. Who would he have given them to but his daughter, Ruth? Then there are those bricks and the hole in the den wall—what about trace evidence? Fibers from Mrs. Wakefield's long-sleeved uniform; hairs, maybe. There was dust on her uniform, too, probably from the masonry work outside. I'm certain the casing and the silencer are inside the wall. Her fingerprints may be on the silencer."

Almost against his will, Joe began to brighten. "There's a lot about this case I don't know. Buck sure doesn't, either. Care to enlighten me?" He reached out to touch Judith lightly on the cheek.

"I haven't had time to tell you everything." She grabbed his hand and pressed it against her face. "All Buck had was one dumb box."

Joe chuckled. "You're going to have to give me all the details. Buck may end up with a mere burglary bust."

Now Judith laughed, too. "Oh, no, he won't. The jewels are right where they belong—in Uncle Boo's safe."

Joe wrapped his free arm around Judith. "What are you talking about?"

"Trixie. Why do you think she came back to Major Manor? She found out what Mason was up to—I'd bet on it. And decided to return the jewels before her latest fiancé got arrested."

"Hunh." Joe stared up at the darkened ceiling. "So Trixie has a conscience after all."

"No, not in the least," Judith replied with certainty. "She just doesn't want to team up with a thief. As ever, Trixie is self-serving. She probably still thinks she can break the wills."

"But she can't." Joe, however, sounded dubious.

"That's right, she can't. Jill should get everything because she's Boo's widow. When she left to use the phone this afternoon, I figure she also called an attorney. Jill's young, but she's not foolish. She loves the house, though I doubt she'll keep it."

"Jill can make another bundle if she sells Major Manor," Joe commented, trying to warm his feet on Judith's. "And the jewels. Or will she give them to her grandmother?"

"I don't know." Judith tried to picture Vivvie Rush with a tiara perched atop her wig. "Jill never cared about the jewelry—it's too stodgy and dated for her tastes. I realize now that the theft upset her at the time, but the loss must have seemed like a drop in the bucket."

"I wouldn't mind meeting Jill," Joe said on a yawn. "Maybe she'd like to invest in the Police Pension Fund."

Enduring Joe's cold feet, Judith chuckled. "Maybe. I think she might give a chunk to Zoe. For all her protests, Zoe would like a second chance at life. Jill's got tons of money and she's not greedy. In the same position, Trixie would never have been so generous."

"Well." Joe sounded bemused. "According to the statements Buck took initially, he never pressed Jill for her I.D. Knowing him, he probably blustered around and told her who she was, instead of asking."

Judith nodded. "Legally, she *was* Boo's niece—great-niece. We all knew that. She'd been adopted so long ago by Derek that nobody ever thought about her not having blood ties to the Lotts and the Majors. She was definitely one of the family. When the will leaving everything to Derek showed up, Jill crowed, which infuriated Toadie and Trixie. Afterward, I wondered about Jill's reaction. All along, she knew she was inheriting the estate. But having put up with lots of Lotts for almost all her life, she was elated to put one over on them. I think she was also afraid that if she let them—or anyone else—know she was Mrs. Bruno Major, the killer might claim another victim."

"Which gave her another reason to take off on a one-way taxi trip out of Major Manor." Joe leaned over, withdrew his feet, and kissed Judith's ear. "Still mad at me?"

Judith considered. "Yes. And you?"

"Definitely."

"How mad?"

"Indescribably."

"Funny, you don't act mad."

"Neither do you."

Judith and Joe could have fooled anybody. Except each other.

Dear Reader:

I hope you enjoyed reading this Large Print mystery. If you are interested in reading other Beeler Large Print Mystery titles or any other Beeler Large Print titles, ask your librarian or write to me at:

Thomas T. Beeler, *Publisher*
Post Office Box 659
Hampton Falls, New Hampshire 03844

You can also call me at 1-800-818-7574 and I will send you my latest catalogue.

Audrey Lesko chooses the titles I publish in Large Print. Our aim is to provide good books by outstanding authors—books we both enjoyed reading and liked well enough to want to share. We warmly welcome any suggestions for new titles and authors.

Sincerely,